William John Courthope

The Liberal Movement in English Literature

William John Courthope

The Liberal Movement in English Literature

ISBN/EAN: 9783337737719

Printed in Europe, USA, Canada, Australia, Japan

Cover: Foto ©Andreas Hilbeck / pixelio.de

More available books at **www.hansebooks.com**

THE

LIBERAL MOVEMENT

IN

English Literature

By WILLIAM JOHN COURTHOPE, M.A.

AUTHOR OF 'THE PARADISE OF BIRDS' ETC.

LONDON
JOHN MURRAY, ALBEMARLE STREET
1885

So tenacious are we of our old ecclesiastical modes and fashions of institution, that very little change has been made in them since the fourteenth or fifteenth centuries, adhering in this particular, as in all else, to our old settled maxim never entirely nor at once to depart from antiquity. We found these institutions on the whole favourable to morality and discipline, and we thought they were susceptible of amendment without altering the ground. We thought they were capable of receiving and meliorating and, above all, of preserving the accessories of science and literature as the order of Providence should successively produce them. And after all, with this Gothic and monkish education (for such it is in the groundwork), we may put in our claim to as ample and early a share in all the improvements in science, in arts, and in literature which have illuminated the modern world as any other nation in Europe. We think one main cause of this improvement was our not despising the patrimony of knowledge which was left us by our forefathers.

BURKE, *Reflections on the French Revolution.*

PREFACE.

THE following papers appeared in the 'National Review,' and, with the exception of a few paragraphs, I have thought it best to republish them in their original form. Their issue at set monthly intervals has given me the advantage of observing the kind of judgments likely to be pronounced on them : on the other hand, it has necessarily prevented my critics from considering them with reference to the argument as a whole. Various and conflicting objections have been made to the opinions expressed in them. I might, of course, reply to these in detail, but, as the papers are now grouped in a volume, I prefer to present them without comment to the impartial consideration of the reader, only adding a few words on a point on which my intention seems to have been very generally misunderstood.

It has been suggested to me that I prejudice my cause by giving to a literary subject a title necessarily carrying with it political associations. I might, indeed, have called the series ' The Romantic Movement in English Literature,' but this would not have expressed all that I had in my mind. Art is the ideal reflection of national life, and owes much of its development to the social and political causes that determine the course of a people's history. Even, therefore, if I had simply intended to illustrate from the poetry of the present century the political effects of the great democratic movement since the French Revolution in 1789, I could, I think, have provided myself with historic materials not irrelevant to the subject. But is it correct to limit the use of the word ' Liberalism ' to politics ? to associate it simply with the events that produced the change in the Poor Law, the extension of the Franchise, the Repeal of the Corn Laws, and the Emancipation of the Press ? Is it not rather the case that these are only the external manifestations of a spirit working in the mind of the people, which has assumed a particular aspect in politics, but which has produced analogous results in the spheres of religion and art? So, at least, it has appeared to others beside myself; and if any are still inclined to question the propriety of my title, I may appeal to the example of so great a master of the English language as Cardinal Newman, in whose 'History of my Religious Opinions' the word 'Liberalism' is employed over and over again to denote a movement in the region of thought.

I have not used the words 'Liberalism' and 'Conservatism' in any invidious or party sense. By 'Liberalism' I mean the disposition which leads men to seek above all things the enlargement of individual liberty : by 'Conservatism' that which makes them desire primarily to preserve the continuity of national development. Between these two principles I can see no essential contradiction, nor do I think that they can be safely separated. At the same time it is perfectly easy to consider each by itself; and indeed, it is sufficiently obvious that, under our

party system, there is an unfortunate tendency
to regard them as if one was exclusive of the
other. Pushed to their logical extremes, each
has a danger peculiar to itself. Excessive Conservatism may doubtless develop into the stag-
nation of Ancestor Worship. On the other
hand, the extravagant pursuit of Liberty ends
in an individualism which strikes at the root of
social and national growth. If, for instance,
the maintenance of rigid commercial restrictions
in favour of a particular interest may have been
injurious to the development of the nation, has
there been no danger in the universal application
of the principle of *laisser faire* without regard
to circumstances ? If the imposition of political
disabilities on those who refused to conform to
the established religion of the country was a
policy which could only be defended under certain conditions of society, is it more reasonable,
in the interests of so-called freedom of thought,
to uproot a religious organisation which has
from time immemorial formed part of the national life ? So in the sphere of creative Imagination. There may be no less error in the

theories of those who, like Wordsworth, make
the individual mind the standard of art, and
defy the rules of tradition and convention, than
in the inflexibility of critics such as Gifford,
who are inclined to yield to prescription an
almost passive obedience.

My intention has been to trace *historically*
the manner in which the movement on behalf
of liberty during the present century has affected
the order established in the sphere of Imagination since the Revolution of 1688. I have
sought to exhibit the constant course of conflict
and reconciliation between the spirit of Authority and the spirit of Freedom, which has
hitherto preserved for us the continuity of our
national life. I have shown how, out of the
ruins of Feudal and Catholic sentiment, arose
a new code of taste, derived from old English
sources, corrected and refined by classical authority; how this assimilated naturally with the
ideas of a ruling aristocracy; how the romantic
element in our language was virtually sup-
pressed ; and how, in the latter part of the
eighteenth century, as the classical spirit began

to languish, the genius of Romance revived, and associated itself in a multitude of subtle forms with the growing spirit of Liberty and Democracy. The subject is a large one, and I have not been able to treat it otherwise than in outline ; but, now that these essays have been collected, I trust it may appear that I have been animated by the spirit of a student rather than of an advocate, and that, according to my lights, I have endeavoured to trace accurately the course of the great conflict of opinion visible in the sphere of taste since the French Revolution. At the same time, I do not for a moment imagine that the account here given of the Liberal and Romantic movement in our literature is wholly dispassionate. The men of genius who played the most prominent part in it lived too near to our own times, and are associated too closely with our own feelings and prejudices, to be judged like Greek and Roman authors, and I can well believe that the impartial reader may detect a bias in my judgments of which I am myself unconscious. If, however, he be inclined to complain that the tribute paid in these essays to the great romantic poets of the present century is short of what justice demands, I would ask him to remember that he is required by Liberal critics to believe that ' Dryden and Pope are not classics of our poetry.' When two writers who have exercised so powerful an influence on the growth of English metrical literature are thus stripped of their laurels by the stroke of a pen, and without any intelligible reason being assigned, it is perhaps not wonderful that those who reverence and admire them as poets should scrutinise closely the claims of the new deities in whose honour they are deposed.

Numerous symptoms, such as the controversy between Mr. Arnold and Mr. Swinburne respecting the merits of Byron and Shelley,[1] show that we have not yet emerged from the party struggle that divided the critical world in the beginning of the century. The relative position in the history of English literature that will finally be assigned to the great poets of the

[1] See Mr. Swinburne's essays on ' Byron and Wordsworth ' in the *Nineteenth Century* for April and May 1884.

present century, has still to be determined by the free conflict of opinion ; and, as I have said in my introductory paper, I pretend simply to describe the Liberal Movement from a Conservative point of view. The description itself may be false or inadequate : but I venture to think it cannot be put aside as unworthy of examination.

CONTENTS.

ESSAY   PAGE

  I. INTRODUCTORY 3

 II. THE CONSERVATISM OF THE EIGHTEENTH CENTURY 35

III. WORDSWORTH'S THEORY OF POETRY 71

 IV. THE REVIVAL OF ROMANCE : SCOTT, BYRON, SHELLEY 111

  V. POETRY, MUSIC, AND PAINTING : COLERIDGE AND

     KEATS 159

 VI. CONCLUSION : THE PROSPECTS OF POETRY . . 197

THE

LIBERAL MOVEMENT IN ENGLISH

LITERATURE

I.

INTRODUCTORY.

EVERYONE who shares the instincts of humanity looks with interest on a quarrel between authors. It arouses excitement of the same kind as that which in old days—for I believe I am speaking of the manners of the past—used to be felt when a whisper ran through the form that there was to be a fight after school was over, or as that which still rises when every corner of the House of Commons fills in anticipation of 'a scene.' We know that there will be an exhibition of human nature as it really is, not merely as it strives to appear. The record of such combats proved a fruitful topic to the industry of Disraeli the elder. But a portion of the subject is still unexhausted, and a chapter of literary history almost equally entertaining might

B 2

be written respecting quarrels *about* authors.   If
a dispute between authors has all the interest
of a duel, the other attains the magnitude of
a battle.   As one thinks of the desperate en-
counters in foot-notes. between rival editors of
the classics, or of all the arguments discharged
by the Academies that fought over the merits of
Tasso and Ariosto, vast materials of literary history at once present themselves.   And all for
the sake of some favourite poet or novelist who
may have been dead and buried a hundred
years !   The matter-of-fact spectator of wars of
this kind is apt to lift up his hands in amaze-
ment at the passions which are excited, and to
wonder whether they might not be composed by
some intervention like that which Virgil recom-
mends for the pacification of belligerent bees.

So, doubtless, wondered many a sober reader
while considering the astounding invectives with
which Mr. Swinburne has lately been endeavouring to befoul Byron's memory.   'Doest thou
well to be angry,' he may have been inclined to
ask, 'because Mr. Arnold has preferred Byron
to Shelley as a poet?'   The question sounds

reasonable enough, yet it would betray but an imperfect appreciation of the real causes of Mr. Swinburne's violence. The fact is that, under a controversy apparently involving only individual preferences, radical antipathies of taste and feeling are latent which are as old as the history of art, and which have, in the present instance, been brought into collision by the operation of historic causes as closely connected with each other as the Thirty Years' War was with the Reformation. If anyone questions the accuracy of this assertion he has but to refer to the controversy about Pope in 1820, and he will find that the respective positions of the disputants of that period are substantially identical with those now severally occupied by Mr. Arnold and Mr. Swinburne.

It is worth while to recall for a moment the outlines of a dispute which attracted great attention in its day, both from the eminence of the combatants and from the intrinsic interest of the issues that were raised. The occasion of the war was the supposed attempt of Bowles to detract from the poetical reputation of Pope, whose works he had edited. Bowles's real intention was to prove that Pope was not a poet of the highest order, a proposition which everyone would have accepted without argument, if he had not thought fit to force an open door by laying siege to it with a whole park of artillery. Nothing would satisfy him but to take the position he desired by slow and regular approaches, and he advanced under cover of two prodigious axioms which he loudly proclaimed to be 'invariable principles' of poetry. These ran as follows: 'All images drawn from what is beautiful and sublime in the works of Nature are more beautiful and sublime than images drawn from Art, *and are therefore more poetical.*' And: 'Subject and execution are equally to be considered ; the one respecting the *poetry*, the other the *art* and *talents* of the poet.' From these he concludes: 'With regard to the first, Pope cannot be placed among the highest order of poets ; with regard to the second, none was ever his superior.'

I think it is obvious that if Bowles's antagonists had fixed their attention on the really weak points in his two positions, he might have suffered instant and disastrous defeat. It is improper to speak of a subject as being intrinsically poetical ; it may be sublime *per se*, but it becomes *poetical* in consequence of the conception and execution of the poet. There is nothing beautiful or sublime in the subject of the ' Rape of the Lock,' and yet few would deny that the subject is treated in an exceedingly poetical manner. It is, in fact, merely begging the question to assume that the sole sources of poetry are the beautiful and the sublime.

Roused, however, to indignation by what they considered an insidious attempt to detract from the reputation of their favourite, Pope's champions either fell upon Bowles at those points where he was really impregnable, or advanced counter-propositions which could not be sustained. Bowles had argued that ' all images drawn from what is beautiful and sublime in Nature are more beautiful and sublime than images drawn from Art.' This is substantially undeniable. Pope, however, drew his images largely from art ; therefore Campbell felt it incumbent on him to dispute an almost self-evident proposition. Bowles, again, insisted that all poetry inhered in the subject; Byron, plunging into the fray, as he says himself, ' like an Irishman in a row, anybody's customer,' maintained, on the other hand, with justice, that it lay rather in the execution ; but he went on to contend that, as Pope's execution was nearly faultless, he was therefore entitled to occupy the same poetical rank as Homer himself ! With his adversaries committing blunders of this kind, Bowles was able partially to disguise his own, and to make so much better a fight than he deserved that a considerable portion of the public fancied he had been victorious all along the line, and had fully established his ' invariable principles.'

Sixty years have gone by, and in the place of Bowles testing the rank of poets by 'images drawn from the sublime and beautiful in Nature,' and deposing Pope from his usurped throne, we have Mr. Arnold telling us : ' It is important, therefore, to hold fast to this : that poetry is at bottom a criticism of life ; that the greatness of

a poet lies in his powerful and beautiful application of ideas to life—to the question : How to
live.' To which question it would appear that,
in Mr. Arnold's opinion, Shelley has not returned a wholly satisfactory answer, and is therefore not to be reckoned a great classical poet.
Whereupon, as was to be expected, Mr. Swinburne takes the field with ' a simple postulate,
or at least a simple assumption, on which,' says
he, 'I would rest my argument. It would be
absolute waste of time for one who assumes it as
indisputable to enter into controversy with one
who regards it as disputable that the two primary
and essential qualities of poetry are imagination
and harmony ; that where these qualities are
wanting there can be no poetry properly so
called, and that where these qualities are perceptible in the highest degree, there, even though
they should be unaccompanied and unsupported
by any other great quality whatever—even
though the ethical or critical quality should be
conspicuous by its absence—there, and only
there, is the best and the highest poetry.' From
which premises we are to conclude that Shelley

is the third, if not the second, in rank of all the English poets.

'Who shall decide when doctors disagree?' Decision is twice as hard in the present disagreement as it was in the great Pope controversy. Then the disputants attacked and resisted according to the established rules of logic. Major, minor, and conclusion were all marshalled before the reader, and the combatants triumphed with or succumbed to unimpeachable syllogisms. Not so our contemporaries. When Mr. Arnold has assured us that poetry in the future will fill the place of religion we are very ready to concede that, if such is to be the case, it is desirable that we should have only such poetry as gives us the truest criticism of life, and that we ought, therefore, to be always studying the best poetical models. But how are we to know these? 'Well,' says Mr. Arnold in effect, with his usual engaging frankness, 'I really can't give you any infallible rules, but perhaps the best way is to carry in your head certain lines and passages about which there can be no mistake, and to be always asking yourself

when you meet with a poem whether it comes
up to this classical mark.' And he gives a
number of such lines as examples, about which
it is only necessary to say that, being selected
by Mr. Arnold, they are of course judiciously
selected, but that the greatness and nobility of
the verses he cites depends entirely upon their
harmonious adjustment to a particular context
from which they have been arbitrarily torn.
And when can a poet be said to have criticised
life in the truest way? Shakespeare and Milton
may pass without much examination. But
Chaucer and Burns? These are not quite up
to the mark. They want ' the σπουδαιότης, the
high and excellent seriousness which Aristotle
assigns as one of the grand virtues of poetry.'
As for Dryden and Pope, ' though they may
write in verse, though they may in a certain
sense be masters of the art of versification,
Dryden and Pope are not classics of our poetry,
they are classics of our prose.'

Surely when a critic of great eminence
thinks it necessary to give such advice to a presumably large number of readers the art of poetry

must have fallen upon evil days. For if there
be any students so extremely cautious and de-
liberative as to fear to trust to their natural
instinct in judging poetry, it is certain that they
might go on applying Mr. Arnold's tests for a
hundred years without being ever able to tell
good poetry from bad. Think of the Greek
rhapsodists whose raptures in reciting Homer
were so strong as to throw them into convulsions: can we imagine men who delight in poetry
in such a way as this balancing their judgments
like wine-tasters and seeking to 'detect the
presence or absence of high quality' in the verse
that they read ? Or the spectators at the festival
of the Dionysia : would Mr. Arnold have had
them distract their imaginations from the great
world of Aristophanic horse-play to reflect
whether the imagery presented to them was
quite worthy of the 'high destinies of poetry' ?
When Shakespeare called upon the assembled
theatre to lift their imaginations to the glories
of Agincourt :

> Suppose within the girdle of these walls
> Are now confined two mighty monarchies,

Whose high upreared and abutting fronts
The perilous narrow ocean parts asunder :
Piece out our imperfections with your thoughts ;
Into a thousand parts divide one man,
And make imaginary puissance ;
Think, when we talk of horses that you see them
Printing their proud hoofs i' the receiving earth,
For 'tis your thoughts that now must deck our kings—

was there an Englishman with the soul of poetry within him who did not answer the appeal in the spirit with which Sir Philip Sidney says that he always read the ballad 'Chevy Chase,' and without the slightest attempt at considering whether the entertainment was quite up to the classical mark ? Or, once more, will Mr. Arnold ever persuade any reader of average sensibility that what ought to be enjoyed in the 'Scholar Gipsy' is rather the moral of the poem, than the beautiful and affecting images of the Oxfordshire landscape with which the poet has surrounded the story ? Never!

In short, I submit with deference, but with confidence, that the ethical standard of judgment which Mr. Arnold proposes as the test of the highest poetry is narrow and arbi-

trary ; that in criticising any poet, nothing is
to be gained by comparing his qualities with
those of some other poet of a perfectly distinct
species ; but that each should be judged on his
own merits, with sole reference to the end proposed, the real question being whether that end
is in itself a just one, and if so, how nearly it is
attained.   True lovers of poetry will, in my
opinion, side with Mr. Swinburne against Mr.
Arnold when the former maintains it to be indisputable that ' the two primary and essential
qualities of poetry are imagination and harmony.'
And that Mr. Swinburne, in his calm moments,
entertains a large and generous idea of the space
that is covered by the terms ' imagination and
harmony,' no one can doubt who reads his
admirably just and appreciative observations on
the poetry of Crabbe.   How comes it, then, that
a critic who can perceive ' imagination and harmony ' in the ' Dutch School ' of English poetry
seems absolutely incapable of detecting either
quality in the verse of Byron ?   How is it
that he does not see that he is not damaging
Byron's poetry, but his own critical reputation,

when he pours out his invective on his victim's 'blundering, floundering, lumbering, and stumbling stanzas,' on his 'gasping, ranting, wheezing, broken-winded verse,' or his 'drawling, draggle-tailed drab of a Muse'? The fact is that Mr. Swinburne, being in a passion at the preference given by Mr. Arnold to Byron over his favourite Shelley, is determined in revenge to lower Byron's reputation by overwhelming him with critical 'Billingsgate,' and by parodying (rather pointlessly) some of his flimsiest and most tawdry verse. But as to settling the question by argument, the 'æsthetic' test which he brings to prove Byron's deficiency in 'imagination and harmony' is every whit as arbitrary as Mr. Arnold's ethical method.

'The test of the highest poetry,' says he, 'is that it eludes all tests. Poetry in which there is no element at once perceptible and indefinable by any reader or hearer of any poetic instinct may have every other good quality; it may be as nobly ardent and invigorating as the best of Byron's, or as nobly mournful and contemplative as the best of Southey's: if all its properties can easily or can ever be gauged and named by their admirers, it is not poetry—above all, it is not lyric poetry—of the first water . . .

> Will no one tell me what she sings ?
> Perhaps the plaintive numbers flow
> For old, unhappy, far off things,
> And battles long ago.

If not another word was left of the poem in which these two last lines occur, those two lines would suffice to show the hand of a poet differing, not in degree but in kind, from the tribe of Byron or of Southey. In the whole expanse of poetry there can hardly be two verses of more perfect and profound and exalted beauty. But if anybody does not happen to see this, no critic of all that ever criticised, from the days of Longinus to the days of Arnold, from the days of Zoilus to the days of Zola, could succeed in making visible the certainty of this truth to the mind of that person.'

In spite of this tremendous affirmation, I venture to think not only that what Mr. Swinburne calls the 'certainty of truth' will be imperceptible to many persons not devoid of poetic sense, but that to any man of plain mind it can be shown to be palpable falsehood. For supposing that the two lines—

> For old, unhappy, far off things,
> And battles long ago,

had been all of the poem which was in existence,

their pathos, and beauty, and harmony would
have been entirely lost. The high quality of the
verses depends upon their association with the
image of the solitary Highland reaper singing
unconsciously her 'melancholy strain' in the
midst of the autumn sheaves : detached from
this image, the lines would scarcely have been
more affecting than our old friends 'Barbara,
celarent,' &c. And as for Mr. Swinburne's
general principle, it will not hold water any
more than his particular instance. 'Poetry,' he
tells us, 'in which there is no element at once
perceptible and indefinable by any reader or
hearer of any poetic instinct is not poetry of the
first water.' It may safely be said of all genuine
poetry that there is something about it which
cannot be analysed or defined, and which is the
genius or character it derives from the poet
himself. So far Mr. Swinburne's proposition
amounts to no more than a truism. And again,
it is true that language is only an imperfect
vehicle for expressing the images which the
mind conceives, and therefore there will always
be something in all imaginative writing which

C

escapes analysis. But if Mr. Swinburne means
to assert that vagueness and indistinctness of
thought and feeling are the characteristics of the
highest poetry, he will have to explain away the
greater part of Homer, and Virgil, and Shakespeare, and Milton ; the fact being that the
greatness of these poets consists in the manly
strength, the distinctness, and the propriety of
the language by means of which they bring
images of things at once sublime and impalpable
before the mind's eye.

I have referred to the controversy between
Mr. Arnold and Mr. Swinburne, not because I
seek presumptuously to intervene in a duel
between two eminent poets and critics, but
because the issues raised by it seem to me to
throw a strong light on the *movement* which gives
the title to this paper. The spectacle of critics
emulously endeavouring to secure precedence in
the poetical Pantheon for Byron, or Wordsworth, or Shelley, or Keats, ought to remind us
that two generations ago three of these claimants
by no means appeared in the light of deities to
those who were then supposed to be the dis-

pensers of fame, but were ruthlessly denounced as impostors and false prophets. Time has brought its revenge; the idols of an older generation have been displaced in favour of the once-despised innovators : we adore what our fathers burned, and burn what they adored. Human justice proceeds in this rough way ; but the catastrophe that has overtaken the able and accomplished critics of the early part of the present century might at least make us modest in anticipating the permanence of our own judgments.

The fact is that though most of us believe in the existence of Absolute Truth in questions of art, it is impossible to measure this by an absolute standard of taste. When any society has passed from the stage of creation into that of criticism, parties develop themselves as naturally in art as they do in politics ; and all critics, consciously or unconsciously arraying themselves on different sides, regard the prepossessions, the prejudices, and even the cant of their own connection as demonstrable truth. This is the experience of all communities that can boast of a

literature. We find a Conservative and Liberal
Party in Art—a Party, that is, adhering to
tradition and authority, and a Party striving
after change and novelty—in Athens under
Pericles, and afterwards; in Rome under Au-
gustus; in France under Louis XIV., and after
the Bourbon Restoration of the present century.
In England the happy Elizabethan period was
an age of creation rather than of criticism; but
Shakespeare and his contemporaries appeared to
the critics of the eighteenth century very nearly
as unsatisfactory, in point of art, as Dryden and
Pope appear to Mr. Arnold and Mr. Swinburne,
and as, perhaps, the great Liberal school of
literature, which has done so much to determine
the taste of the present generation, will appear
to the times that shall be hereafter.

For it is plain enough to all who consider
the matter that the dispute between Mr. Arnold
and Mr. Swinburne about Wordsworth and
Byron is of an internecine character. Both
critics are Liberals : the poets they are writing
about were Liberals : their criticisms are made
on Liberal principles. The Conservatives are

out of the quarrel altogether. Not that either of
the two critics is intolerant enough to deny to
the Conservatives a certain *raison d'être*. Mr.
Arnold has the charity, in his own manner, to allow the eighteenth century to have
been 'excellent and indispensable,' though he
will not admit the great typical writers of the
period to enter his charmed poetical circle. Mr.
Swinburne, as we have seen, goes farther, and is
even ready to praise the poetry of Crabbe, and to
concede that Byron and Pope were poets ' after
a fashion.' Nor is either critic blind to the imperfections of the poets whom he most admires.
Twenty years ago, when the tide of Liberalism
was still running strong, the Liberal critic who
declined to accept the ' Excursion ' as one of the
canonical books of the art of poetry would have
been regarded as a heretic. But now Mr. Arnold
admits that ' although Jeffrey completely failed
to recognise Wordsworth's real greatness, he
was yet not wrong in saying of the " Excursion "
as a work of poetic style, " This will never do." '
When a concession of this kind can be made, it
may be hoped that we have approached a time in

which it will be again possible to examine, in something like a judicial temper, poetical qualities that have been obscured by a passionate dislike or an equally passionate admiration. But the proper balance of judgment will not be attained until Liberal critics leave off regarding Conservative principles from the heights of contemptuous superiority, and consider whether in some respects the ages we have been taught to disparage ought not rather to be regarded as our masters in the art of expression. It is with the hope that I may be able, however inadequately, to stimulate inquiry in this direction, that I propose, in a short series of papers, to trace from the Conservative point of view the course and the character of the Liberal movement in our literature.

Let me say, by way of preface, that by the word 'literature' I mean imaginative literature, and especially poetry; and by 'Liberal movement,' the writings of those who, in point of time, followed the French Revolution, and who founded their matter and style on the principles to which that Revolution gave birth. It may, I

think, be regarded as no less certain that the
democratic upheaval has developed a Liberal
movement in art than that it caused a Liberal
movement in politics and a Liberal movement
in religion.   In all three spheres, as I have said
in a previous paper, optimism, the fundamental
principle of Liberalism, is ever at work, firing
men's fancies with the idea of a constant expansion of the human powers of morality and
imagination.   Thus Mr. Arnold tells us :

> The future of poetry is immense, because in poetry,
> where it is worthy of its high destinies, our race as
> time goes on will find an ever surer and surer stay.
> There is not a creed which is not shaken, not an
> accredited dogma which is not shown to be question-
> able, not a received tradition which does not threaten
> to dissolve.   Our religion has materialised itself in the
> fact, in the supposed fact ; it has attached its emotion
> to the fact, and now the fact is failing it.   But for
> poetry the idea is everything ; the rest is a world of
> illusion, of divine illusion.   Poetry attaches its emotion
> to the idea ; the idea *is* the fact.

This is only saying in other words what
Wordsworth said at the beginning of the century :

> Poetry is the first and last of all knowledge—it is

as immortal as the heart of man. If the labours of men of science should ever create any material revolution, direct or indirect, in our condition, and in the impressions which we habitually receive, the Poet will sleep then no more than at present; he will be ready to follow the steps of the man of science, not only in those general indirect effects, but he will be at his side, carrying sensation into the midst of the objects of the science itself.

In both these passages the influence of the principle of optimism is sufficiently apparent. The Conservative, on the other hand, whose principles lead him to believe in the radical imperfection of all mortal nature, and in the inherent taint of evil in man, takes a far less sanguine view of the prospects of the art of poetry. He is more inclined to Macaulay's conclusion :

We think that as civilisation advances poetry almost necessarily declines. . . . In an enlightened age there will be much intelligence, much science, much philosophy, abundance of just classification and subtle analysis, abundance of wit and eloquence, abundance of verses, and even of good ones; but little poetry. Men will judge and compare, but they will not create.

It will be observed that in these three

passages the word 'poetry' is used in substantially the same sense, as meaning, that is
to say, 'poetical sentiment,' or the raw stuff
out of which poems are made. And using it in
this sense, I confess I do not understand how it
is possible to dispute the truth of Macaulay's
proposition. Science and poetry are antagonistic
forces, since the advance of science narrows
the kingdom of imagination, which is the source
of *creative* poetical life. Wordsworth, it is true,
credited imagination with a transmutative power
which, in some mysterious way, enables it to
change objects of knowledge into something different from themselves. ' The remotest discoveries,' says he, ' of the chemist, the botanist, or
mineralogist, will be as proper objects of the
poet's art as any upon which it can be employed,
if the time should ever come when these things
shall be familiar to us, and the relations under
which they are contemplated by the followers of
these respective sciences shall be manifestly and
palpably material to us as enjoying and suffering
beings.' Well, we boast, and with justice, of
the vast discoveries which have been made in all

these sciences, and of the extent to which they
are studied by the people : but I would put it
to any plain man who shall glance at the charming dialogues of Izaak Walton, or at the ' Vulgar
Errors ' of Sir Thomas Browne, whether he does
not find ten times as much material for poetical
creation in the views about natural objects which
prevailed even two hundred years ago as in all
the enlightenment of Darwin and Lyall.   It
must be so.   Where fact and science come,
imagination must depart.   Like some ancient
indigenous race it retires before the irresistible
forces of well-equipped invaders : inaccessible
mountain-peaks and tracts of impenetrable forest
remain in its possession ; but the rich and open
country of every-day life, over which it once
roamed with the freedom of unquestioned owner-
ship, is lost to it for ever.

Against the optimist views of the Liberals
as to the inexhaustible resources of poetry, it
appears to me, then, that Macaulay's position is
unassailable.   It is not a question what the
poet would like to do, or what he ought to do,
with his imagination, but what the inexorable

laws of Nature and Society will allow him to do. On the other hand, I do not think that Conservatives are at all bound to follow Macaulay to the extreme limits of his pessimist conclusion. If his reasoning were sound, the greatest poems ought to be produced in the rudest ages, whereas we know that this is contrary to experience. It is obvious that even the age of Homer was one of considerable artistic refinement, and it would have been quite impossible for a barbarous stage of society to have produced ' The Æneid,' ' The Divine Comedy,' or ' Paradise Lost.' The reason is obvious. For the making of all great poetry not only is abundant imagination and sentiment required, but judgment, knowledge of composition and proportion, a language rich, full, and harmonious, and, in a word, all the resources of *art*. These qualities are not found in an infant community. Such a community will provide the raw material, the poetical elements, which the great poet will afterwards use, but it will not produce the great poem. It is not the peasant creator of the fairies, but Shakespeare the artist, who invents the incomparable machinery of the 'Midsummer Night's Dream :' the imagination of Cædmon may, in some respects, vie even with that of Milton ; but the harsh crudities of the Anglo-Saxon language would have overpowered the genius of Milton himself. Long ages of refinement and philosophy were wanted to prepare for the glories of 'Paradise Lost.'

It seems to me that half the confusion that prevails in the discussion of the subject is due to the ambiguous sense attaching to the word 'poetry.' When Macaulay says that 'an enlightened age will have little poetry,' he really means that it will have no widespread imaginative feeling. But the only just and precise sense in which the word can be used is to signify the Art of Poetry as opposed to the other imitative arts of Painting, Sculpture, and Music. Macaulay carries his confusion of thought into his definition of the art of Poetry.

'By poetry,' he says, 'we mean not all writing in verse, nor even all good writing in verse. Our definition excludes many metrical compositions which, on other grounds, deserve the highest praise. By poetry we mean the art of employing words in such a manner as to produce an illusion on the imagination, the art of doing by means of words what the painter does by means of colours.'

But plainly, on this principle, we should have to deny the title of painter to many who have expressed their thoughts by means of colours. It can scarcely be said that the pictures of Teniers, for instance, 'produce an illusion on the imagination.' But can we, without abuse of language, say that Teniers is less a painter (not a lesser painter, observe) than Tintoretto because he does not rise above the representation of Dutch fairs, while the other depicts the most sublime scenes of Scripture history ? Macaulay's definition is framed to cover only poems of the highest order of creative invention. It will not even suit lyric poetry, the end of which is not to produce an illusion, but to touch the feelings in the most direct and immediate manner. It will not include such a poem as the 'Georgics,' and he would be a bold man indeed who should deny the 'Georgics' to be poetry. It naturally excludes all satiric and epigrammatic verse ; but what are we to do with this large class of composition which, for some reason or other, is expressed in a manner that is not prose ? The common sense of the world has assigned to such writers the title of poet. Johnson asks, ' Who is a poet if Pope is not ? ' and I do not know that anyone has ever been able to answer his question.

I venture in the face of Macaulay's definition, and in the face of the speculations of modern philosophers who have thrown contempt on such a simple view of the matter, to affirm that all *good* writing in verse—in other words, good composition in metre—is good poetry in its own kind. By poetry I mean the art of producing pleasure by the just expression of imaginative thought and feeling in metrical language. There are many kinds of feeling—sublime, pathetic, serious, ludicrous—which can be better expressed in metre than they can in prose. One kind of feeling is doubtless much higher than another ; therefore the poet who produces pleasure by satisfying men's ideas of the sublime belongs to a higher order than he who merely pleases their

sense of the gay or the ludicrous. But the test
of the standard rank of any poet is simply his
capacity for producing lasting pleasure by the
metrical expression of thought, of whatever kind
it may be ; and therefore Horace, and Dryden,
and Pope, have as good a title to be considered
classical poets as Teniers has to be ranked
among the masters of painting. On the other
hand, there may be poets finely endowed with
gifts of imagination and harmony, who may yet
fail in many of their works to produce that lasting pleasure which is the test of classical poetry,
either because they have squandered their powers
on the treatment of subjects which lie beyond
the just range of imagination, or have used them
for the expression of imaginative ideas which do
not possess an enduring interest. I shall attempt,
then, by reference to this standard, to determine
in the next paper what were the aims and ideals
of those English writers who constituted the
tradition established during the eighteenth century ; then to examine in what respects the
great writers of the present century, who have

produced the movement in literature that I have called Liberal, departed from this tradition; and in conclusion, to consider what kind of a prospect the movement, now that it is fully developed, seems to disclose to us.

THE

CONSERVATISM OF THE EIGHTEENTH

CENTURY

II.

THE CONSERVATISM OF THE EIGHTEENTH CENTURY.

I WOULD ask the reader who follows my argument to consider that it rests on two assumptions. The first is, that poetry is a *social* art; that the creations of the greatest poets are not mere isolated conceptions of their individual minds, but are the products of influences which are felt by all their contemporaries, though the poet alone has the power of expressing them. 'There must,' says Shelley, 'be a resemblance which does not depend on their own will between all the writers of any particular age. They cannot escape from subjection to a common influence which arises out of an infinite combination of circumstances belonging to the

times in which they live, though each is in a
degree the author of the very influence by which
his being is thus pervaded. Thus the tragic
poets of the age of Pericles ; the Italian revivers
of ancient learning ; those mighty intellects of
our own country that succeeded the Reformation, the translators of the Bible, Shakespeare,
Spenser, the dramatists of the reign of Elizabeth,
and Lord Bacon ; the colder spirits of the in-
terval that succeeded ; all resemble each other,
and differ from every other in their several
classes. And this is an influence from which
neither the meanest scribbler nor the sublimest
genius of any era can escape ; and which I have
not attempted to escape.' The second assumption is that the general spiritual imagination of
society, which is the source of all poetry, is less
free in a refined than in a rude age, just as the
imagination is far more at liberty in each of us
during childhood and youth than after we have
acquired the judgment and experience of mature
life. Wordsworth illustrates this truth by two
very beautiful images. One is in the ' Ode to
Immortality ' :

Heaven lies about us in our Infancy!
Shades of the prison-house begin to close
Upon the growing boy,
But he beholds the light, and whence it flows,
He sees it in his joy.
The youth who daily farther from the East
Must travel, still is Nature's priest,
And by the vision splendid
Is on his way attended;
At length the man perceives it die away,
And fade into the light of common day.

And he expresses the regret which so many experience in a period of materialising science when they look back upon the ages of free and simple imagination :

Great God! I'd rather be
A Pagan suckled in a creed outworn,—
So might I, standing on this pleasant lea,
Have glimpses that would make me less forlorn;
Have sight of Proteus rising from the sea;
Or hear old Triton blow his wreathèd horn.

It is obvious that a remarkable evolution, alike in the imaginative life of the individual and in that of society, is described or suggested in these lines. Yet although both assumptions are thus severally supported by the authority of

two of the greatest poets of the present century
(in the face, it is true, of Wordsworth's own
critical theory) ; although Plato, in his dialogues,
insists over and over again on the essential
antagonism between science and imagination ;
although I was most careful to disavow all
sympathy with Macaulay's pessimist doctrine
— that, ' as civilization advances, *poetry* necessarily
declines,' the opinions I expressed in the last
paper written on the subject were assailed in
many Radical quarters as novel, heretical, per-
verse, and depressing. A very practical proof
was thus afforded that Conservatives are much
more in sympathy, than are Radicals, with the
scientific doctrine of Evolution. It is natural
that it should be so. Life, in the Radical view,
is simply change ; and a Radical is ready to
promote every caprice or whim of the numerical
majority of the moment in the belief that the
change which it effects in the constitution of
society will bring him nearer to some ideal state
existing in his own imagination. Life, according to the Conservative belief, on the other hand,
is growth, and all real growth must be con-

tinuous.   Conservatism, in whatever sphere,
consists in preserving and expanding the stream
of traditional national life which has come down
to us from our fathers. Conservatism, in politics,
as Burke says, bids us act upon the maxim,
'never wholly or at once to depart from antiquity.' Conservatism in art and literature, if
we are to believe Sir Joshua Reynolds, lies in
discovering the principles that inspired the great
masters of early times, and in applying them to
our own circumstances. 'It is from a careful
study of the works of the ancients,' says he,
'that you will be enabled to attain to the real
simplicity of nature ; they will suggest many
observations that would probably escape you if
your study were confined to nature alone. And,
indeed, I cannot help suspecting that in this instance the ancients had an easier task than the
moderns. They had probably little or nothing
to unlearn, as their manners were nearly approaching to this desirable simplicity ; while the
modern artist, before he can see the truth of
things, is obliged to remove a veil with which
the fashion of the times has thought proper to

cover her.'　Here we have an expression of the
true doctrine of Conservative Evolution.

In this sense the eighteenth century, which
is the subject of the present paper, seems to me
to have played a highly Conservative part in
the history of English religion, politics, art, and
literature.　To many, no doubt, the statement
will sound paradoxical.　The eighteenth century
has been constantly represented to us in modern
criticism as the pioneer of the great Revolution
in thought and manners, which has been pro-
ceeding on the Continent since 1789, and which
has, of course, exercised an important influence
on our own history.　But, as far as England is
concerned, I think it may be demonstrated that
the work of the eighteenth century consisted in
providing a safe mode of transition from the
manners of mediæval to those of modern society.
Suppose, for a moment, that this century were
eliminated from our history, and that we were
obliged to carry back our thoughts, without
halting-place, to the ideas and sentiments embodied in Sir Philip Sidney's 'Arcadia,' the
' Faery Queen,' or the fashionable 'metaphysical'

poetry of the seventeenth century ; would any plain man hesitate to acknowledge that though, in other points besides language, he could detect a certain kinship and sympathy between past and present, yet that they were divided from each other by a wide gulf of imagination and sentiment ?   But fill in the gap with the eighteenth century, and we feel not only that, in spite of obvious superficial divergencies of taste and perception, we and they occupy a common intellectual ground, but also that, looking back on the sixteenth and seventeenth centuries, through the light of the eighteenth, the nature of many of the sympathies which we are dimly conscious of sharing with those ages, is ex- plained by modifications of manners effected in the intermediate period.   The natural inference is that the eighteenth century, far from being a time of destruction and revolution, was a neces- sary link in a long chain of historic national development.

To discuss adequately the Conservatism of the eighteenth century would be the work of a volume rather than of a magazine article.   I can

but indicate or suggest what appears to me to be
the general 'lie' of the ground, and illustrate my
view by reference to the opinions of some of the
most representative Englishmen of the century.
For the purposes of my argument the great
point to remember is that there has been no
breach in the continuity of our social history.
Though our annals are sufficiently stained with
violence and bloodshed, though we have never
shrunk from settling with the sword differences
too radical to be composed with the tongue, we
have never cut ourselves off, after the manner of
France at the end of the last century, from the
sources of our national life. We have, therefore,
as yet experienced no convulsions arising out
of the complete separation between Church and
State ; till recently there has been no wide-spread
confiscation of property ; no one has hitherto
called for a Code Napoléon. If the Reformation
produced sharp conflicts in consequence of the
dispute about the Headship of the Church, the
life-blood of the parochial system continued to
circulate almost as quietly as it circulated in the
days of the 'Canterbury Tales.'   A violent

collision between the extreme principles of Monarchy and Republicanism no doubt overthrew, for a short period, the constitution in Church and State ; but the foundations of society remained unimpaired, and the nation, finding itself completely out of harmony with the order that had been imposed on it, restored the old Constitution in 1660, and defined it in 1688. It can scarcely be doubted that the continuity of tradition has been thus preserved, because our best minds have enlisted themselves in the cause of order, and have made it the object of their deepest study how to reconcile this with the claims of rational liberty. If, therefore, we can see how Butler, for instance, sought to advance the cause of Christianity in his age, how Burke interpreted the Constitution, and how Pope developed the traditions of English poetry, we shall have a fairly clear conception of the nature of English Conservatism, religious, political, and literary, in the eighteenth century. It may be objected that it is fantastic to look for a common principle running through so many different spheres of activity. But it

appears to me that in all of them the same
intellectual tendency may be traced—namely, an
instinctive acknowledgment of the truth that all
spiritual, political, and artistic development must
proceed in conformity with an ancestral *law*, the
authority of which is not to be questioned, and
which must be frankly obeyed by every individual who wishes to be completely free.

To begin with Butler, whose attitude in this
respect often causes his reasoning to be misunderstood. The modern assailants of Christianity assume that ever since the Renaissance
an intellectual movement has been going on
which has little by little been undermining the
cause of revealed religion. The Reformation,
they argue, took away so much ; the eighteenth
century destroyed so much more ; the fall of the
fortress before the historical and scientific criticism of modern days is inevitable. Singularly
enough they point to the attitude of the great
divines of the eighteenth century as evidence in
favour of their argument. Look at Butler, they
say ; it is plain that he has the depressed air
of a beaten man ; the low ground on which he

rests his arguments is a proof of what we say. Who would believe in a *probable* God ? And, of course, it is undeniable that Butler's whole method of argument gives a handle to anyone who chooses to reason in this captious and superficial manner. Such an opportunity is obviously offered in the following typical passage :

The evidence of religion then being admitted real, those who object against it as not satisfactory, *i.e.* as not being what they wish it, plainly forget that this is the very condition of our being; for satisfaction, in this sense, does not belong to such a creature as man.

Only a man, urges the agnostic philosopher, who is conscious that he has very little to say for himself, would resort to a pessimistic argument in defence of such a high matter as revealed religion. But those who reason like this show a strange inability to recognise the relative strength of their own and their adversary's position. They seem to regard Christianity merely as a speculative system which must stand or fall on purely intellectual grounds. But as a matter of fact the vast power of Christianity is derived from a practical and moral source. It is *in* possession of men's souls and spirits. Nineteen centuries have established its dominion over the conscience of the greatest nations of the world. The members of those nations have had their moral ideas formed in infancy on the assumption of the truth of Revelation long before it was possible for them to examine the testimony by which the authority of Revelation is supported. The opponents of Christianity must therefore undermine the *conscience* of Christendom, before they can hope to weaken materially the belief in the divine authority of revealed religion. The burden of proof lies with them. And of this fact the defenders of Christianity have always shown themselves to be perfectly aware. As they have been, naturally, men of ardent piety and devotion, the real argument that has weighed with them has been the spiritual experience of mankind. They see the necessity, no doubt, of defending the credibility of the testimony by which the truth of Revelation is established. On the other hand, they know that it is not incumbent on them to persuade the Christian

world of the truth of Revelation, but rather on
their adversaries to prove its falsehood, and that
this is a physical impossibility. The moral
obligations imposed by Christianity on the conscience can never, therefore, be disregarded.
'Religion,' says Butler, 'is a practical thing, and
consists in such a determinate course of life, as
being what, there is reason to think, is com-
manded by the Author of Nature.' Relying,
then, on the strength of their moral and spiritual
position, Christian writers have often made use
of intellectual weapons calculated to give their
adversaries wrong ideas as to their belief.
Jeremy Taylor, in his ' Liberty of Prophesying,'
employs a purely sceptical line of argument in
order to establish the right of freely interpreting
Scripture. Locke, in his ' Reasonableness of
Christianity,' followed a course of reasoning
which Toland afterwards developed into an
argument for Deism. As for Butler, no one
who reads the following passage can mistake, except designedly, the purpose of the
' Analogy ' :

I desire it may be considered with respect to the

whole of the foregoing objections, that in this Treatise I have argued upon the principles of others, not of my own; and have omitted what I think true and of the utmost importance, because by others thought unintelligible or not true. Thus I have argued upon the principles of the Fatalists, which I do not believe; and have omitted a thing of the utmost importance which I do believe—the moral fitness or unfitness of actions prior to all will whatever; which I apprehend as certainly to determine the Divine conduct, as speculative truth and falsehood necessarily determine the Divine judgment.

Put into a summary form, what I may, I hope without offence, call the Conservative position of the Anglican divines of the eighteenth century seems to be something of this kind: —The fact that the Christian law, eighteen hundred years after its institution, continues to exercise a living power over the conscience of men, is the highest proof that can be afforded of its divine origin. But this divine authority is denied by some on purely speculative grounds: let us, therefore, meet them on the grounds of speculation, and test the arguments on which they rely, so that, by proving their unsoundness, we may deprive them of the right of resisting the claims of conscience by the voice of so-called reason. ' The design of this Treatise,' says Butler, speaking at the conclusion of his ' Analogy,' ' is not to vindicate the character of God, but to show the obligations of men ; it is not to justify His providence, but to show what belongs to us to do.'

If we turn from religion to the sphere of politics, probably everyone will readily allow Burke to be the best representative that could be selected of the broad Conservatism of the eighteenth century. He is the most eminent of the Whigs or Moderate Liberals before the — French Revolution. Since that epoch there has been a constant tendency in the leaders of the Whig party to gravitate towards Revolutionary Radicalism. They have shown the greatest ingenuity in appropriating to their faction abstract principles, as when Fox drank to ' The Sovereignty of the People,' and his successors to ' The cause for which Hampden perished in the field, and Sidney on the scaffold.' Such Platonic enthusiasm is harmless enough, so long as it is confined to animating the Liberal party to exertions sufficient to turn out the Tories when they happen to be in power. But now that it is being employed to persuade the people of the congenital virtue of the Liberals, and the inbred wickedness of the Tories, it is well to remember that old-fashioned Whiggism was something fundamentally different in character from anything that at present disguises itself under the name. Whiggery, in Burke's days, meant simply adherence to the principles of the Revolution of 1688, and the Whig Party meant the connection of noblemen and gentlemen associated in Parliament to control the still preponderant power of the Crown. And because it meant this, and only this, there was scarcely a Tory statesman or writer of distinction in the eighteenth century who would have hesitated, so far as principle was concerned, to call himself a Whig. Oxford and Bolingbroke, as well as Pitt and Canning, started in their political careers in connection with the Whig Party; Bolingbroke avowedly bases his political theories on the old Whig principles; Swift, long after writing his 'Examiners,' declares that he is still, what he always was, a

Whig of the Revolution settlement ; Pope bitterly denounces Walpole in glowing lines which
Warton declares to be the incarnation of Whiggism. What, then, made it so easy for rival
statesmen in the last century to occupy common
ground of principle ? Two or three passages
from Burke will set the matter in the plainest
light.

'In the 1st of William and Mary,' says he, 'in the
famous statute called the Declaration of Right, the two
houses utter not a syllable of "a right to frame a
government for themselves." You will see that their
whole case was to secure the religion, laws, and liberties
that had been long possessed, and had been latterly
endangered. "Taking into their most serious consideration the best means for making such an establishment,
that their religion, laws, and liberties might not be in
danger of being again subverted," they auspicate all
their proceedings, by stating as some of those best
means, "in the first place to do as their ancestors in
like cases have usually done for vindicating their
antient rights and liberties, to declare ; " and then they
pray the king and queen " that it may be declared and
enacted, that all and singular the rights and liberties
asserted and declared are the true antient and indubitable
rights and liberties of the people of this kingdom."

'You will observe,' Burke continues, 'that from
Magna Charta to the Declaration of Right, it has been

the uniform policy of our Constitution to claim and assert our liberties, as an *entailed inheritance* derived to us from our forefathers, and to be transmitted to our posterity, as an estate specially belonging to the people of this kingdom, without any reference whatever to any other more general or prior right. By this means our Constitution preserves an unity in so great a diversity of its parts. We have an inheritable crown, an inheritable peerage, and a House of Commons and a people inheriting privileges, franchises, and liberties from a long line of ancestors.'

And again :

We wished at the period of the Revolution, and do now wish, to derive all we possess *as an inheritance from our forefathers.* Upon that body and stock of inheritance we have taken care not to inoculate any scion alien to the nature of the original plant. All the reformations we have hitherto made have proceeded upon the principle of reference to antiquity ; and I hope, nay, I am persuaded, that all those which possibly may be made hereafter, will be carefully formed upon analogical precedent, authority, and example.

There is not a syllable in these utterances to which a modern Conservative would not cheer-fully subscribe. But how many leagues away do they carry us from the Liberal-Radicalism now crying out for the abolition of the hereditary branch of the Legislature, because it appeals to the people against the arbitrary will of the dominant faction in a House of Commons which is approaching the term of its constitutional existence !

It may seem at first a more difficult and obscure matter to trace the Conservative movement, distinctive of the eighteenth century, in its literature ; but I think that a little consideration will show it to be very visible in the work of Pope, whom I have chosen as the natural representative of the poetry of the period. If we go back to the poetry of Chaucer, we find very clearly shown in it the beginnings of two separate streams of inspiration, each of which may be traced in a distinct course through the history of our literature, the poetry of Romance and the poetry of Manners. The former had its source in the institutions of Chivalry and in Mediæval Theology. It makes its first appearance in many of the ' Canterbury Tales,' and in poems like ' The Romance of the Rose' and ' The Flower and the Leaf'; it runs strongly through our national ballad poetry ; it attains a

large and noble flow in the 'Faery Queen,' and
then, wasting itself among the refinements and
gallantries of the seventeenth century, may be
said to run underground till it reappears in a
new and unexpected shape in the romantic outburst of the early part of the present century.
The other poetical river has been fed by the life,
action, and manners of the nation. After showing itself in full flow in the admirable Prologue
to the 'Canterbury Tales,' it almost vanishes
from sight for two centuries, when it is suddenly
discovered again in the satires of Hall, and the
comedies and historical plays of Shakespeare,
being carried on through the series of noble
historical portraits in 'Absalom and Achitophel,'
through the moral satires of Pope, the didactic
poems of Johnson and Goldsmith and the Tales
of Crabbe—and in prose through the novels of
Fielding, Smollett, Madame D'Arblay, and Miss
Austen, as late as the generation that produced
'Vanity Fair.'

Now, if we trace the course of the romantic
stream of our poetry, we shall find that it affords
a very remarkable illustration of what has been

already said about the exhaustibility of poetical
materials.   In Chaucer and in our ballad poetry
the volume of imagination is swift and strong ;
but in the poetry of succeeding generations the
impulse is far feebler, and even in the 'Faery
Queen' the reader feels, in spite of the genius of
the poet, that as springs of social action, Medi-
aevalism and Feudalism are losing their force.
The poem is an *allegory* : of dramatic life and
movement it is entirely devoid.   When we come
to the seventeenth century, the source of inspiration seems almost to have run dry.   Here and
there a genuine note of chivalry is heard in
poetry, as in the noble lines of Lovelace :

> I could not love thee, dear, so much,
>   Loved I not Honour more ;

or in the monarchical fancy of the gallant Mont-
rose :

> My dear, my only love, I pray
>   That little world of thee
> Be governed by no other sway
>   Than purest Monarchy.
> For if Confusion have a part,
>   Which virtuous souls abhor,
> And call a synod in thy heart,—
>   I'll never love thee more.

The muse of Herrick, too, seizes with the felicity of real inspiration, and adorns with delightful fancy and humour, old Catholic customs still lingering in the country districts. But these are exceptions. No doubt the poets of the seventeenth century seem in many respects to be more gifted than those of the eighteenth. They try to get farther away from common life ; they show a more curious invention, more ingenious flights of fancy. But they have one fatal defect : take them as a whole, it is impos- sible to read them. Pope, with his usual piercing insight, passes just judgment on the seventeenth- century style in the four verses in which he sums up the merits of Cowley, a really noble and elevated spirit :

> Who now reads Cowley ? If he pleases yet,
> His moral pleases, not his pointed wit.
> Forgot his epic, nay, Pindaric art ;
> But still I love the language of his heart.

There is the truth of the matter. The poetry of the seventeenth century ' wants heart.'[1] Two

---

[1] I am, of course, only speaking of poetry peculiar to the age in which it was written. The poetry of Shakespeare and Milton belongs, in the literal sense, to the seventeenth century,

thoroughly representative passages, showing the manner in which the distinguished poets of the period treated questions of love and religion—their favourite topics—will illustrate what is meant. The first is an extract from Cowley's 'Mistress,' and is called 'Counsel':

> Gently, ah! gently, madam, touch
>   The wound which you yourself have made;
> That pain must needs be very much
>   Which makes me of your hand afraid.
> Cordials of pity give me now,
> For I too weak for purgings grow.
>
> Do but awhile with patience stay
>   (For counsel yet will do no good)
> Till time, and rest, and Heaven allay
>   The violent burnings of my blood.
> For what effect from this can flow,
> To chide men drunk for being so?
>
> Perhaps the physic's good you give,
>   But ne'er to me can useful prove;
> Med'cine may cure but not revive;
>   And I'm not sick, but dead in love.
> In Love's Hell, not his world, am I,
> At once I live, am dead, and die.

but the interest of each is universal; it is not the product of a particular fashion of thought.

Of writing like this we may say with certainty that a lover, sufficiently master of himself to discover so many ingenious fancies, could not have been so ill as he would have us suppose: it is evident that he is not speaking 'the language of the heart.' A still more remarkable specimen of unreality is furnished in Crashaw's poem called 'The Weeper,' on Mary Magdalene, of which the following is an extract:

> Hail, sister springs,
> Parents of silver-footed rills,
> Ever-bubbling things!
> Thawing crystals! snowy hills,
> Still spending, never spent! I mean
> Thy fair eyes, sweet Magdalene.
>
> Heavens thy fair eyes be,
> Heavens of ever-falling stars;
> 'Tis seed-time still with thee,
> And stars thou sowest, whose harvest dares
> Promise the earth to countershine
> Whatever makes Heaven's forehead fine.
>
> Upwards thou dost weep;
> Heaven's bosom drinks the gentle stream;
> Where the milky rivers creep
> Thine floats above, and is the cream.
> Waters above the heavens, what they be
> We are taught best by thy tears and thee.

Mary Magdalene's tears the cream of the Milky Way! In its own age this contortion of fancy was supposed to give proof of a fine poetical genius; but time has taught us that men only write in such a style when they have really nothing to say.

It is indeed evident that unless poetry were recruited by new and abundant waters, it was in danger, in the seventeenth century, of perishing in a marsh. The eighteenth century brought the much-needed supply. Everyone knows that Pope, the most thoroughly representative poet of the age, aimed at 'correctness' in writing, but what the exact quality was that is signified by this word, is by no means generally understood. The common belief, that he sought to attain nothing but a mechanical regularity of versification, is, it is almost unnecessary to say, very wide indeed of the mark. Correctness in metrical composition, as I understand Pope to mean, implies obedience to the *laws* of imaginative thought, and, therefore, not only precision of poetical expression, but justice of poetical conception. In this sense, the fashionable metrical

writing of the seventeenth century was astonish-
ingly incorrect. The poets of the age sought to
invest with fanciful and romantic forms, thoughts
and feelings which had long ceased to move
the imagination of society. Pope perceived this,
and he understood that the quibbles, refinements, and affectations that mark their style,
were the product of imaginative exhaustion. His
criticism on their work is sweeping, but few will
deny it to be just.

> As for the wits of either Charles's days,
> The mob of gentlemen who write with ease,
> Sprat, Carew, Sedley, and a hundred more,
> Like twinkling stars the Miscellanies o'er,
> One simile, that solitary shines
> In the dry desert of a thousand lines,
> Or lengthened thought that gleams through many a
> page,
> Has sanctified whole poems for an age.

Vividly attracted as his own keen and sensi-
tive nature was to the romantic traditions of
English literature, his instinct told him that
these had, for the time at least, lost their
vitality, and that the true course of poetical
development lay in the direction which Dryden

had given to our poetry in ' Absalom and
Achitophel,' and other satiric and didactic compositions. Accordingly, though he had set out
in his own career on the high romantic road, he
takes credit to himself in the full maturity of his
judgment—

> That not in Fancy's maze he wandered long,
> But stooped to Truth and moralized his song.

Addison prided himself on having ' brought
philosophy out of closets and libraries, schools
and colleges, to dwell at clubs and assem-
blies, at tea-tables and in coffee-houses,' and
so Pope, in the true spirit of his ancestor,
Chaucer, taught poetry to come down from her
romantic heights to sympathize with the thoughts
and to elevate the language of men busily
engaged in establishing for themselves new
traditions of political and social order. The
ancient spring of inspiration derived from
national life and manners was renewed, and a
long succession of poets—Thomson, Collins,
Gray, Goldsmith, Johnson, and Crabbe—carried
on the ethical impulse communicated to poetry
by Pope.

There is something equally Conservative in the development of the metrical form in which the new movement clothed itself. No one, I think, can doubt that the colloquial form of the heroic couplet, as it is handled first by Chaucer, and afterwards by Dryden and Pope, affords admirable scope for the expression of those thoughts and feelings which lie properly within the sphere of imagination, and yet not far from the sympathies of common social life. Mr. Arnold, it is true, speaks of the style of eighteenth-century verse as if it were not poetical at all; but it is evident that he has no sympathy with the writers of the period, or he would scarcely have selected one of the poorest couplets Pope ever wrote as a good specimen of his manner.[1] When we think, however, of the distinctness with which writers of varying genius have stamped their own character on the heroic couplet, and the manifold themes of which it is made the vehicle, it seems to me impossible not to regard it as a noble and harmonious

[1] To Hounslow Heath I point, and Banstead Down :
Thence comes your mutton, and these chicks my own.

poetical instrument.   Let us remember how
social were the aims of the great writers of the
age.   'The proprieties and delicacies of the
English,' says Dryden, the immediate father of
the whole line, 'are known to few ; 'tis impossible even for a good wit to understand and
practise them without the help of a liberal education, long reading and digesting of those few
good authors we have among us, the knowledge
of men and manners, the freedom and habitude
of conversation with the best company of both
sexes ; and, in short, without wearing off the
rust he has acquired while laying in a stock of
learning.'   This is an excellent description of
that union of traditional metrical language with
the forms and idioms of modern society which
is the groundwork of the 'poetical diction' of
the eighteenth century ; and it may be supple-
mented by what Pope tells us of the capacities
of the heroic couplet as the vehicle of expression
for such a poem as the 'Essay on Man.'

'This,' says he, 'I might have done in prose : but
I chose verse, and even rhyme, for two reasons.   The
one will appear obvious that principles, maxims, or

precepts so written, both strike the reader more strongly at first, and are more easily retained by him afterwards ; the other may seem odd, but it is true : I found I could express them more shortly this way than in prose itself; and nothing is more certain, than that much of the force, as well as of the grace, of arguments or instructions depends on their conciseness. I was unable to treat this part of the subject more in detail without becoming dry and tedious, or more poetically without sacrificing perspicuity to ornament, without wandering from the precision, or breaking the chain, of reasoning. If any man can unite all these without diminution of any of them, I freely confess he will compass a thing above my capacity.'

It would be impossible to find a passage indicating better than this the general aims of 'correctness' in poetry, namely, a clear perception in the poet of what it is just to express in metre ; a severe exclusion of whatever is not subsidiary to the end in view ; and a determination not to be satisfied with any form of metrical language short of that which is exactly required for the forcible, concise, and harmonious expression of the thought.

These illustrations will, I hope, suggest in outline the nature of the Conservatism of the eighteenth century. So far from being the destructive period that its critics represent it to be, such revolutions of thought and manners as took place in England were accomplished in the sixteenth and seventeenth centuries, and the task of the eighteenth was to recombine the shattered forms of the old national life into a system suited to modern circumstances. The Reformation had destroyed the external unity and absolute authority of the Church; Protestantism generated a multitude of sects, the most extreme of which questioned the foundations of Revelation itself. Such rebellion could no longer be put down by interdict and excommunication, but Butler met it by asserting the supremacy of conscience; and the authority of the continuous Christian tradition. The Revolution of 1688 overthrew the last remains of Monarchical Feudalism, but the aristocracy carried on the best traditions of the old into the new *régime*, and, as has been said, Burke contended with justice that the Revolution gave Englishmen no rights which they did not previously possess under the law of their country.

In the sphere of thought the decay of Mediæval and Feudal influences had exhausted those romantic imaginations on which men's minds had once loved to linger. But to renew the sunken springs, Dryden, Pope, and their followers introduced a generous fountain of fresh inspiration by reviving and developing Chaucer's old satiric methods of portraying life and character. Everywhere we see signs of development with a constant reference at the same time to the most ancient sources of national tradition ; everywhere we are reminded of Wordsworth's lines:

> O joy ! that in our embers
> Is something that doth live,
> That nature yet remembers
> What was so fugitive.

The general result of all this is that, in spite of certain debasing aspects of the eighteenth century, in spite of the wide-spread corruption of Politics, the worldliness of the Church, the realism of Art, it is impossible to study the theology, the oratory, the poetry, the fiction, or the painting of the age, without coming to the conclusion that the ancient spirit of religion and

chivalry is still an operant influence in the English nation. Retrenched of its old splendour and
picturesqueness, subordinated to the growing
element of commerce, it is still there, not merely
as an image flashing before the fancy of the
individual, but as a living power affecting the
faith and manners of the people. For though the
predominant characteristic in eighteenth century
art and literature is its strong perception of the
realities of life, and the vividness with which it
portrays the evil side of human nature, it still
shows itself alive to man's nobler aspirations.
If it has created for us Tom Jones, and Moll
Flanders, and Sporus, and Jonathan Wild, it
has also created Sir Roger de Coverley, the
Man of Ross, the Vicar of Wakefield, Robinson
Crusoe, and Uncle Toby, together with that air
of grace and high-breeding visible in the work of
the great portrait-painters of the age. Its types
are limited and to some extent formal, but as far
as they go they are manly and natural. The
very limitation of its ideal gives an added distinctness to the form in which it is expressed.
Style and method are, in all the arts, the objects

of constant consideration, and Pope's principles of correctness in versification find a counterpart in the rules of painting elaborated by Sir Joshua Reynolds in his 'Discourses' to the Royal Academy. In second-rate artists and writers this strict attention to propriety often leads, no doubt, to stiffness and bombast, but even in them it acts as a salutary preventive against vulgarity, obscurity, and inaccuracy of expression.

WORDSWORTH'S THEORY OF POETRY

III.

WORDSWORTH'S THEORY OF POETRY.

Not that I think the amiable bard of Rydale shows judgment in choosing such subjects as the popular mind cannot
sympathize in. I do not compare myself in point of imagination
with Wordsworth, far from it ; for his is naturally exquisite,
and highly cultivated from constant exercise. . . . But I cry
no roast-meat. There are times a man should remember what
Rousseau used to say : 'Tais-toi, Jean Jacques, car on ne
t'entend pas.' . . . The error is not in you yourself receiving
deep impressions from slight hints, but in supposing that precisely the same sort of impressions must rise in the minds of
men, otherwise of kindred feeling ; or that the commonplace
folk of the world can derive such inductions at any time or under
any circumstances.—*Scott's Journal,* January 1, 1827.

IN the last paper I said that one of the most
marked features of the imaginative genius of
the eighteenth century was its limitation. ·When
the range of thought and feeling in the ' Canterbury Tales,' the ' Faery Queen,' Shakespeare's
plays, and ' Paradise Lost,' is compared with the
subject matter of Dryden and Pope's satires, of
the ' Vanity of Human Wishes,' the ' Elegy in

a Country Churchyard,' the 'Bard,' and the
'Progress of Poesy,' the 'Odes on Liberty,' and
the 'Passions,' the 'Deserted Village,' and the
'Traveller,' everyone must perceive within how
narrow a tract the imagination of the later
period is circumscribed, and that the mines of
poetry which the region contains, though pre-
cious, are not inexhaustible.

The causes of this limitation are readily discoverable by the light of history. Chaucer had
at his disposal all the resources of a social
system highly stimulative to the imagination,
which was not peculiar to one country, but prevailed over the whole of Europe. His successors, after the period of the Reformation,
drew inspiration from still deeper wells. With
minds dramatically excited by the spirit of religious liberty and by ardent patriotism, they
employed the materials afforded by the still vivid
traditions of romantic chivalry, together with
the wealth of ideas and the beauty of form discovered in the revival of classical letters. All
these opposite veins of thought may easily be
detected in the wonderfully compounded work

of Spenser, Shakespeare, and Milton.   But after —
the civil war, religious, political, and social influences turned the imagination of the English
people exclusively upon their own manners.
The old modes of mediæval thought had lost
their power over the mind : the spirit of religious fanaticism which rose up in opposition to
them seemed hostile to every form of creative
art.   In the sphere of politics the ancient
traditions of Monarchical Government were subverted first by the Rebellion and afterwards
by the Revolution.   Everywhere men were asking themselves wherein consisted the foundations
of society, what were the limitations of liberty,
and how they were to recognise the first principles of art.   And, these being the questions
which agitated the mind of the nation above all
others, it was these for which a natural, an irresistible instinct drove men of genius to provide
an answer, either in a philosophic or in an imaginative shape. ⸱The poetry of the eighteenth —
century is the poetry of Society and Manners.

So long as a powerful necessity compelled
men to think and act for themselves, their work

was marked by a vital originality of matter and form, and hence in literature almost everything of imaginative value belonging to what may be broadly called the eighteenth-century movement came into existence between the Restoration and the accession of George III. Dryden, Pope, Thomson, Gray, Johnson, among the poets; Swift, Steele, Addison, Fielding, and Smollett, among the essayists and novelists, had written their all or their best before 1760. The 'Deserted Village,' the 'Traveller,' the 'Vicar of Wakefield,' Crabbe's 'Village,' and Miss Burney's novels, are nearly all the works of genius or talent, peculiarly characteristic of the eighteenth century, produced after this date and before the French Revolution. When the liberties of the nation were finally secured, and the principles of taste and manners advocated in the 'Tatler' and 'Spectator' had met with general acceptance, the creative impulse of the age seems to have ceased. Faction reigned supreme in politics: the Church sank into slumber: artifice in poetry prevailed over thought. We see a Junius succeeding a Swift as a controversialist; a War-

burton following a Butler in theology ; for Pope
as a satirist we have to put up with Churchill ;
and the pure Horatian style of the 'Epistle to
Arbuthnot' is exchanged for the sonorous empti-
ness of the 'Botanic Garden.'

I endeavoured to illustrate the decay of
mediævalism in the seventeenth century by
citing two poems of Cowley and Crashaw ; a
comparison of a passage from Thomson's 'Seasons' with one from Darwin's poem mentioned
just above, will be equally suggestive of the
exhaustion of the inspiring impulse of the eighteenth century. The following extract from —
'Winter' shows the creative spirit of the age
still in its vigour :

What art thou, Frost ? and whence are thy keen stores
Derived, thou secret all-invading power
Whom even the illusive fluid cannot fly ?
Is not thy potent energy, unseen,
Myriads of little salts, or hooked, or shaped
Like double wedges, and diffused immense
Through water, earth, and ether ? hence at eve,
Steamed eager from the red horizon round,
With the fierce rage of Winter, deep suffused,
An icy gale, oft shifting, o'er the pool
Breathes a blue film, and in its mid career

Arrests the bickering stream.   The loosened ice
Let down the flood, and half-dissolved by day
Rustles no more ; but to the sedgy bank
Fast grows, or gathers round the pointed stone,
A crystal pavement by the breath of heaven
Cemented firm ; till, seized from shore to shore,
The whole imprisoned river growls below.
Loud rings the frozen earth, and hard reflects
A double noise ; while at his evening watch
The village dog deters the nightly thief;
The heifer lows ; the distant waterfall
Swells in the breeze ; and with the hasty tread
Of traveller, the hollow-sounding plain
Shakes from afar.   The full ethereal round,
Infinite worlds disclosing to the view,
Shines out intensely keen, and, all one cope
Of starry glitter, glows from pole to pole.

In the following from the 'Botanic Garden '
the same spirit is seen in its decay :

Nymphs, your fine forms with steps impassive mock
Earth's vaulted roofs of adamantine rock;
Round her still centre tread the burning soil,
And watch the billowy lavas as they boil :
Where in basaltic waves imprisoned deep
Reluctant fires in dread suspension sleep ;
Or sphere on sphere in widening waves expand,
And glad with genial warmth the incumbent land.
So when the Mother-bird selects their food
With curious bill, and feeds her callow brood,

Warmth from her tender heart eternal springs,
And pleased she clasps them with extended wings.
You from deep cauldrons and unmeasured caves
Blow flaming airs, or pour vitrescent waves,
O'er shining Ocean ray volcanic light,
Or hurl innocuous embers to the night;
While with loud shouts to Etna Hecla calls
And Andes answers from his beaconed walls:
Sea-wildered crews the mountain-stars admire,
And Beauty beams amid terrific fire.

There is evidently a common element in these two passages. In both (though only in the first few lines of Thomson) the description is, to some extent, scientific, and, as far as it is so, would find a more fitting expression in prose; in both the frequent use of Latin words and the Latin method of linking epithets to substantives is observable; but while Thomson has conceived his subject with enthusiasm, and imparts his enthusiasm to the reader, Darwin thinks throughout in a matter-of-fact spirit, and uses metre merely for decorative purposes; so small is his sense of sublimity that he does not perceive anything ridiculous in imagining one volcano hallooing to another.

Wordsworth lamented that he could not 'hear old Triton blow his wreathèd horn.' Darwin feigns, without a blush, that the operations of Nature are performed by a whole army of nymphs, sylphs, and gnomes, yet in the very same breath describes with scientific coldness the mechanical forces to which they owe their origin!

Poetry of this kind is as sure a symptom as the lethargy of the Church or the prevalence of petty faction in politics that the vigorous and constructive Conservatism of the eighteenth cen- tury, the nature of which I attempted to describe in the last paper, has become crystallized in lifeless forms and conventions. Side by side, however, with these indications of exhaustion in the established order of society there are many signs of the activity and progress of the demo- cratic spirit. Wilkes in the field of politics, Wesley in the sphere of religion, and Burns in the realms of poetry, all, though with very dif- ferent intentions, strike the same note :

The rank is but the guinea stamp,
The man's a man for a' that.

At the same time, the centrifugal movement of the individual away from society, which appears to be a natural accompaniment of democracy, and which manifests itself in France in the philosophy of Rousseau, is seen in the blended Methodism and love of Nature in Cowper's poetry. Many influences thus combined to prepare the way for that strife between the spirit of aristocracy and the spirit of democracy both in politics and art, the outbreak of which was hastened by the incidents of the French Revolution.

In Literature the battle began with the controversy excited by the publication of Wordsworth's ' Lyrical Ballads.' To prevent the historical accuracy of this assertion being questioned, let me quote what Coleridge, who had every means of knowing, says in his 'Biographia Literaria,' about the origin of the volume, and the influence it exerted on the taste of the times :

The thought suggested itself (to which of us I do not recollect) that a series of poems might be composed of two sorts. In the one, the incidents and agents were to be, in part at least, supernatural ; and the excellence aimed at was to consist in the interesting of the affections by the dramatic truth of such emotions as would naturally accompany such situations, supposing them real. . . . For the second class, subjects were to be chosen from ordinary life; the characters and incidents were to be such as will be found in every village and its vicinity where there is a meditative and feeling mind to seek after them, or to notice them when they present themselves. In this idea originated the plan of the ' Lyrical Ballads'; in which it was agreed that my endeavours should be directed to persons and characters supernatural, or at least romantic; yet, so as to transfer from our inward nature a human interest and a semblance of truth sufficient to procure for these shadows of imagination that willing suspension of disbelief for the moment, which constitutes poetic faith. Mr. Wordsworth, on the other hand, was to propose to himself, as his object, to give the charm of novelty to things of every day, and to excite a feeling analogous to the supernatural, by awakening the mind's attention from the lethargy of custom, and directing it to the loveliness and the wonder of the world before us; an inexhaustible treasure, but for which, in consequence of the film of familiarity and selfish solicitude, we have eyes yet see not, ears that hear not, and hearts that neither feel nor understand.

Coleridge accordingly wrote the 'Ancient Mariner' with a view to its insertion in a volume of poems composed upon this double principle, but it was eventually determined that Words-

worth's poems should be published by themselves, and they therefore appeared under the
title of ' Lyrical Ballads.'

' To the second edition,' says Coleridge, ' he added
a preface of considerable length, in which, notwith-
standing some passages of apparently a contrary import,
he was understood to contend for the extension of this
style to poetry of all kinds, and to reject as vicious and
indefensible all phrases and forms of style that were
not included in what he (unfortunately, I think, adopt-
ing an equivocal expression) called the language of real
life. From this preface, prefixed to poems in which
it was impossible to deny the presence of real genius,
however mistaken its direction might be deemed, arose
the whole long-continued controversy. For from the
conjunction of perceived power with supposed heresy, I
explain the inveteracy, and in some instances, I grieve
to say, the acrimonious passions, with which the controversy has been conducted by the assailants.'

Here, then, is an announcement made on the
very highest authority that ' Lyrical Ballads '
sounded the first note of the ' new departure '
which I have called ' The Liberal Movement in
English Literature.' I have not selected this
title without deliberate purpose. Before Wordsworth's time it had been the acknowledged

function of the poet to give definite form and coherence to the ideal conceptions which floated vaguely and without consistency in the mind of society at large. But, as we see from the foregoing passages, Wordsworth held that the object of poetry was to 'awaken the mind from the lethargy of custom,' and to reveal to it truths which it could not perceive without the mediation of the 'sacer vates.' The poet, as he describes him in his preface, is a man exalted, not only in his powers of conception and expression, but in his moral faculties, far above his fellows, 'rejoicing more than other men in the spirit of life that is in him,' and therefore qualified to act as the interpreter to them of the mysteries of Nature. To suppose that a being of this kind should submit himself to ancient traditions and conventions of the art, would be unreasonable ; rather it is for society to wait for such oracles as may be vouchsafed to it by the poet, and be thankful. Hence the main contention of Wordsworth in his theory of poetry is to assert the right of the individual poet, by virtue of his superior endowments, to exercise his imagination as he chooses, without reference to the imagination of society.

In this contention there is an element of truth :

Pictoribus atque poetis
Quidlibet audendi semper fuit *æqua* potestas.

Wordsworth gave expression, with greater power and feeling than any other poet, to certain universal perceptions in the English mind, to which society during the prevalence of urban habits in the eighteenth century had become insensible. He was therefore fully justified in asserting his own liberty against the conventional canons of criticism, in so far as these helped to dull the sense of natural beauty. But he went much further, and, in the preface of which Coleridge speaks, endeavoured to establish a code of abstract principles by which the value of all poetry might be tested. As his reasoning largely influenced his own practice and the subsequent course of English poetry, I shall attempt in this paper to examine how far it is in harmony with the fundamental principles of the art.

In the first place, however, in order to test

the character of Wordsworth's theory, it is important to recall the circumstances under which
it was evolved. What roused him into rebellion
against the canons of criticism generally accepted
in his day was undoubtedly the style of 'poetical
diction' then considered to be the indispensable dress of all true poetry. He saw that the
mode of expression employed by Darwin in his
' Botanic Garden' was widely admired, yet the
colouring of this poem appeared to him, as to
most men of just and manly taste, to be false
and gaudy. Looking back to the earlier poets
of the century, he found that germs of the same
diction were discoverable in them ; as, for instance, in Pope's 'Messiah,' in some of Johnson's
verses, and, indeed, in almost all the characteristic poems of the age. Instead of reasoning that the defect might spring from the
natural corruption of some true principle of art,
he inferred from his observations that it arose
from a false ideal of composition, consciously
adopted by the poets. And, as so often happens
to men of a combative turn, his violent sentiments of dislike led him to argue that all true

poetry must be composed on a system exactly opposite to the style which he condemned. Darwin seemed to withdraw himself deliberately from the common sympathies of humanity; true poetry, Wordsworth argued, should, therefore, look for its subjects in the objects and incidents of every-day life. Darwin's diction was artificial in the highest degree ; it follows that the genuine language of poetry should resemble as closely as possible the language of the peasantry. Darwin wrote in a style which was the antithesis of prose; hence Wordsworth would have us believe that there is no essential difference between the language of prose and verse, and that the fact of poems being written in metre is merely to be regarded as an accident of the art.

In considering the justice of these views I suppose that everybody would be on Wordsworth's side as far as he was opposed to Darwin. Almost any species of verse-writing, if it show sincere feeling, is better than a style inspired simply by pomposity and affectation. To enlarge the spiritual experience of an artificialised society by imaginative representations of the beauty of

Nature and common life was a just and noble aim for poetry, but it was not a new one. To take only a few examples which at once occur, Virgil had written the 'Georgics,' Thomson the 'Seasons,' Gray the 'Elegy in a Country Churchyard,' Goldsmith the 'Deserted Village.' All these were 'subjects chosen from ordinary life,' just as much as 'Peter Bell,' the 'Idiot Boy,' 'Alice Fell,' 'Beggars,' or the 'Sailor's Mother.' The real innovation introduced by Wordsworth was one of poetical *form*, and lay in the manner in which he employed the imagination to present objects to the reader with a view of producing pleasure. On this point it is ·best to let him speak for himself.

The principal object, then, proposed in these poems was to choose incidents and situations from common life, and to relate or describe them, throughout, as far as was possible in a selection of language really used by men, and at the same time to throw over them a certain colouring of imagination, whereby ordinary things should be presented to the mind in an unusual aspect; and further and above all, to make these incidents and situations interesting by tracing in them, truly though not ostentatiously, the primary laws of our nature: chiefly as far as regards the manner in which we associate ideas in a state of excitement.

Here we have a compendious statement of the radical difference between the practice of Wordsworth and that of preceding poets who had dealt with 'subjects chosen from ordinary life.' Neither Virgil, nor Thomson, nor Gray, nor Goldsmith, had attempted to present the objects they described 'to the mind in an unusual aspect.' They trusted to produce pleasure by associating qualities inherent in these objects with other beautiful ideas, naturally connected with them, and expressed in a noble and harmonious form of verse. With them the subject matter of poetry lay in associations of ideas existing in their readers' imaginations equally with their own. With Wordsworth, on the other hand, all depended on the perception of the poet himself, and his power to displace and recombine the ordinary association of ideas so as to 'present them to the mind in an unusual aspect.' And, of course, if he had been able to produce great and permanent pleasure on the principles he lays down, all objection would have been silenced, and the only thing to be said would be that he had discovered principles of art which had hitherto been unknown or neglected.

Fortunately Wordsworth's works comprise poems composed on the old principles as well as on his own, so that we are able to compare the two systems at work in the same mind, with the result that his finest poetical effects are seen to be produced when he is most flagrantly violating his own rules.

Comparing 'Lucy Gray,' for instance, which everyone will admit to be a perfect work of art, with 'The Idle Shepherds,' which is one degree less successful, and, again, with 'The Sailor's Mother,' or ' Peter Bell,' which are not successful at all, it will be found that the pleasure excited arises from the simple association, in a beautiful metrical form, of ideas that naturally affect the feelings, and that this pleasure diminishes in proportion as the poet intrudes his personality upon the reader, and endeavours to eke out the tenuity of his subject by analysis and reflection. In ' Lucy Gray ' the narrative is of the most direct kind ; there is no sort of mental analysis employed ; the exquisite charm of the workman- ship comes from the simple description of pa- thetic objects, and the admirable and unexpected

turns of the ballad style in which the story is
told. In 'The Idle Shepherd Boys' the real
beauty of the poem consists in the delightful
landscape presented to the imagination in the
first three stanzas, particularly the third :

> Along the river's stony marge
>   The sand-lark chants a joyous song ;
> The thrush is busy in the wood,
>   And carols loud and strong.
> A thousand lambs are on the rocks,
>   All newly born! both earth and sky
> Keep jubilee, and more than all
>   Those boys with their green coronal ;
> They never hear the cry,
>   That plaintive cry which up the hill
>   Comes from the depth of Dungeon-Ghyll.

There is no analysis here ; nothing but a
musical combination of images that produce
immediate pleasure in the mind and heart ; such
incidents as the narrative contains are redeemed
from meanness only by falling in naturally with
the beautiful pastoral scene called up before the
imagination ; and, even as it is, several stanzas
are so prosaically expressed as to jar on the
effect of the melodious opening. But take ' The
Sailor's Mother,' and it will be seen that the

occasional flatness of expression, which mars the completeness of 'The Idle Shepherd Boys,' prevails from the first line to the last, with the exception perhaps of the second stanza.

> One morning (raw it was and wet,
> A foggy day in winter-time),
> A woman in the road I met,
> Not old, though something past her prime;
> Majestic in her person, tall and straight;
> And like a Roman matron's was her mien and gait.
>
> The ancient spirit is not dead;
> Old times, thought I, are breathing there;
> Proud was I that my country bred
> Such strength, a dignity so fair:
> She begged an alms like one in poor estate;
> I looked at her again, nor did my pride abate.
>
> When from these lofty thoughts I woke,
> 'What is it,' said I, 'that you bear,
> Beneath the covert of your cloak,
> Protected from the cold damp air?'
> She answered soon as she the question heard,
> 'A simple burden, Sir, a little singing-bird.'
>
> And thus continuing, she said,
> 'I had a son, who many a day
> Sailed on the seas, but he is dead;
> In Denmark he was cast away:
> And I have travelled weary miles to see
> If aught which he had owned might still remain for me.

' The bird and cage they both were his ;
'Twas my son's bird ; and neat and trim
He kept it : many voyages
The singing-bird had gone with him ;
When last he sailed he left the bird behind,
From bodings, as might be, that hung upon his mind.

' He to a fellow-lodger's care
Had left it to be watched and fed,
And pipe its song in safety ; there
I found it when my son was dead ;
And now, God help me for my little wit !
I bear it with me, Sir, he took so much delight in it.'

I suppose that there is scarcely anyone largely acquainted with poetry who would not say, on first reading it, that there was an incongruity between the matter of this poem and the metrical form in which it is expressed. But, ' Hold, hold ! ' we may imagine Wordsworth to reply ; ' you are wrong to judge in this way ; for, if you think about the poem, you will see that the simple incident it records puts you upon a train of the most suggestive thought respecting the unseen spiritual world and the nature of the affections. The imagination has therefore discharged its functions properly. As I say in " Peter Bell," another poem of the same kind :

' The dragon's wing, the magic ring
   I shall not covet for my dower,
If I along that lowly way,
With sympathetic heart may stray,
   And with a soul of power.
These given, what more need I desire
   To stir, to soothe, or elevate ?
What nobler marvels than the mind
May in life's daily prospect find,
   May find or there create ?

' And that the imagination has this creative
power of " conferring additional properties upon
an object, or abstracting from it some of those
which it actually possesses," [1] I can prove to you
by the language which poets use. For instance,
take the use of the word " hang " in poetry :

' Non ego vos posthac viridi projectus in antro
   Dumosâ *pendere* procul de rupe videbo.—VIRGIL.

' Half way down
' *Hangs* one who gathers samphire.—SHAKESPEARE.

' As when, far off at sea, a fleet descried
   Hangs in the clouds.—MILTON.

' In all these passages it is obvious that the
quality of hanging does not really inhere in the
object, but is conferred on it by the imagination,

[1] Preface to the edition of 1815.

which I have, therefore, properly employed analytically, though in a different direction, to suggest a train of feeling connected with the incident of the sailor's mother.   And as to your complaint that there is an incongruity between the nature of the thought and the mode of its expression, that arises from the false ideas of poetical diction which you have derived from your study of the poets.   True, I might have said what I had to say in prose, but " why should I be condemned for attempting to add to such description the charm which, by the consent of all nations, is acknowledged to exist in metrical language? " ' [1]

To this, however, the reader may reply confidently : ' Your reasoning, no doubt, is very fine and ingenious, but the matter is one not for argument but for perception.   If the association of ideas is so strongly rooted in my mind that no exercise of your imagination is able to overcome the repugnance I feel at finding a subject which seems to me naturally prosaic treated in metre ; while, on the other hand, you are often

[1] I have endeavoured in the above passage to condense the argument of Wordsworth's Prefaces to the Editions of his Poems published in 1805 and 1815.

able to produce the highest pleasure in my mind
by your metrical treatment of more imaginative
subjects ; and if, besides, this latter is evidently
the way in which all great standard poets produce pleasure, is it not possible. that on this
occasion you have been employing your imagination improperly?' Wordsworth seems to have
thought that a poet could always write poetically
by the mere exercise of his will. But the evidence
of the greatest creative poetry proves that the
imagination must, in the first place, be over-
mastered and possessed by an impulse from
without, and Scott describes universal experience
in the following passage of one of his letters :

Nobody knows that has not tried the feverish trade
of poetry, how much it depends upon mood and whim :
I don't wonder that in dismissing all the other deities
of Paganism the Muse should have been retained by
common consent, for, in sober reality, writing good
verses seems to depend upon something separate from the
volition of the author. I sometimes think my fingers
set up for themselves, independent of my head ; for
twenty times I have begun a thing on a certain plan,
and never in my life adhered to it (in a work of imagination, that is) for half an hour together.

This is a vivid description of the working of

the ' estro ' or ' afflatus,' without which Byron so often declares in his letters that he cannot write well in metre ; of that ' Eros ' which Plato tells us, in the ' Symposium,' seizes and inflames the imagination of the poet. Nor is it the first act of poetical conception alone which is performed in this manner ; in all the imaginative arts the form of the work produced is largely determined by fortune and inspiration. I remember, among the studies of the painters preserved at Florence, a rough design of (I think) Parmigiano, in which the artist, desiring to represent the image of terror on a man's face, has left on the paper three or four unsuccessful attempts, showing that he only attained by degrees the expression of the exact idea that he had conceived. Milton, we know, had originally resolved to cast ' Paradise Lost ' into the form of a drama. Nor can anything be more suggestive than the account which Lockhart gives of the growth of ' The Lay of the Last Minstrel.'

Sir John Stoddart's casual recitation, a year or two before, of Coleridge's unpublished ' Christabel,' had fixed the music of that noble fragment in his memory ;

and it occurs to him that by throwing the story of
Gilpin Horner into somewhat of a similar cadence, he
might produce such an echo of the later metrical
romance as would serve to connect his 'Conclusion'
of. the primitive Sir Tristram with his imitations of the
popular ballad in 'The Grey Brother' and 'Eve of St.
John.' A single scene of feudal festivity in the hall
of Branksome, disturbed by some pranks of a non-
descript goblin, was probably all that he contemplated;
but his accidental confinement in the midst of a volun-
teer camp gave him leisure to meditate his theme to
the sound of a bugle; and suddenly there flashes on
him the idea of extending his simple outline, so as to
embrace a vivid panorama of that old border-life of war
and tumult, and all earnest passions, with which his
researches on the 'Minstrelsy' had by degrees fed his
imagination, until every the minutest feature had been
taken home and realised with unconscious intenseness
of sympathy; so that he had won for himself in the
past another world, hardly less complete or familiar than
the present. Erskine or Cranstoun suggests that he
would do well to divide the poem into cantos, and
prefix to each of them a motto explanatory of the
action, after the fashion of Spenser in the 'Faery
Queen.' He pauses for a moment—and the happiest
conception of the framework of a picturesque narrative
that ever occurred to any poet—one that Homer might
have envied—the creation of the ancient harper starts
to life. By such steps did the 'Lay of the Last
Minstrel' grow out of the 'Minstrelsy of the Scottish
Border.'

When the imagination is in this exhilarating atmosphere, as it requires some larger and bolder means of expression than is afforded to it by prose, it seizes on metre as naturally as a bird takes to the air, and employs the vivid metaphorical forms of language which led Wordsworth into his fallacious views about its methods of analysis and transmutation.   Unless a man's imagination is inspired from without, and his design is conceived when the mind is in that excited state, he will do wrong to choose metre as his instrument of expression.   Hence it is — that so much of Wordsworth's verse seems to be written in violation of the laws of poetical art. In the 'Excursion,' for instance, though it is full of the most noble incidental passages, evidently written under the influence of direct inspiration, yet, as the design of the whole poem is certainly formed by a process of cool meditation, we are constantly haunted by a sense that we are in an atmosphere unfavourable to the movement of metre.   I have opened the 'Excursion' at random, and I light at once on the following passage :

> Forgive me if say
> . That an appearance which hath raised your minds
> To an exalted pitch (the self-same cause
> Different effect producing), is for me
> Fraught rather with depression than delight;
> Though shame it were could I not look around
> By the reflection of your pleasure, pleased.[1]

It is plain that these thoughts would be much more fittingly expressed in prose than they are in verse. Nor is this simply because the substance of them is philosophical and didactic, for so is the substance of the ' Essay on Man,' and yet the thought in the ' Essay on Man ' is (for the reason given by Pope, and quoted in my last paper) expressed better in metre than it could be in prose. The reason is, as everyone can see, that the writer of the above passage is not in a mood for the expression of thoughts for which metre is adapted. Even in pathetic narrative poems like ' Michael,' the prosy effect is often reproduced.

> A good report did from their kinsman come
> Of Luke and his well-doing; and the boy
> Wrote loving letters, full of wondrous news,
> Which, as the housewife phrased it, were throughout,

---

[1] *Excursion,* Book iii.

' The prettiest letters that were ever seen.'
Both parents read them with rejoicing hearts.
So many months passed on : and once again
The shepherd went about his daily work
With confident and cheerful thoughts ; and now
Sometimes when he could find a leisure hour,
He to that valley took his way, and there
Wrought at the sheep-fold. Meanwhile Luke began
To slacken in his duty ; and at length
He in the dissolute city gave himself
To evil courses ; ignominy and shame
Fell on him, so that he was driven at last
To seek a hiding-place beyond the seas.

Is any charm superadded to this narrative
by the employment of metre ? I imagine that
the story told as Mrs. Gaskell, for instance,
might have told it in prose, would have been
more pathetic, simply from the fact that the
artifice would have been less felt. But now
compare with this the noble opening stanza in
' Laodamia ' :

With sacrifice before the rising morn
Vows have I made by fruitless hope inspired ;
And from the infernal gods, 'mid shades forlorn
Of night, my slaughtered Lord have I required :
Celestial pity I again implore,
Restore him to my sight—great Jove, restore !

How could this passionate invocation have
been given in prose ?   And why could it not ?
Because the imagination is moving in a world
of its own : it is exhilarated by the atmosphere ;
and it seeks for unusual forms in which to express its enthusiasm.   Or take, again, the magnificent lines on ' Yew Trees ' :

There is a Yew-Tree, pride of Lorton Vale,
Which to this day stands single in the midst
Of its own darkness, as it stood of yore :
Not loth to furnish weapons for the bands
Of Umfraville or Percy ere they marched
To Scotland's heaths ; or those that crossed the sea
And drew their sounding bows at Azincour,
Perhaps at early Crecy or Poictiers.
Of vast circumference and gloom profound
This solitary tree ! a living thing
Produced too slowly ever to decay ;
Of form and aspect too magnificent
To be destroyed.   But worthier still of note
Are those fraternal four of Borrowdale,
Joined in one solemn and capacious grove ;
Huge trunks, and each particular trunk a growth
Of intertwisted fibres serpentine,
Up-coiling and inveterately convolved ;
Nor uninformed with Phantasy, and looks
That threaten the profane ; a pillared shade
Upon whose grassless floor of red-brown hue,

By sheddings from the pining umbrage tinged
Perennially—beneath whose sable roof
Of boughs, as if for festal purpose decked
With unrejoicing berries—ghostly Shapes
May meet at noontide; Fear and trembling Hope,
Silence and Foresight; Death the Skeleton,
And Time the Shadow; there to celebrate,
As in a natural temple scattered o'er
With altars undisturbed of mossy stone,
United worship; or in mute repose
To lie and listen to the mountain flood
Murmuring from Glaramara's inmost caves.

These lines, read in the light of his theory, seem to me to suggest vividly the source of Wordsworth's greatness and weakness as a poet. His formulated creed was that the imaginative mind, by an act of meditation, can make any subject, however trivial, poetical. But his practice proves that a poet only writes poetically when he is under an overmastering external influence, directing his mind to a subject congenial to his powers. The yew-trees that inspired the above noble verses were certainly not such an object ' as will be found in every village,' nor could any ' meditative and feeling mind ' have given such splendid utter-

ance to the emotions they excite. No : the
forces that made Wordsworth a poet were far
different from those conscious reasonings on
Man and Society of which he gives an account
in the ' Prelude ' : his inspiration sprang from
mysterious sources which, as he shows us in the
first book of his curious metrical autobiography,
had been *unconsciously* pouring images into his
mind from his earliest childhood. The religious
ideas excited by the unseen life of Nature, the
sublime outlines of mountain and valley, the
blending of wood and water, the changes of
light and shadow, the spirit-like movements of
birds, the simple manners and passions of the
peasantry, mingled so suggestively with the
historic monuments of the past, these were the
romantic fountains at which other poets had
drunk in passing, but to which Wordsworth
was constantly returning for deep draughts of
inspiration.

When he is completely under the direction
of his Muse he illustrates as happily as any man
the truth of Horace's observation,

Cui lecta potenter erit res,
Nec facundia deseret hunc, nec lucidus ordo.

His theory, on the other hand, shows him to have been under the impression that he merely *chose* to express himself in verse in order to give a certain additional charm to his thought, and that he purposely selected a style of diction approaching as nearly as possible to the manner of prose. And, no doubt, this sufficiently describes his case in his uninspired moments, which are frequent enough. But when the 'afflatus' is upon him it turns his genius naturally into ancient traditional channels of expression, and prompts him, like all great poets, to *develop* metrical movements which certainly did not originate with himself. His use of the Ballad form, for instance, was largely due to the publication of Percy's 'Ancient Reliques'; Bowles had previously revived and popularised the use of the Sonnet; Wordsworth's style of writing blank verse is unmistakably his own, but no one can read his lines on 'Yew-Trees' without perceiving how greatly he was influenced by Milton, while at other times the example of Cowper seems not to have been without its effect.

Again, Wordsworth in his theory lays the foundations of poetry in the perceptions of the individual poet. But all his best work is based on universal associations, and its merit comes from the beauty of the form in which a general feeling is expressed. If one recalls those poems of his which have taken the deepest root in the national mind, the 'Ode on Immortality,' 'Lucy Gray,' 'the 'Song at the Feast of Brougham Castle,' 'The Boy of Windermere,' numerous sonnets, of which 'Westminster Bridge' and · 'It is a beauteous evening calm and free,' are types ; and such characteristic lines as—

> The light that never was on sea or land,
> The consecration and the poet's dream ;

or—

> Love had he found in huts where poor men lie ;
> His daily teachers had been woods and rills ;
> The silence that is in the starry sky ;
> The sleep that is among the lonely hills—

one is aware immediately that the poet has put · into the best possible form of musical words a feeling which had hitherto been lying chaotically indistinct in the heart. Wordsworth's genius moved with a large and expanding power in the midst of a society accustomed to town life, limited, refined, highly artificialised, and exclusively occupied with the contemplation of its own manners ; he extended men's social ideas by showing with unsurpassed power what beautiful, pathetic, and sublime associations were connected with the natural life of their country. Hence, in so far as he was genuinely a poet, the Liberalising influence he exerted on literature was, in the deepest and truest sense, Conservative.

On the other hand, his solitary habits led him in theory, and often in practice, to principles which, as far as the art of poetry is concerned, may be called thoroughly Jacobinical. Perpetually occupied with the contemplation of his own mind, he forgot that it was said that those who measure themselves by themselves and compare themselves with themselves are not wise. Incessant introspection increased his intellectual arrogance and impaired his judgment. He could not appreciate the genius of others who had written as well of men and

society as he had written of external nature ;
and when Scott sent him his edition of Dryden,
he avows in his letter of acknowledgment that
he considers the latter to be no poet. Everything, however, that passed into his own mind
appeared to him to become possible material for
poetry. He never said to himself, ' Tais-toi,
Jean Jacques, on ne t'entend pas ; ' but imagined
that each experience interesting to himself would
be of equal interest to the world. This over-
weening estimate of his own genius caused him
to undervalue tradition, and, as far as he could,
to obliterate and level the distinctions which the
practice of the best poets had created between
the style of poetry and prose.

Summarised briefly, what I have endeavoured .
to establish in the present and in the preceding
papers comes to this. Reason shows that
there are certain subjects as incapable of just
expression in metrical language as others are
by the arts of painting, sculpture, and music.
Experience proves that the sources of all great
poetry are to be sought far back in the annals,
traditions, and religion of the people ; and the

history of English literature further indicates
that the stream of national creative imagination
flows from two main sources, the poetry of
romance and the poetry of manners. Wordsworth's great and truly Conservative achievement consists in his having given to the poetry
of romance, the existence of which during the
eighteenth century had come to be almost forgotten, a large and surprising development. But
in his hatred of the canons of criticism, which
had prevailed through that century, he committed himself in theory, and often in practice,
to principles revolutionary of the whole character
of the art.

In brief, the great changes in English
poetry which he initiated in opposition to the
rules of art prevailing in the eighteenth century
were these : he taught that poetry was the ideal
of the Individual not the ideal of Society ; he
therefore removed the art from the sphere of
social action to that of individual reflection and
mental analysis ; and he insisted that as any
object may become a fit subject for poetry,
provided that it be sufficiently modified by the

imagination of the poet, so the language in which
the subject is presented should not be regulated
by the mixed literary and social standard sanc-
tioned by tradition, but should as closely as possible follow the diction of real life, particularly
that of the peasantry. It is not difficult to see
that if Wordsworth's views on these points be
correct, then the practice of the great classical
poets in all nations must have been completely
wrong.

THE REVIVAL OF ROMANCE:

SCOTT, BYRON, SHELLEY

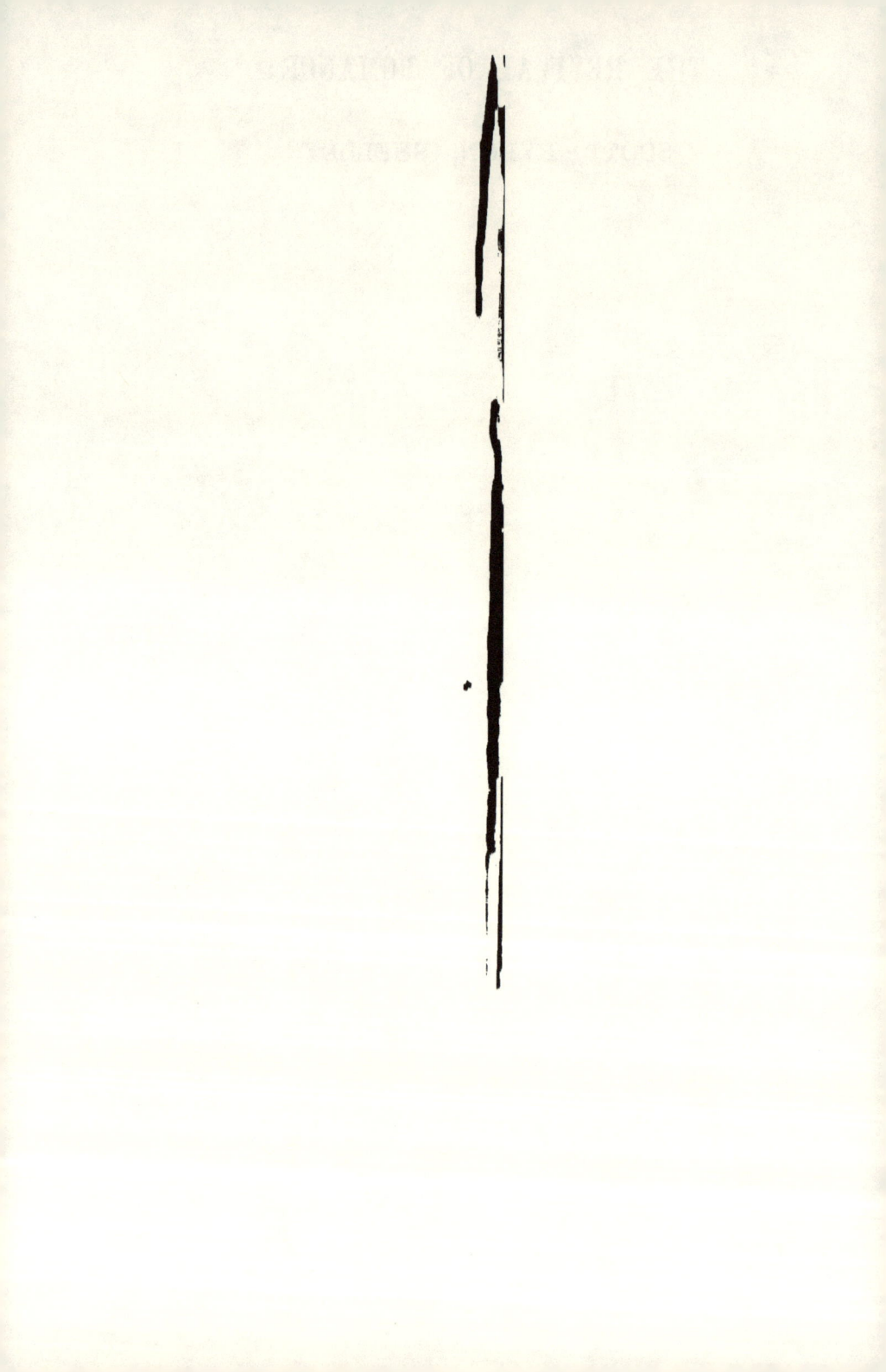

*THE REVIVAL OF ROMANCE: SCOTT, BYRON,
SHELLEY.*

By his habits of severe and lonely meditation
and of philosophical analysis, Wordsworth was
well qualified to become the apostle of the new
movement which, as Coleridge tells us, was in-
augurated by the publication of ' Lyrical Ballads.'   On the other hand, his remoteness from
social life and action, and the studied prosiness
of much of his versification, prevented his poems
from making an immediate impression on the
taste of an age imbued with reverence for the
classical models of poetical diction.   The shock
which was felt by the imagination of society at
the end of the eighteenth century, and which
produced the vast development or the complete
subversion of so many deeply-rooted feelings and
ideas, exhibits its effects most distinctly in the

work of those great writers whose names stand
at the head of this paper. In this paper I
shall endeavour to trace the rise of the new
school of Romance in English Literature, its connection with the classical school of the eighteenth
century, and the various channels into which it
was directed by Scott, Byron, and Shelley.

The genius of the eighteenth century in England was hostile to Romance in all its shapes.
Almost every writer of the period is a disciple
of Cervantes. The early part of the century
produced the most exquisite and delicate satire
on feudal Toryism in the person of Sir Roger
de Coverley. Chivalrous feeling could scarcely
breathe in the same atmosphere as Gulliver.
Pope, whose mind was very open to the influences of the old-fashioned sentimental gallantry, boasts, nevertheless, that he soon aban-
doned 'Fancy's maze' to 'moralize his song.'
Fielding found the inspiring motive for his own
novels in his contempt for the sentimentalities
of Richardson. Goldsmith, the finest artist of
the school of Addison, shows himself utterly insensible to the influences that were operating on

the genius of Gray. As for Johnson, perhaps the most thoroughly representative man of letters in the century, his opinion on the matter, manifested in almost every page of Boswell's Life, is well illustrated by his recorded criticism on 'La Nouvelle Héloïse.' '*Boswell*.—" I don't deny, Sir, but that his novel may perhaps do harm ; but I cannot think his intention was bad." *Johnson*.—" Sir, that will not do. We cannot prove any man's intention to be bad. You may shoot a man through the head, and say you intended to miss him, but the judge will order you to be hanged. An alleged want of intention, when evil is committed, will not be allowed in a court of justice. Rousseau, Sir, is a very bad man. I would sooner sign a sentence for his transportation than that of any felon that has gone from the Old Bailey these many years. Yes, I should like to have him work in the plantations." '

It is to be hoped that we have so far outlived the sickly dreaminess of the revolutionary period as to own that the manly Doctor was in the main right. He saw that Rousseau's view

I

of life, however attractive to the imagination, *had no basis of reality*, and that without the established order which this sense of reality implies, civilised society cannot exist. The view that Johnson propounded in his direct ' knock-down ' style was shared by all his great contemporaries. The sons, grandsons, or great grandsons of men who had learned from many disappointments to distrust all fanaticism and enthusiasm, they had seen the old principle of feudal monarchy, upheld by Plantagenets and Tudors, dwindle in the feeble keeping of the Stuarts ; the knightly rule of devotion to women travestied by the adoration of such ' mistresses ' as sprang out of the brain of Cowley or Waller ; the lofty and beautiful imagery of the ' Faery Queen ' replaced by the gallantries of a Suckling, a Rochester, and even of an Afra Behn. The Feudal Ideal was, for the time, extinct as a social force. Yet the void thus created was far from being filled by the principle of Puritanical or Deistic democracy. Sour, gloomy, bigoted, tyrannical, or at best dry and pedantic, the reign of the Saints and of the Philosophers was scarcely more tolerable than that of the Atheists. In this arid social desert, where could men who desired a manly and moderate Freedom find a national standard of political order, good breeding, and good taste, which should be in touch with the traditions of the past, and yet conformable to the growth of modern society? This was the problem which the Conservatism of the eighteenth century had to solve, and I confess that when I think, on the one hand, of the anarchy of extremes into which the imagination of the English people had fallen after the Restoration, and, on the other, of the masculine, unaffected, straightforward habits of thought, as well as of the finish and perfection of style, achieved by the great writers of the post-Revolution period, no words seem to me too strong to express the debt of gratitude which the nation owes to Steele, Addison, Pope, Gray, Fielding, Johnson, and Goldsmith. Critics of the present day are apt to talk in a superior and patronising tone of the eighteenth century. They say it is 'unpoetical,' unromantic, sceptical, utilitarian. But surely the wonder is that, after the Revolution through which it had passed, English society was able to construct an ideal life of any kind. The best answer to those who disparage the eighteenth century is the question, ' What should we have done without it ? '

The attitude of the great representative writers of the eighteenth century towards Romance is very intelligible. It expresses the contempt of men trained in the stern school of experience for the Quixotism of visionaries who think it an easy thing to reconstitute society after ideas existing only in their own mind. Having themselves struggled manfully with all kinds of physical and moral ill, they know the extreme difficulty of establishing a social *modus vivendi*. Hence their distrust of mere sentiment and enthusiasm. Undoubtedly, however, their ingrained pessimism exercises a contracting influence on their understandings. A keen sense of reality in the external order of nature and of human society causes them to disregard the spiritual wants of the individual. No one knew better than Johnson the reality of the inward life, but he looked with apprehension on its consequences when converted into action. All attempts to change the established order in the fond hope of reaching an ideal state of things seemed to him equally blameworthy; hence he comprehended in a common anathema Wilkes and Washington in politics, Behmen and Wesley in religion, Macpherson and Gray in literature.

For the same reason he overlooked the obvious danger to society that the *modus vivendi* might come to be mistaken for the life itself—which was, indeed, precisely what happened in the last part of the eighteenth century. There was real value in the form and order constituted by the statesmen, artists, and men of letters who grappled with the confusion and anarchy produced by the downfall of the old *régime*, but they were valuable only because they were an outward expression of vigorous life and thought. When the new order was once established, natural indolence prompted society to be content with mere rules, without looking for the living spirit of things, and a period of torpor accord-

ingly supervened in Church, State, and Literature. Anglican theology lapsed into formalism ;
the Whiggery of the Revolution declined into
petty factiousness under the Pelhams and many
of their successors ; while the standard of ' correctness,' which had once been represented by
the energy and conciseness of Pope, was con-
founded—as, indeed, Macaulay himself confounds it—with the mechanical regularity of
Hayley and Pye.

Apprehending that the new literary movement was based, as he says of Methodism, on ' a
principle utterly incompatible with social or civil
security,' Johnson miscalculated the true nature
of the tendencies of taste disclosed in the
poetry of Gray and Collins, and in the popular
favour shown to Percy's ' Reliques.' He had
taken an active part as a combatant in the
political and literary struggle which ended in
the re-establishment of order, and, having fought
his way through all kinds of obstacles to a
dictatorship in the world of letters, he regarded
the classical Settlement as final. But now that
the battle was done, others were less content

with the fruits of victory. They were at leisure to contemplate critically what had been accomplished, and as the fervid atmosphere, which had been so favourable to the production of satirical and controversial writing, cooled, a feeling of *ennui*, and of the melancholy which always accompanies it, gradually spread through society. Comparing the new social idea with the old, men could not fail to see that the former had many imperfections and the latter many advantages. The dry light of judgment and common sense approved of the existing standard as the best that circumstances permitted, but, judged side by side with the comprehensiveness of the Catholic Church and the Feudal System, it appeared colourless and uninspiring. Conscious of this deficiency, the creative faculty of the age accepted the principles of the established *régime* as constituting the code of practical conduct, but set itself eagerly to search for fresh materials wherewith to amuse, to stimulate, to enrich, and to amplify the life of the Imagination.

Out of this new spirit in Society arose what may be called the 'Dilettante school of English

literature—a school which branches into many
departments, and comprehends artists as different
in excellence as Gray and Della Crusca, but the
chief representatives of which are Gray, Collins,
Horace Walpole, and the two Wartons. Gray
and Collins are the poets of the movement.
The leading characteristics of their poetical work
—and of Gray's more especially—are a pervading
melancholy, an inclination to select romantic
subjects, and at the same time an adherence to,
and even an accentuation of, the classical forms
of diction which had been naturalised in the
language by the genius of Pope. Horace Walpole is the *virtuoso* pure and simple. Without a
spark of genius, he has a taste, bright and intelligent, for the arts ; he understands their principles, and dabbles in them all. He revives
Gothic architecture in Strawberry Hill—a toy
house ; he makes an experiment in romance in
‘ The Castle of Otranto ’—a toy novel ; he
writes sketchy Lives of the Painters, and com-
poses an ingenious ‘ Essay on Landscape
Gardening.’ The brothers Joseph and Thomas
Warton exercised considerable influence on the

public taste by their powers of criticism. Joseph's
'Essay on the Genius of Pope,' while showing a
scholar's appreciation of Pope's wonderful skill
in expression, reminded the reader of what had
been long forgotten, the superior qualities of the
older and more imaginative style of poetry.
Thomas had himself a genuine vein of romance,
and his fine 'History of English Poetry'
awakened general interest in the early sources of
our metrical literature. Towards the close of
the eighteenth century the taste for the supernatural and the marvellous was quickened by
German influences, which inspired the fictions
of Monk Lewis and Mrs. Radcliffe; and the
stream of romance added to its volume the
French Revolutionary ethics advocated in the
imaginative and philosophical works of William
Godwin. In all these writers two leading characteristics are manifest; a Conservative adherence to classical form, and a Liberal tendency
to encourage romantic feeling; a tendency which,
it is evident, may be either so chastened by judgment and reflection as simply to intensify the
pleasures of the imagination, or, if unchecked

by reason, may ripen into revolt against the whole order of existing society. Examples of both results are seen in the writers who are the special subject of this paper.

It seems to me an undeniable fact, looking at the question in its relation not to morality but simply and solely to art, that the most enduring creations of the romantic school are the work of the man who adhered most tenaciously to the social common sense and the inherited life of his nation, and kept the firmest check upon the caprices of his own individual genius. I need hardly say that I allude to Scott. In his patriotism, his passionate love of the past, and his reverence for established authority, literary or political, Scott is the best representative among English men of letters of Conservatism in its most generous form. Conservatism, indeed, penetrates his whole being to such an extent that our Radical Diogenes will not even admit that he possesses the quality of greatness.

He had nothing (says Carlyle) of the martyr; into no 'dark region to slay monsters for us' did he, either led or driven, venture down: his conquests were for his own behoof mainly, conquests over common market labour, and reckonable in good metallic ·coin of the realm. The thing he had faith in except power, power of what sort soever, and even of the rudest sort, would be difficult to point out. One sees not that he believed in anything; nay, he did not even disbelieve; but quietly acquiesced and made himself at home in a world of conventionalities: the false, the semi-false, and the true were alike true in this, that they were there, and had power in their hands more or less. It was well to feel so; and yet not well! We find it written 'Wo to them that are at ease in Zion;' but surely it is a double wo to them that are at ease in Babel, in Domdaniel. On the other hand he wrote many volumes, amusing many thousands of men. Shall we call this great? It seems to us there dwells and struggles another sort of spirit in the inward parts of great men.

And so on through a long tirade full of an envious admiration, an extorted enthusiasm, a reluctant love, that make Carlyle's Essay on Walter Scott one of the most interesting pieces of *autobiography* and one of the worst pieces of literary criticism in the English language. For what does this censure amount to? That Scott was a Conservative, and that he amused the people. But the question is not whether Scott was a great man, but whether he was a great writer ; and if Carlyle's standard of measurement is adopted, the most famous poets must all be excluded from the category of greatness. What was there of ' the martyr ' in Homer, Virgil, or Shakespeare ?   May we not even say, in a sense, that Milton and Dante are ' at ease in Zion ' ?   But if the real greatness of artistic achievement consists in that grandeur and serenity of soul which enables the creator to merge himself in his work, then beyond all question Scott was great, and great not in spite of, but because of, his Conservatism.

It was precisely his calm acceptance of the facts of life that furnished Scott with his broad basis of dramatic romance.   He was ready to work with any tools that came to his hand.   He found romance in the keeping of the *dilettanti*, and society rejoicing in the supernatural machinery of the Minerva Press.   Nevertheless, while he was perfectly alive to the childishness of the prevalent taste, he never speaks but with respect of his predecessors, Horace Walpole and Mrs. Radcliffe, to whom he ungrudgingly acknowledges his obligations.   Indeed, his own name and fame seem to be the last things he desired to thrust into prominence. His early adventures in the semi-civilized society of Scotland had provided him with sufficient individual experience for an interesting autobiography; yet, though the incidents of his own life are worked into his tales with the finest dramatic skill, the author of the 'Waverley Novels' remained through the whole wonderful series 'the Great Unknown.'

With all his enthusiastic love of the past, Scott's practical instinct told him that the 'common sense' of the eighteenth century was the best rule of modern life; hence the ideal world that he has created for us has its foundations on a sound and sober conception of reality. His heroes are often complained of as unheroic; but examine a little closer, and it will be seen that the weaknesses of their disposition are necessary to the development of the action, and to the grouping of the stronger and more interesting characters required for the construction of the story. What can be better adapted to its end than the character of Waverley himself? 'My

intention,' says Scott, ' is not to follow the steps
of that inimitable author (Cervantes) in describing such total perversion of intellect as mis-
construes the objects actually presented to the
senses, but that more common aberration from
sound judgment, which apprehends occurrences
indeed in their reality, but communicates to them
a tincture of its own romantic tone and colouring.'   So, too, in his renderings of history.
Nothing would have been easier for him in ' Old
Mortality,' for instance, than to throw the whole
balance of the reader's sympathy on the Stuart
side.   And yet with what delicate art is that
sympathy secretly instilled without any positive
violation of historic truth ; how dexterous the
conception of making the Presbyterian Morton
the hero of the story ! how generous the representation of the heroism of the Covenanters !
how unfaltering the delineation of their brutal
judges !   Think, again, of the masterly skill
with which, in ' The Antiquary,' all the shades and
gradations of a complex feudal society are brought
together upon a single canvas ; the shrewd
pedantry of Oldbuck, the vagrant license of

Edie Ochiltree, the criminal devotedness of Elspeth Mucklebackit, and the asceticism of Lord Glenallan. See the fine contrasts of character; Claverhouse and Balfour of Burley; Jeanie Deans and the Duke of Argyll; Rob Roy and Bailie Nicol Jarvie; the Master of Ravenswood and Bucklaw: or the blending of the humorous with the pathetic; Dandie Dinmont with Meg Merrilies; Cuddie Headrigg with Ephraim Macbriar; and Evan Dhu Maccombich with the Baron of Bradwardine. How utterly impossible would this power of producing vivid impressions of reality have been to a man who had not accepted the standard of faith and morals established in the historic society to which he belonged, and who would, therefore, have been unable to impart dramatic consistency to the creatures of his imagination!

All this, however, we are given to understand, is in truth but flimsy stuff, very far, indeed, from being genuine ideal creation.

'We might say,' continues Carlyle, 'in a short word, which means a long matter, that your Shakespeare fashions his characters from the heart outwards; your Scott fashions them from the skin inwards, never

getting near the heart of them. The one set become
living men and women; the other amount to little
more than mechanical cases, deceptively painted auto-
matons. . . . To the same purport, indeed, we are to
say that these famed books are altogether addressed to
the every-day mind; that for any other mind there is
next to no nourishment in them. Opinions, emotions,
principles, doubts, beyond what the intelligent country
gentleman can carry along with him, are not to be
found. It is orderly, customary, it is prudent, decent;
nothing more.'

Nothing more! The enlightened Radical
mind can find nothing more than what is ' decent
and customary' in Jeanie Deans, Meg Merrilies,
Dandie Dinmont, Nicol Jarvie, Dugald Dalgetty,
Cuddie Headrigg, Edie Ochiltree; James I.
and Louis XI. seem to it ' little more than
mechanical cases, deceptively painted auto-
matons'; the grief of Saunders Mucklebackit
over his drowned son; the wild-animal attach-
ment of Meg Merrilies; the devotion of Gurth
and Wamba to their master; the heroism of
Ephraim Macbriar: this is painting men 'from
the skin inwards, never getting near the heart
of them.' Heaven and earth! But the secret
of this astonishing judgment is to be found in

the fact that 'these famed books are altogether addressed to the every-day mind.' There lay the offence. It mattered not that the marvellous world called into existence by the Great Magician had enchanted the imagination of hundreds of thousands of men and women who, amid the prosaic and often sordid conditions of their actual life, caught far-off glimpses of the noble, the heroic, and the beautiful, in the ideal reproduction of the life of their ancestors. In the serene atmosphere of this imaginary sphere there was no introspection, no self-torturing, no mental analysis. Hence Radical philosophy finds that imagination has failed in its proper duty. But the 'every-day mind' which has tasted the nectar and ambrosia of romance will continue to lavish its tribute of passionate affection on the memory of Scott for having preserved an ideal world, pure from the smoke and din of 'common day,' and will bow before him as, after Shakespeare and Milton, the greatest *creator* in the English language.

I say 'creator' and not 'poet' advisedly; for, as a poet in the strict technical sense of the

K

word, Scott evidently stands on a lower level
than Byron, Wordsworth, and Shelley. His
metrical romances, admirable as *tours de force*,
and full of passages of effective rhetoric and
striking description, do not compel the imagination to that complete 'suspension of disbelief'
which is the mark of the highest kind of poetry.
The reason is obvious. Scott's genius was for
historical romance ; and, as Aristotle tells us,
the poet deals with what is general, the historian
with what is particular. Skilfully as the character of Marmion has been constructed, the
reader cannot help feeling that it has been put
together ; hence we never quite breathe in the
story, as we do in the ' Iliad ' or the ' Odyssey,'
the ideal atmosphere which is produced by the
perfection of metrical writing. Prose alone
could secure the large and unfettered liberty
that historical romance requires : when Scott
employs his magic powers to clothe the spirit
of the Past in the language of real life the verisimilitude of his creation is complete.

A vehicle of a very different kind was

required for the romance of Byron : indeed, it would be difficult to find two writers belonging to the same school with so many features in common yet opposed to each other in so many essential particulars as Byron and Scott. Scott was, in the highest sense of the word, a creator ; he lives in a hundred beings of his own invention. Byron's poetical faculty was mainly lyrical, not dramatic : Macaulay says of him, with justice : ' Lord Byron never wrote without some reference, direct or indirect, to himself.' Scott used his individual experience as the basis of his ideal creations : Byron employed ideal forms to invest his own person with a poetical atmosphere. Scott was, heart and soul, a Conservative : Byron's mind was the battle-field of contending impulses, the aristocratic sense of order and the democratic love of liberty ; sentiment and cynicism ; religious instinct and sceptical philosophy. Hence, while all Scott's romantic characters are obviously creatures of the imagination pure and simple, the difficulty with Byron's representations of himself is to discover how much of them belongs to the world of reality and how much to the world of romance.

This curious twofold nature of his genius has been the cause of stumbling to critics like Macaulay and Carlyle, who endeavour to explain it on a single principle. Macaulay, looking exclusively at the romantic aspect of his poetry, disparages it in a well-known passage, describing its effects on undergraduates and medical students, as if it were mere affectation—the expression of a transitory fashion of feeling. But he does not attempt to explain the cause of the extraordinary intensity of this contemporary feeling, or of the power with which the poetry of Byron still affects the imagination. Carlyle, on the other hand, with a truer perception of the spirit and reality of the emotions excited by his verse, describes them as *Werterism*, ' a class of feelings,' to use his own words, ' deeply important to modern minds ; *feelings which arise from passion incapable of being converted into action*, which belong to an age as indolent, cultivated, and unbelieving as our own.' But the character of the drivelling German—

> Whose passion boiled and bubbled,
> Till he blew his silly brains out,
> And by it no more was troubled—

is something different in kind from the character of Byron. There is very little of impotence in 'English Bards and Scotch Reviewers.' Even Byron's romantic heroes know how to find a vent for their vapours in some sort of action. Childe Harold himself seeks to obtain self-forgetfulness by incessant travel. Conrad gets rid of his *ennui*, misanthropy, and self-contempt, by piracy. Don Juan is anything but a dreamer. Carlyle's explanation, in short, if less superficial than Macaulay's, is quite as incomplete.

It seems to me that throughout Byron's poetry three main elements of feeling may be traced : the romance of the *dilettante*, the indignation of the satirist, and the lyrical utterances of the man himself. Moreover, looking at his works historically and biographically, it is possible to observe these elements alternately predominating, or blending with and absorbing each other in his poetical creations, according as

his genius was affected by external circumstances. In the 'Hours of Idleness,' as is
natural, we find them all in embryo, separate
and distinct. The romantic sentiment of the
dilettante is plainly visible in numerous love-
poems, in melancholy musings over the decayed
halls of his ancestors, and in recollections of the
Highland home of his childhood. Satire, in a
crude and boyish form, exhibits itself in the
portrait of Pomposus. But the note of genuine
personal unhappiness sounds unmistakably in
the following stanzas :—

> Few are my years, and yet I feel
>   The world was ne'er designed for me :
> Ah! why do darkening shades conceal
>   The hour when man must cease to be ?
> Once I beheld a splendid dream,
>   A visionary scene of bliss.
> Truth! wherefore did thy hated beam
>   Awake me to a world like this ?
>
> I loved—but those I loved are gone ;
>   Had friends—my early friends are fled.
> How cheerless feels the heart alone
>   When all its former hopes are dead !
> Though gay companions o'er the bowl
>   Dispel awhile the sense of ill ;
> Though pleasure stirs the maddening soul,
>   The heart—the heart—is lonely still.

Igneus est ollis vigor et cœlestis origo. It is
pathetic to trace the consistency of Byron's
genius in these lines, the utterances of boyhood,
and in those written at Missolonghi on the completion of his thirty-sixth year :—

> My days are in the yellow leaf;
>   The flowers and fruits of love are gone ;
> The worm,.the canker, and the grief
>   Are mine alone !
>
> The fire that on my bosom preys
>   Is lone as some volcanic isle ;
> No torch is kindled at its blaze—
>   A funeral pile.
>
> The hope, the fear, the jealous care,
>   The exalted portion of the pain
> And power of love, I cannot share,
>   But wear the chain.

In *English Bards and Scotch Reviewers* we see
the poet, stung into resistance by the injustice
of the reviews on his first volume, casting aside
the cloak of the *dilettante* and pouring forth his
scorn alike on the romanticism and on the
pedantry of his age. Dilettantism resumes its
sway in 'Childe Harold,' and in all that series
of romantic poems which, on his return from

his travels, made his name so rapidly famous in
every country of Europe, and himself the darling
of English society. It is dilettantism, blended
with the deep vein of personal melancholy which
had shown itself separately in his early poems,
and is, therefore, something very different from
the conceits of a posing sentimentalist. Still, the
' unreality ' of the following is transparent :

I now leave Childe Harold to live his day, such as
he is ; it had been more agreeable, and certainly more
easy, to have drawn an amiable character. It had been
easy to varnish over his faults, to make him do more
and express less, but he never was intended as an example further than to show that early perversion of mind
and morals leads to satiety of past pleasures, and dis-
appointment in new ones, and that even the beauties of
nature and the stimulus of travel (except ambition, the
most powerful of all excitements) are lost on a soul so
constituted or, rather, misdirected.

If Byron had attempted to make his hero
' an amiable character,' or anything but what he
is, his poem would have been a failure. The
merit of the work lies in the description of the
Pilgrimage, not in the character of the Pilgrim ;
but the latter is admirably designed for giving
human interest to a series of pictures, otherwise

unconnected, which, without this central figure,
would have been utterly wanting in poetical life
and unity.

The same self-conscious air reappears in the
preface to ' The Corsair.'

> With regard to my story, I should have been glad
> to have rendered my personages more perfect and
> amiable, if possible, inasmuch as I have been sometimes
> criticised and considered no less responsible for their
> deeds and qualities than if all had been personal. Be
> it so—if I have deviated into the gloomy vanity of
> ' drawing from self,' the pictures are probably like,
> since they are unfavourable; and, if· not, those who
> know me are undeceived, and those who do not I have
> little interest in undeceiving.

By this mixture of romance with reality he
exactly hit the public taste.

In his later poems all this is changed. Society
has now condemned the poet to banishment : he
leaves England for ever. The effect of his exile
on his genius is prodigious. The bored *dilettante*,
with his transparent dramatic disguises, dis-
appears : in the third canto of ' Childe Harold '
and in ' Manfred ' the identity of the poet with
his characters is scarcely concealed. Romance

is discarded ; he bares his heart, and fiercely insists on the sole reality, universal suffering. The intensity of his feelings imparts to his style a splendour and passion that raise it far above the diction of his earlier poems, and yet in the midst of it all the predominant note discovers the author of ' Hours of Idleness '—' the heart, the heart, is lonely still.' Nor is he satisfied with simply stripping off his ideal trappings. In his recoil from society the spirit of the satirist revives, and in ' Don Juan ' he pours forth a flood of cynical contempt on the high-strung, romantic, and sentimental fancies dear to that popular taste which he had himself done so much to encourage.

If, then, passing from the remarkable mixture of romance, cynicism, and natural feeling in the genius of the poet, we search for the special quality that gives his work its enduring interest and its strange power over the imagination, I think it will be found to be *reality* ; reality in description, reality in feeling, reality in style.

1. In spite of his habits of morbid introspection, Byron always sees with the greatest

clearness the objects he describes. He never confounds his own wishes, fancies, and dreams with external truth. He is, in fact, a pessimist; and the two last cantos of ' Childe Harold,' the high-water mark of his poetical achievement, are a new and splendid variation of the always fascinating old theme, ' vanity of vanities.' Nothing can be more brilliant than his illustrations from nature and history of the truths which the writers of the books of Job and Ecclesiastes, as well as Virgil and Heraclitus, had told before him :

Omnia fatis

In pejus ruere.

Rebel and sceptic though he is, no Christian, no Conservative, could wish to have his case stated on stronger natural premisses than in ' Childe Harold,' and in many passages of ' Don Juan.'

2. His romantic representations of his own sufferings are qualified by a kind of common-sense of the imagination. I am far from seeking to defend his conduct on moral grounds. I admit fully that what Carlyle calls his Werterism,

his· practice of procuring materials for poetry
from his own sufferings, was unmanly. I am
equally sensible that his egotism was prejudicial
to his art; that it impaired his sense of proportion, and disqualified him from being either
a good dramatist or a good story-teller. But,
looking at his poetry in its purely lyrical aspect,
it is surely impossible for any man not to be
carried away on the tide of its power and
passion.

> To each his sufferings: all are men,
> Condemned alike to groan,
> The tender for another's pain,
> The unfeeling for his own;

and if Byron's perpetual references to his own
pain betray a want of feeling, they at least compel universal sympathy. Nay, even when his
Werterism expresses itself in its most theatrical
forms, in his Conrads, his Alps, and his Laras,
we are conscious that he is discharging not
merely the torrent of his private unhappiness,
but a pent-up volume of social emotion. These
characters are the ideal spokesmen of an ancient
and still chivalrous society turning its imagina-

tion fondly back to the ages of arms, love, and
adventure, and rebelling against the tame utilitarian standards imposed on it by the growth of
industrial civilization.

3. But perhaps the most powerful factor in
Byron's poetical genius is his style.   Alone
among his contemporaries he understood how
to swell the stream of English poetical diction
as it had come down to him from the eighteenth
century, so as to make it an adequate vehicle of
expression for romantic thought and feeling.
Wordsworth speaks the language of philosophers, Shelley of spirits, but Byron of men.   Of
this superiority he was himself conscious.   'The
pity of these men,' says he, in one of his letters
to Murray, speaking of certain contemporary
poets, 'is that they never lived in high life, nor
in solitude : there is no medium for the knowledge of the busy or the still world.   If admitted into high life for a season, it is merely as
spectators—they form no part of the mechanism
thereof.   Now Moore and I, the one by circumstances and the other by birth, happened to be
free of the corporation, and to have entered into

its pulses and passions *quarum partes fuimus.*' He had, in fact, served the apprenticeship which Dryden, in a passage I have previously quoted, declares to be necessary for the poet, viz. : ' a liberal education, long reading and digesting of those few good authors we have among us, the knowledge of men and manners, the freedom and habitude of the best company of both sexes, the wearing off the rust one has acquired while laying in a stock of learning.' Since his boy-hood his reading, though not deep, had been wide and various, and he had formed his taste on the best authors of the eighteenth century. Even in his early poems we see that he is master of a mould and manner of poetical diction, in-herited from the school of the *Dilettanti*, which if conventional, is plain and vigorous. As the glow of his thought and feeling intensified, his style expanded ; but the traditional manner with which he started remained the groundwork of his versification. The lines on the battle of Waterloo, some of the soliloquies in ' Manfred,' the description of the shipwreck in ' Don Juan,' and such a lyric as ' She Walks in Beauty,' show

that he had the power of clothing his most
sublime and fiery thoughts in language as lucid
and precise as Pope's. Macaulay's estimate of
his poetical position is admirable :—

> He belonged half to the old and half to the new
> school of poetry. His personal taste led him to the
> former; his thirst of praise to the latter; his talents
> were equally suited to both. His fame was a common
> ground on which the zealots on both sides—Gifford,
> for example, and Shelley—might meet. He was the
> representative, not of either literary party, but of both
> at once, and of their conflict, and of the victory by
> which the conflict was terminated. His poetry fills
> and measures the whole of the vast interval through
> which our literature has moved since the time of
> Johnson. It touches the 'Essay on Man' at one ex-
> tremity and 'The Excursion' at the other.

The absence of this element of reality is
mainly what distinguishes the romance of Shelley
from that of Byron. Shelley's poetry is scarcely
less personal than his friend's. He, himself, is
the poet in 'Alastor;' Laon in the 'Revolt of
Islam;' 'Prometheus Unbound;' and 'Prince
Athanase;' in all his longer poems the incidents of his own life are reproduced in an ideal
form; like Byron, too, he is constantly dwelling

upon his own feelings. But Byron had a fine tact and business-like instinct as to the kind of feelings which were available for treatment in poetry. As the impulse seized him he threw these off in a poetical form, finding relief from his suffering in the art of composition. But, the moment of inspiration gone, he relapsed into himself: in him the poet made only a portion of the man. He never attacked the foundations of religion and society; his quarrels were with men as individuals. Shelley, on the other hand, is the Don Quixote of poetry. He is the poet *par excellence*, ' of imagination all compact.' The visions of his own mind are to him the real system of the universe, and, full of the Revolutionary philosophy of the period, he tilts at the existing order of society as the knight at the windmills, and much with the same result.

Mr. Arnold would have us conclude that the cause of the unsubstantial character of Shelley's longer compositions is his false ' criticism of life.' It seems to me it would be juster to say that the cause is his imperfect perception of the limits of art. For, after all, in this world of mere sense it

is difficult to say what criticism of life is absolutely true.   Besides, many poems which philo-
sophically are based on a false criticism of life,
such as Pope's 'Essay on Man,' have, as works
of art, achieved enduring fame.   Shelley's 'Ode
to Liberty' is full of the same political spirit as
his 'Revolt of Islam;' but it is an admirable
composition, which the other is not.   What is
the reason?   In poetry the goodness or badness
of the central conception depends not on its
philosophical truth, but on its fitness for the
purposes of art.   Though the theory of life
maintained in the 'Essay on Man' is false, it
forms a convenient backbone for the poem, and
serves for a support to all those brilliant aphor-
isms and epigrams in which Pope's genius shone
with unrivalled lustre.   In the same way
Shelley's political enthusiasm found its just
vehicle of expression in the ode.   But in those
forms of poetry which depend upon the representation of character and action his unchecked
imagination destroys his sense of order and proportion, and of the proper boundaries between
romance and reality.   I have already dwelt upon

L

the advantages which Scott derived from his
Conservatism, in being able to take the established order of things as the basis of his romance.
Shelley wished to upset the established order,
and to reconstruct society on an ideal foundation.
He describes himself in the character of Julian :
' Without concealing the evil in the world, he is
for ever speculating how good may be made
superior.   He is a complete infidel, and a scoffer
at all things reputed holy.'   What were the consequences of these Revolutionary opinions upon
his art ?

If greatness in poetry consisted in a succession of dazzling images, and a rapid flow of
splendid verse, Shelley would be entitled to
almost the first place in English literature.   In
an elegiac poem like ' Adonais,' these qualities
produce a magical effect.   What can be more
sublime than the following :

> Life, like a dome of many-coloured glass
> Stains the white radiance of Eternity.

The same greatness of imagery is visible in
the ' Revolt of Islam,' as, for example :

> The King with gathered brow and lips
> Wreathed by long scorn, did inly sneer and frown,
> With hue like that when some great painter dips
> His pencil in the gloom of earthquake and eclipse:

and in 'Prometheus Unbound,' as in the marvellous picture of the Dream:

> What shape is that between us? Its rude hair
> Roughens the winds that lift it, its regard
> Is wild and quick, yet 'tis a thing of air,
> *For through its grey robe gleams the golden dew*
> *Whose stars the noon has quenched not.*

But in all the higher qualities of epic and
dramatic construction his work is defective.
Take the 'Revolt of Islam,' for instance. Homer,
Virgil, and even Ariosto, make us sympathise
with their heroes and heroines, ideal creatures,
no doubt, but always acting and suffering in a
manner befitting the imaginary circumstances in
which they are placed. In Shelley's poem we
are in constant doubt what is romance and what
is reality. The hero and heroine are young
philosophers of the modern French school, who
contrive a social revolt, somewhat after the
ancient Greek pattern, from which, however,

they retire at the most critical moment, to relate their experiences to each other, and indulge in rapturous embraces. The action of the poem is involved in the greatest perplexity. We have a suspicion that what the poet intends to describe, or to allegorise, is the conflict between the French and the armies of the Allied Sovereigns, but the supernatural machinery of the fable seems to carry us back to the plains of Troy. Laon and Cythna speak like disciples of Condorcet, while at the same time they are involved in adventures resembling those of the 'Arabian Nights.'

Precisely the same defects exhibit themselves in 'Prometheus Unbound,' where Shelley has borrowed a Greek legend as the vehicle of expression for his private beliefs. As a whole, in spite of its splendid passages, it is a tiresome poem. The imagery blazes without relief; the action flags amid the cloying sweetness of the melodies; the characters are mere empty abstractions employed on a monotonous repetition of a tale of pain, misery, and oppression which cloaks the dialect of the French Revolution.

How different is the method of the genuine dramatist, as shown in the 'Prometheus Vinctus'; how simple—indeed, how matter-of-fact—is the treatment of the myth; how straightforward the plot; how well distinguished and how justly balanced the characters—the cheery manliness of Prometheus, the feminine sympathy of the Oceanides, the humorous fussiness of Oceanus, and the gentlemanly good breeding of Hermes! The reason of the difference in result is obvious enough. Shelley's conception has its foundation in French sentimentalism : Æschylus built on Attic common-sense.

Whenever, then, Shelley endeavours to cast his romantic ideas of human nature into an epic or dramatic form his art fails. Even in ' The Cenci,' where he has to deal with a subject of matter-of-fact which he has conceived with great power, the horrible and monstrous nature of his theme prevents that free play of natural human action and passion which is characteristic of the highest kind of tragedy. It is not till he works his lyrical or elegiac vein, and gives utterance to his own personal feeling, that we feel he is indeed in contact with reality. And the character of his lyrical poetry is the best comment on the soundness of his philosophical principles. As we see in ' Julian and Maddalo,' he scoffed at the doctrine of the weakness of the human will, which is the fundamental doctrine of Christianity : though Plato, Ovid, and his own friend Byron were as convinced of the truth of this doctrine as St. Paul himself, he held that it was responsible for most of the ills of humanity : he insisted that men were sole masters of their destinies. And yet all his most impassioned lyrics are charged with the expression of his own suffering. Like Byron, he shows himself a complete pessimist. Such poetical *abandon* may have been unmanly ; it was certainly not what was to be expected of one who revived the old Stoic doctrine of the self-sufficiency of the will ; but it is impossible to deny the extraordinary beauty and intensity of the language in which it is expressed. It is in poems of this sort that Shelley deeply touches the heart, and makes us feel the reality of his own nature. When he says in dejection sitting by the sea at Naples :

I could lie down like a tired child,
　And weep away the life of care
Which I have borne and yet must bear,
　Till death like sleep might steal on me,
And I might feel in the warm air
　My cheek grow cold, and hear the sea
Breathe o'er my dying brain its last monotony:

when he cries to the West Wind :

If I were a dead leaf thou mightest bear ;
If I were a swift cloud to fly with thee ;
A wave to pant beneath thy power and share ˙

The impulse of thy strength, only less free
Than thou, O uncontrollable !   If even
I were as in my boyhood, and could be

The comrade of thy wanderings over heaven,
As then when to outstrip the skiey speed
Scarce seemed a vision, I would ne'er have striven

As thus with thee in prayer in my sore need.
Oh ! lift me as a wave, a leaf, a cloud !
I fall upon the thorns of life ! I bleed !

A heavy weight of hours has chained and bowed
One too like thee: tameless and swift and proud :

when, above.all, he exclaims, on hearing the
sky-lark :

We look before and after
  And pine for what is not:
Our sincerest laughter
  With some pain is fraught:
Our sweetest songs are those that tell of saddest
  thought.

Yet if we could scorn
  Hate, and pride, and fear;
If we were things born
  Not to shed a tear,
I know not how thy joy we ever could come
  near—

when we read verse so full of music and anguish,
we wonder how the poet failed to perceive that
the power of Christianity lies not in superstition,
but in the hope which it offers to the unsatisfied
longings of the soul,

  The desire of the moth for the star,
    Of the night for the morrow;
  The devotion to something afar
    From the sphere of our sorrow.

I have endeavoured in this and in the preceding paper to trace the causes that gave rise
to the Liberal Movement in English Literature,
and the relation of the new Romantic school to
the Classical school of art and letters dominant

after the Restoration. The Revolution of 1688 saved constitutional liberty, but saved it by the sacrifice of much that was picturesque, loyal, and enthusiastic in the semi-Catholic and semi-feudal England of the seventeenth century. Similarly, the standard of taste formed mainly by the influence of the ' Tatler ' and ' Spectator ' involved a virtual suppression of the romantic element which had figured so prominently in early English literature. It struck a mean between the immorality and conceit fashionable in the poetry of the seventeenth century and the austere barrenness of Puritan democracy. It speedily commended itself to the perception of the educated and refined classes, the exclusive possessors at that time of political power, familiar with the best models of classical writing, and with the rules of politeness current in modern society, and capable of enjoying the conversational brilliancy produced by the keen encounter of wits in clubs and coffee-houses. On the other hand, it provided an inadequate ideal for the great middle class throughout the nation, which, excluded from any direct participation in the government, began, nevertheless, to acquire a definite sense of its own growing power. The solitary thinker who compared the actual condition of things with some image in his own mind, the democratic malcontent inspired with a passion for equality, the man of fashion wearied with monotony and convention, the religious devotee alienated by the semi-Erastianism of the Established Church, all failed to find satisfaction in the social ideal of the age. A great ferment was, therefore, working in the heart of the nation long before the outbreak of the French Revolution, moving some to seclude themselves from company, others to seek for an expansion in the sources of rational pleasure, others to rebel against the restrictions of law and morals, and a few to aim at the reconstruction of society on new and abstract lines.

All these motives were at work in the movement we know under the name of Liberalism, and all disclose themselves in the poetry of the great writers who have just been passing under review. In Wordsworth we see reflected the natural tendency of the imaginative mind to withdraw itself from the sphere of social action, and to solace itself with pure contemplation. Scott, Byron, and Shelley, on the other hand, represent the various forms of social action in which the new movement sought to find imaginative expression.   The work of Scott is a symbol of the natural healthy desire for expansion in the heart of society, which, while strongly attached to the ancient order, is conscious in itself of abounding vitality, and delights to find a reflection of its own spirit of boldness and adventure in the stirring narratives of the life of its ancestors.   Byron speaks rather the feelings of an ancient aristocracy, who find this inherited spirit of adventure still strong within them, and not being able under the conditions of modern society to give it all the scope they desire, end by openly defying the moral laws and restrictions by which that society is cemented.   Shelley is at the pole of Romance opposite to Scott.   The one appeals to the instinct of Reverence, the other to the passion of Hope.   Scott was passionately attached to the institutions of his country, not only because they secured to him a large share.

of personal happiness and liberty, but on account
of the free access which, through them, his spirit
obtained to the ideal region of the past.   Shelley
hated them because he saw in them only a brute
barrier between mankind and the happy state he
imagined for it in the future.   The varied creations of Scott, therefore, are based on experience,
common sense, and the continuity of tradition ;
the creations of Shelley rest on the hopes which
he built in his aerial and splendid imagination, in whose rainbow colours the taint of evil
that ever debars men from the sense of complete
ideal satisfaction, is lost or transfigured.   As to
the soundness of this foundation for the purposes
of art, many suggestive inferences may be drawn
from the character of Shelley's own work, and
others from the nature of the parallel movement
in poetry initiated by the genius of Coleridge
and Keats.

POETRY, MUSIC, AND PAINTING

COLERIDGE AND KEATS

POETRY, MUSIC, AND PAINTING: COLERIDGE AND KEATS.

IN a passage of his 'Life of Byron,' interesting as giving a poet's estimate of the inspiring forces of his age, Moore describes the effects of the drama of the French Revolution on contemporary imagination.

'There are those,' says he, 'who trace, in the peculiar character of Lord Byron's genius, strong features of relationship to the times in which he lived; who think that the great events which marked the close of the last century, by giving a new impulse to men's minds, by habituating them to the daring and the free, and allowing full vent to the "flash and outbreak of fiery spirits," had naturally led to the production of such a poet as Byron; and that he was in short as much the child and representative of the Revolution, in poesy, as another great man of the age, Napoleon, was in statesmanship and warfare. Without going the full length of this notion, it will, at least, be conceded, that the free loose which had been given to all the passions and

energies of the human mind, in the great struggle of
that period, together with the constant spectacle of
such astounding vicissitudes as were passing, almost
daily, on the theatre of the world, had created, in all
minds, and in every walk of intellect, a taste for strong
excitement, which the stimulants supplied from ordinary
sources were insufficient to gratify;—that a tame deference to established authorities had fallen into disrepute,
no less in literature than in politics, and that the poet
who should breathe into his songs the fierce and passionate spirit of the age, and assert, untrammelled and
unawed, the high dominion of genius, would be most
sure of an audience toned in sympathy with his strains.'

Dull, indeed, must the spirit have been
which failed to catch some inspiring fervour from
the atmosphere of those extraordinary times.
The ages of knight errantry seemed to have revived. While historic dynasties were overthrown
in a single night, while every common soldier
felt that he might carry his marshal's *bâton* in
his knapsack, while obscure adventurers seated
themselves on the most ancient thrones of
Europe, it would have been strange if imagination had been anything but romantic. Byron
may be the best poetical representative of the
Revolutionary forces of the period, but he is by

no means the only one. Their influence is equally visible in the fire and flow of Shelley's verse. The romantic spirit, indeed, makes itself felt in the work of those whose temper is most opposed to the Revolutionary movement. Campbell, who in another age would probably have had to rest content with such reputation as he might have acquired from the 'Pleasures of Hope,' is inspired with 'The Battle of the Baltic' and 'Hohenlinden ; ' while if Byron may be claimed as the special child of Cosmopolitanism, Patriotism can at least boast of having informed the better part of the genius of Scott.

But while the French Revolution quickened the spirit of romantic action in poetry, it also gave birth to the more enduring movement of romance in philosophical thought. The outburst of Liberty and the expansion of genius, coinciding as they did with the advance of democracy, encouraged the spread of the Optimism cherished by all the philosophers who derived their descent from Rousseau. A belief in the unlimited progress of the human race took possession of most reflecting minds. The vast development of

M

physical science, and the revolution which this
entailed in man's *circumstances*, were supposed
to be accompanied by a corresponding enlargement of his virtue, his wisdom, and of his cor-
poral powers. Condorcet assured his disciples
that they might hope for the unlimited prolon-
gation of life. Shelley, treading in the steps of
his French masters, insisted that, if we could
only get rid of the debasing superstitions of
Christianity, we might expect to become perfectly good and happy. Others, to heighten the
charms of the smiling prospect, indulged the
idea that, as man was destined in this life to develop moral and physical capacities far in advance
of anything he could at present conceive, so he
might look forward to the conquest and possession of untold treasures of art, latent in a new
world of imagination.

Prominent among these sanguine prophets
was Wordsworth. Like many other enthusiastic
young men of talent he had hailed the beginning
of the French Revolution, and had excused as
natural its bloody excesses. Even when its
true nature dawned on his mind, and he saw

that the Jacobin movement was directed against the cause of Liberty, he retained a chastened faith that the future would behold the realisation of the glowing hopes and visions in which he had indulged. So noble a principle as Liberty, he felt sure, could not fail to be the pioneer of moral progress, and always in the van of human movement he saw the poet's imagination cheering on the race to fresh conquests. Arguing against those who entertained a contracted and artificial view of the nature of Poetry, and who adhered to the current theories of poetic diction,—

'The objects,' he cried, ' of the poet's thoughts are everywhere ; though the eyes and senses of man are, it is true, his favourite guides, yet he will follow wherever he can find an atmosphere of sensation in which to move his wings. . . . The remotest discoveries of the chemist, the botanist, or mineralogist, will be as proper objects of the poet's art as any upon which it can be employed, if the time should ever come when these things shall be familiar to us, and the relations under which they are contemplated by the followers of their respective sciences shall be manifestly and palpably material to us as enjoying and suffering beings.'

In these words we find the first application to Poetry of the Revolutionary theory of perpetual

Progress. The belief is an amiable one, but it can scarcely be entertained without ignoring facts in the history of art which raise an entirely different presumption. Could Wordsworth have pointed to a single nation in which poetry of the highest order had been produced in the full maturity of philosophy and natural science ? Plato declared that there was an old-standing quarrel between philosophy and poetry, and resolved to banish the poets from his ideal Republic. It would be difficult to name a Greek or Latin poet of the highest creative order who arose after Aristotle had produced his ' Physics ' or Pliny his ' Natural History.' Galileo was an enthusiastic student of Tasso's poetry, but I never heard of any Italian poet who derived his inspiration from the scientific discoveries of Galileo.

And, again, if Wordsworth had been asked to account, on his hypothesis of constant progress in poetry, for the extreme regularity of the phenomena that mark the rise, development, and decline of the art, it is difficult to see what answer he could have returned. The golden

age of poetical production is as a rule confined
within well-marked epochs of national history.
Greece has its great epic period ; its great lyrical
period ; its great dramatic period ; afterwards
comes the age of decadence, brightened by the
genius of Theocritus, and closing with the
Anthology. Rome produces her Lucretius and
Catullus ; then her Horace and Virgil ; then
her Juvenal, and, of course, the inevitable epi-
grammatist, Martial. Dante in Italy is followed
by Ariosto and Tasso, but in the next generation the rage is for Marini. Spain's genius was
less fertile in poetry, but she was the land of
chivalry and romance, out of which rose the
beautiful idiom of Cervantes, only to be succeeded, however, by the *estilo culto* of Gongora.
If poetry in England survived the euphuism,
the mannerism, and the affectation which dis-
figured the poetry of those whose attempts to
combine the spirit of Mediævalism with the
spirit of the Renaissance rival the contortions of
the Marinis and Gongoras of the Continent, this
was chiefly thanks to the manly genius of Dryden,
who brought fresh vitality into the art by deal-

ing with life and manners according to the
tradition of Chaucer.   And yet, genuine as the
Conservative movement of Dryden and his followers was, the English imagination felt that
something was gone, that 'there had passed
away a glory from the earth.'   Look at the conclusion of the ' Ode on the Poetical Character,'
and see how Collins, the most romantic representative of the Classical school in the eighteenth
century, felt as he gazed backwards on the
vanished ages of imagination.

I view that oak the fancied glades among,
By which, as Milton lay, his evening ear,
From many a cloud that dropped ethereal dew,
Nigh sphered in heaven, its native strains could hear;
On which that ancient trump he reached was hung !
    Thither oft, his glory greeting,
    From Waller's myrtle shades retreating,
With many a vow from Hope's aspiring tongue,
My trembling feet his guiding steps pursue ;
    In vain—such bliss to one alone
    Of all the sons of soul, was known ;
And Heaven and Fancy, kindred powers,
Have now o'erturned the inspiring bowers,
Or curtained close such scene from every future view.

Such being the feelings of one of Words-

worth's immediate predecessors—and Collins'
complaint is repeated in various forms by Gray
and Cowper—it seems strange that the founder
of the new Romantic school should have cherished
so firm a persuasion of the boundless resources
of poetry. A closer examination of his views,
however, renders his conclusions less surprising.
He believed that the English poets had been
long following a false track, and that he had
himself discovered the only true principles of
poetical composition. The old-fashioned poet
may be said to resemble the Demiurgus of Plato's
' Timæus.' Creator as he is, he creates not the
subject matter of his art, which he finds already
existing chaotically in the mind of his nation,
but the ideal form and order in which those
scattered ideas must be presented to the people.
This realm of national imagination has a natural
tendency to contract. Scientific methods of
thought deprive it of much ground over which,
in the infancy of society, it was accustomed to
range with perfect freedom. The growth of
commerce, and of artificial manners, extinguishes
the local life, customs, and traditions out of

which, during the active, warlike ages, are woven
ballad poetry and romance.   And not only does
the ground of imagination contract before the
encroachment of external forces, but it is occupied as property by the elder poets, so that La
Bruyère has some reason for his complaint:
' Les anciens ont tout dit ; on vient aujourd'hui
trop tard pour dire des choses nouvelles.'

To these considerations, however, Wordsworth's answer was simple.   He held that the
real source of poetry is the mind of the individual poet, and that *all* feelings and impressions
which it receives from the outside world become
proper subject matter for poetry after passing
through the crucible of imagination.   Hence his
conclusion : ' Poetry is immortal as the heart of
man,' since Nature is boundless, and the poet is
at perfect liberty to cast his impressions into an
imaginative mould just as his individual caprice
may dictate.   Of course, if this be really so,
cadit quæstio ; because, as the impressions of
every individual are different, the number of
metrical combinations in which they can be
expressed will be infinite.

But is it so ?   Look at the poetry of Wordsworth himself, and see how his theory works
out.   If all the poems included in his published
works were composed on his own principle, and
were valuable in themselves, his reasoning would
be colourable, for in mere bulk his metrical
writings are weighty enough.   When, however,
these are classified, we find that one large group,
containing among others such noble poems as
' Laodamia,' and the ' Ode on Immortality,' is
composed on the old lines, the poet having
founded his subject on universal associations,
and simply cast them into an ideal form.   Of
another large class, such as ' The Excursion,'
' The Prelude,' ' The White Doe of Rylstone,'
and ' Peter Bell,' we may say that they are so
entirely wanting in the primary qualities of
poetical design, unity, and proportion, that,
whatever individual beauties they may possess,
they have no title to be considered works of art.
Wordsworth himself pronounces judgment on
compositions of this kind when he says that
their chief justification lies in their *moral* purpose.   Mark, however, his admission : ' *Not that*

I always began to write with a distinct purpose formally conceived.' But no extensive work of art is worth anything that is not so conceived, because it is impossible that it can be an ideal whole. And yet once more, observe that striking characteristic which Coleridge notes in Wordsworth's poetry :

'I affirm,' says he, 'that from no contemporary writer could so many lines be quoted without reference to the poem in which they are found for their own independent weight and beauty. From the sphere of my own experience, I can bring to my recollection three persons of no every-day powers and acquirements, who had read the poems of others with more and more unalloyed pleasure, and had thought more highly of their authors as poets ; who have yet confessed to me that from no modern work had so many passages started up anew in their minds at different times, and as different occasions had awakened a different mood.'

Coleridge satisfies himself with recording this phenomenon without attempting to account for it, and yet the explanation of it is full of interest from the light it throws on Wordsworth's Theory of Poetry. Of all the great English poets, Wordsworth has, it seems to me, least of the faculty of the Demiurgus. Endowed with an imagination of remarkable power and beauty, he is deficient in the highest of all poetical qualities, Invention. His method of writing in verse is unlike that of almost all his predecessors. Poetry he defines to be ' the *spontaneous* overflow of powerful emotion '; and this, no doubt, sufficiently describes his own principle of composition which led him, after receiving a hint or impulse from the external world, immediately to give it expression in metre. But to the operations of the presiding faculty of the mind which shapes impressions into an ideal whole, admitting some and rejecting others, according as they are related to a central design, he was almost a stranger. His ideas were quickly received and sharply returned, in individual and isolated forms. Hence, as I have already said, his longer poems are without form and void : on the other hand, no man ever employed with more force and felicity that mould of poetry which is specially adapted for the expression of individual thought, namely, the Sonnet.

If Wordsworth's poetry vividly illustrates the practical worth of his theory, Coleridge's

work shows us the natural development of the
Romantic movement in the hands of a genuine
Inventor. The latter had embraced Wordsworth's philosophy of poetry, of which indeed
he was the joint author, but being a born artist,
he dissented from his friend's application of it.
He agreed with him in deriving all poetry from
the mind of the individual poet, and his love of
metaphysics induced him to believe that he
could penetrate behind the veil of sense, and
establish a transcendental basis for the Law of
the Association of Ideas. Like Wordsworth,
too, he was transported with a belief in the
boundless range of the Imagination, and was an
enthusiast for its perfect Liberty. ' How oft,'
he cries, in the fine opening of his ' France '—

How oft, pursuing fancies holy,
My moonlight way o'er flowering weeds I wound,
Inspired, beyond the guess of folly,
By each rude shape and wild unconquerable sound !
O ye loud waves ! and O ye forests high !
    And O ye clouds that far above me soared !
Thou rising sun ! thou blue rejoicing sky !
    Yea, everything that is and will be free !
    Bear witness for me wheresoe'er ye be,
    With what deep worship I have still adored
        The spirit of divinest Liberty !

And yet the recipient of all these varied impressions has left only four poems with which his name will be for ever associated, 'The Ancient Mariner,' 'Christabel,' 'Kubla Khan,' and (on a lower level) 'The Dark Ladie.' What is the cause of this comparative sterility in the midst of such abundant resources? Partly, no doubt, the one usually assigned, want of will and resolute purpose. Coleridge wasted his powers on a multiplicity of designs which he had never sufficient perseverance to carry into execution. The dream of Pantisocracy on the banks of the Susquehanna, the 'Watchman,' and a hundred vast projects of theology and metaphysics, all tell the same tale. In poetry, however, it is only fair to remember that Coleridge always declared the cause of the paucity of his productions was not idleness but impotence. In the Preface to 'Christabel,' published in 1816, he says : ' Since 1800 my poetic powers have been till lately in a state of suspended animation ; ' and with his peculiar poetical aims, I hold that the statement is deserving of entire credit. He considered, as I

have said, that the object of poetry was to
excite subtle trains of imaginative associations;
but he was not satisfied, like Wordsworth, with
simply analysing the impressions of his own
mind. Feeling in himself the impulse of the
Inventor and Creator, he was always searching
after new 'Forms.' Cowper, in 'The Task,'
had been the first to show how a poem might
be written, by simply following out a train of
ideas, not embodied in a definite subject, but
naturally connected with each other, and united
by a moral purpose. To Coleridge's keen
artistic perception this plan had not enough
of unity, and he sought, as he tells us in his
'Biographia Literaria,' to improve on it, by
taking as his subject a Brook which he conceived might be treated, with all its associations
of ideas, as it widened into a river and made its
way to the sea. His genius, however, was of
far too weird and romantic an order to succeed
in didactic poetry, and soon abandoning his
enterprise, he set himself to look for 'fresh
woods' in other directions. Though, of course,
he would not have admitted anything of the

kind, I think it is evident that he next began
to reason on the subtle affinities between sound
and sense, and to perceive that isolated romantic
images might be so linked together by mere
metrical movement as to produce the effect of
unity which the mind requires in an ideal
creation. He resolved, in fact, deliberately to
compose as a *Musician*. We see this very plainly
in the beautiful fragment entitled ' The Knight's
Grave,' which was confessedly composed as an
experiment in metre.

Where is the grave of Sir Arthur O'Kellyn ?
    Where may the grave of that good man be ?
By the side of a spring, on the breast of Helvellyn,
    Under the twigs of a young birch tree !
The oak that in summer was sweet to hear,
And rustled his leaves in the fall of the year,
And whistled and roared in the winter alone,
Is gone,—and the birch in its stead has grown.
        The Knight's bones are dust,
        And his good sword rust ;—
        His soul is with the saints, I trust.

There is very little necessary logical connection between the images contained in these
verses, and yet I should think scarcely anyone

could read them without being affected by their
subtle pathos.   Probably the motive of the
composition was the word ' Helvellyn,' which
is musical in its sound, and, as the name of a
mountain, carries with it romantic associations.
To connect these with the grave of a knight
was a natural sequence of thought, and the
disappearance of the oak which had once grown
in the place of the young birch tree, as chivalry
had preceded the modern order of society, is
beautifully suggestive.   But the unity of the
piece lies in the dactylic movement of the
metre, which probably came into the poet's
mind in connection with the name which he
invented to rhyme with Helvellyn, and which
is admirably . adapted to convey the desired
feeling.

So little does the effect of Coleridge's poetry
depend upon the logical sequence of ideas, that
of his four really characteristic poems, three,
viz. ' Christabel,' ' Kubla Khan,' and ' The Dark
Ladie,' are fragments ;   one, ' Kubla Khan,' is
said to have been composed in a dream, while
' The Ancient Mariner ' was founded, so far as

the bulk of the story is concerned, on the dream
of a friend. All this is the almost inevitable
result of his method of composition. He declared, indeed, that he had always intended to
finish ' Christabel,' the story being complete in
his mind, but, had he done so, the result must
have been unsatisfactory, for, while in the poem,
as it is, the mind passes on satisfied from one
image to another, it is impossible that so wild a
tale could ever have had a conclusion more
rational than a dream. ' The Ancient Mariner '
is complete, but we do not read it, nor was it
composed, for the sake of the action or the
moral. As we know, it was put together piece-
meal after the manner of ' The Knight's Grave,'
and the effect, both in this poem and in
' Christabel,' is produced by the combination
of isolated weird and romantic images in a
strange elfin metre. We are not affected by any
human interest in either story, but by the vivid
pictures of

> The one red leaf, the last of its clan,
> That dances as often as dance it can,
> Hanging so light, and hanging so high,
> On the topmost twig that looks up at the sky ;

N

or of

> The chamber carved so curiously,
>> Carved with figures strange and sweet,
> All made out of the carver's brain,
>> For a lady's chamber meet :
> The lamp with two-fold silver chain
>> Is fastened to an angel's feet :

or by such melodies as—

> And the good south wind still blew behind,
>> But no sweet bird did follow ;
> Nor any day for food or play,
>> Came to the mariner's hollo !

and

> Oh sleep ! it is a gentle thing,
>> Beloved from pole to pole !
> To Mary Queen the praise be given !
> She sent the gentle sleep from heaven,
>> That slid into my soul.

Coleridge is in fact the great Musician of the romantic school.of English poetry. His practice is the exact antithesis of Wordsworth's theory that there is no essential difference between the language of poetry and the language of prose. In him metrical movement is all in all. He was the first to depart from the lofty severe iambic movement which had satisfied the feeling of the

eighteenth century, and, by associating picturesque images and antique phrases in melodious
and flowing metres, to set the imagination free
in a world quite removed from actual experience.
His invention exercised a profound influence
upon the course of English verse-composition.
' Christabel,' as we know, inspired the metrical
movement in the ' Lay of the Last Minstrel,'
and since the ' Siege of Corinth,' and ' Parisina,'
are obviously prompted by the ' Lay of the Last
Minstrel,' Byron's repudiation of plagiarism, in
the ' Siege of Corinth,' from ' Christabel,' which
had only just been published, must be taken as
applying to the thought, and not to the music of
the poem.

An analogous movement, though quite in
another direction, is observable in the poetry
of Keats. Keats' method of composition was,
in every principle, opposed to that of the Lake
School. Wordsworth and Coleridge regarded
Liberty as the mainspring of all human action,
and the latter, though he was far from putting
his moral principles into practice, justifies the
movement of the French Revolution, as I have

shown in the passage quoted from his ' France,'
by the operation of the laws of external Nature.
Similarly it was Wordsworth's object in poetry
' to choose incidents and situations from common
life . . . and at the same time to throw over
them a certain colouring of imagination whereby
ordinary things should be presented to the mind
in an unusual aspect.' For this purpose the
Imagination required the sovereign liberty and
transmutative power which Wordsworth claimed
for it, and which it could exert with little difficulty in the midst of the romantic associations
of the Lake district. But to Keats, the child of
London parents, and accustomed from infancy to
the mean and sordid routine of city life, Nature
imparted none of those philosophical and moral
ideas which she aroused in the poet of the
Cumberland mountains. The Liberty of the
Imagination meant for him something very
different from the Revolutionary yearnings of
the period.

Though I do not know
The shiftings of the mighty winds that blow
Hither and thither all the changing thoughts
Of men ; though no great ministering reason sorts

Out the dark mysteries of human souls
To clear conceiving, yet there ever rolls
A vast idea before me, and I glean
Therefrom my liberty; thence, too, I've seen
The end and aim of Poesy.

To the future of humanity which occupied so
large a part of Shelley's thoughts he was pro-
foundly indifferent.   Fame,—

Fame the last spur that the clear spirit doth raise
To spurn delights and live laborious days—

was the object of his scornful ridicule; human
action of any kind—even of the romantic ballads
that had stirred the heart of Sir Philip Sidney
' like the sound of a trumpet,' and of history that
had inspired some of the noblest of Shakespeare's
dramas—was nothing to him compared to the
emotion of an ideal love-scene :—

Hence pageant history! hence gilded cheat!
Swart planet in the wilderness of deeds!
Wide sea that one continuous murmur breeds
Along the pebbled shore of memory!
Many old rotten-timbered boats there be
Upon thy vaporous bosom magnified
To goodly vessels; many a sail of pride,
And golden-keeled is left unlaunched and dry.
But wherefore this ?   What care though owl did fly.

Above the great Athenian admiral's mast ?
What care though striding Alexander past
The Indus with his Macedonian numbers ?
Though old Ulysses tortured from his slumbers
The glutted Cyclops, what care ?   Juliet leaning
Amid her window flowers—sighing—weaning
Tenderly her fancy from its maiden snow
Doth more avail than these : the silver flow
Of Hero's tears, the swoon of Imogen,
Fair Pastorella in the bandit's den,
Are things to brood on with more ardency
Than the death-day of Empires.

One cause and one alone can explain and excuse this unblushingly-avowed preference for the feminine over the masculine motives of composition,—namely, physical debility.   To this indulgence Keats is entitled : and yet when we think of the fiery spirit that has fretted out many a puny body, it is difficult to read without disgust the following confession of an apparently contented materialist :—

This morning I am in a sort of temper indolent and supremely careless ; I long after a stanza or two of Thomson's 'Castle of Indolence'; my passions are all asleep, from my having slumbered till nearly eleven, and weakened the animal fibre all over me to a delightful sensation about three degrees on this side faintness.

If I had teeth of pearl, and the breath of lilies, I should call it languor; but as I am, I must call it laziness. In this state of effeminacy the fibres of the brain are relaxed in common with the rest of the body, and to such a happy degree, that pleasure has no show of enticement, and pain no unbearable frown; neither Poetry nor Ambition nor Love have any alertness of countenance; as they pass by me they seem rather like those figures on a Greek urn, two men and a woman, whom no one but myself could distinguish in their disguisement. *This is the only happiness, and is a rare instance of advantage in the body overpowering the mind.*

We have in this passage a clear index of Keats' motive when he was in the comparatively active mood of poetical composition. To the vivid and powerful imagination which worked within his diseased frame, 'the vast idea,' 'the end and aim of Poesy,' of which he speaks in his lines on 'Sleep and Poetry,' was to escape from the detested surroundings of actual life into the ideal world which was ever floating before his mind's eye. In his earlier poems he seems to be haunted by the fear lest he should die before he had time to execute his purpose. The difficulty was to find a form of metrical composition

adapted to the expression of his conception.
Though, in its repugnance to the actual and the
real, his imagination is akin to that of Coleridge,
yet the mind of the latter was of a much more
energetic and manly order, while the metrical
music which he invented had too much of continuous action to depict adequately the steadfast
and isolated images which Keats' fancy loved to
evoke.   Nor could the younger poet make anything of an extended narrative in verse.   As a
story, ' Endymion ' deserves all that its worst
enemies ever said of it.   ' Hyperion ' shows a
remarkable advance, but it is well that Keats
left it a fragment, for it is plain that, with his
effeminate notion of Apollo, he could never have
invented any kind of action which would have
interested the reader in learning how the old
Titan Sun-God was turned out of his kingdom.
The poem, in its language, challenges comparison
with ' Paradise Lost,' where Milton is confronted
with the same difficulty, yet even he, with all
his skill in construction and his noble power of
representing character, often contends vainly
against the poverty of human interest and incident inherent in his subject.

Keats evidently felt that in ' Endymion ' he had not reached his 'end and aim of poesy.' But he was on the right track. In ' Sleep and Poetry ' he lets us see very plainly, though he is himself scarcely conscious of the fact, that the source of his inspiration is Sculpture and Painting. In looking on a picture by Titian, or on the reliefs on a Grecian Urn; his Fancy lit on objects which carried him away into a world entirely remote from his actual circumstances, and we see him in 'Endymion' constantly trying to reproduce, in words, the image of some landscape or figure which he remembers in painting. These isolated pictures, indeed—everyone will recall the description of Adonis asleep, of Cybele drawn by her lions, and the beautiful processional song of the Bacchanals—are the only successful parts of the poem. But in his later works he had found his foothold, and in ' St. Agnes' Eve,' the ' Ode to the Nightingale,' the ' Ode on the Grecian Urn,' and other short poems of the same kind, he shows that he has discovered a group of sculpturesque and picturesque subjects—subjects, that is to say, which

suggest permanent forms in the midst of constant material change—on which his imagination
can work with perfect happiness and freedom.
He has realised his own ideal. As he says in
the last stanza of the 'Ode on the Grecian
Urn '—

> O Attic shape ! Fair Attitude ! with brede
>   Of marble men and maidens overwrought
> With forest branches and the trodden weed;
>   Thou silent form dost tease us out of thought
> As doth Eternity : cold Pastoral !
>   When old age shall this generation waste,
>   Thou shalt remain in midst of other woe
> Than ours, a friend to man, to whom thou sayst
>   ' Beauty is Truth, Truth Beauty '—that is all
>   Ye know on earth, and all ye need to know.

With what skill he had learned to call up a
picture in all its distinctness of form and colour
before the imagination, is best seen in the opening stanzas of ' St. Agnes' Eve,' and in the unrivalled description of the painted window in the
same poem :—

> A casement high and triple-arched there was,
> All garlanded with carven imag'ries
> Of fruits, and flowers, and branches of knot-grass,
> And diamonded with panes of quaint device

Innumerable of stains and splendid dyes,
As are the tiger-moths' deep-damasked wings,
And in the midst, 'mong thousand heraldries
And twilight saints and dim emblazonings,
A shielded scutcheon blushed with blood of queens and
    kings.

It is, in fact, evident that, just as Coleridge,
by an instinctive process, learned how to produce musical effects in language by combinations of metrical sounds, so Keats came gradually
to perceive the analogy between painting and
poetry latent in the picturesque associations of
individual words.   We see the tendency betray-
ing itself early, in his sonnet on Chapman's
' Homer ' ; in its maturity, in the beautiful
lines—

Charmed magic casements opening on the foam
Of perilous seas, in faery lands forlorn ;

in the passage that follows :

Forlorn ! the very word is like a bell
To toll me back from thee to my sole self ;

and in the lines in ' Lamia '—

Then once again the charmèd god began
An oath, and through the serpent's ears it ran,
Warm, tremulous, devout, psalterian.

And it is carried to its height in the wonderful description immediately connected with these lines—a passage in which the distinctness of the painting is equalled by its loathliness—depicting the agony of the serpent during her transformation into a woman.

These are remarkable achievements which only those who are insensible to the power of genius are likely to underrate. Both Coleridge and Keats must be regarded as *inventors* in the art of poetry, and, as we know, Virgil gives inventors of all kinds a place beside the poets in Elysium.

Quique pii vates et Phœbo digna locuti ;
. Inventas aut qui vitam excoluere per artes.

I think it will not be contended that I have sought grudgingly to deprive the romantic poets of the honours that are justly their due. On the other hand, it would be the mark of a feeble or a servile mind to shrink, either in deference to the authority of genius, or in gratitude for the boon of novelty, from inquiring whether those who in this century have discovered

fresh arts of metrical composition, have always
' spoken things worthy of Phœbus.' I must go
one step farther. I think that men of impartial
judgment will not deny that whatever results
may be achieved by the new methods must be
achieved by the sacrifice of some principle which
lies at the foundation of what the world has
agreed to regard as the highest kinds of poetry.

Look at Wordsworth's method, for instance.
There can be no doubt that, by carefully watch-
ing the individual impressions made on his own
mind by objects in the external world, it may
be possible for a man of genius and imagination
to notice many subtle beauties which may have
escaped general observation, and to record them
in a striking metrical form. But it is absolutely
essential that if he adopt the principle of analysis,
he should forego the principle of action ; since
he cannot form his conception in the sphere of
imagination pure and simple, nor can he give
to his creation that extension and proportion
which is indispensable to any great ideal whole.
Moreover, by basing poetry solely on the analysis
of his own impressions, he necessarily deprives

the art of its ancient *social* influence, because, as
Scott justly says, he can have no guarantee that
a record of his individual experience will have
power to arouse in the minds of his hearers
those universal associations to which the great
masters of verse appeal.

Again, a man may follow in the track of
Coleridge and Keats, and make it his chief aim
to touch the imagination by discovering new
associations of metrical sound, or fresh combinations of picturesque words. But do not let
it be argued that those who devote themselves
to this pursuit are enlarging the boundaries of
the art, when in fact they are sensibly contracting them. Poetry contains in itself the principles of painting, sculpture, and music, but, in
its highest forms, it only develops and employs
these for the representation of some human interest and action. For instance, the passage in
the ' Penseroso '—

> Oft on a plot of rising ground
> I hear the far-off curfew sound,
> Over some wide-watered shore,
> Swinging slow with sullen roar;

> Or if the air will not permit,
> Some still removed place will fit,
> Where glowing embers through the room
> Teach light to counterfeit a gloom ;
> Far from all resort of mirth,
> Save the cricket on the hearth,
> Or the bellman's drowsy charm
> To bless the doors from nightly harm.

Here is the Law of Association at work in all its power, a number of apparently unconnected images being combined, as in 'Christabel,' in a musical metre ; but, unlike 'Christabel,' the unity of the poem lies, not in the music, but in the thought, namely, the description of the features of Melancholy.

As to painting, there is almost as much highly wrought imagery to be found in a *simile* of Homer or of Ariosto, as in a whole poem of Keats, and yet with them the simile is merely a halting-place for repose in the midst of a swift narrative of ideal action. Is there anything in Keats that can match the following as a picture ?—

> And at a stately side-board, by the wine
> That fragrant smell diffused, in order stood
> Tall stripling youths rich-clad, of fairer hue

Than Ganymed or Hylas ; distant more
Under the trees, now tripped, now solemn stood,
Nymphs of Diana's train, and Naiades
With fruits and flowers from Amalthea's horn,
And ladies of th' Hesperides, that seemed
Fairer than feigned of old or fabled since
Of faery damsels met in forest wide
By Knight of Logres or of Lyones,
Lancelot, or Pelleas, or Pellenore ;
And all the while harmonious airs were heard
Of chiming strings, or charming pipes, and winds
Of gentlest gales Arabian odours fanned
From their soft wings, and Flora's earliest smells.

But will anybody say that this most noble passage was the motive of 'Paradise Regained' in the sense that the desire to produce gorgeous word-colours was the motive of 'St. Agnes' Eve?'

The nearer Poetry approaches to Painting, the farther must it depart from action, because a picture can only represent an action suspended in a single moment of time. And if you sacrifice action in poetry, you sacrifice all that makes it the noblest of the arts, since it alone is able to convey to the mind in a rational form an idea of the most lofty and energetic passions that sway the human heart. Of these Keats knew nothing.

With his brilliant pictorial fancy, he was able to conjure up before his mind's eye all those *forms* of the Pagan world which were, by his own confession, invisible to Wordsworth ; but, on the other hand, to the actual strife of men, to the clash and conflict of opinion, to the moral meaning of the changes in social and political life, he was blind or indifferent. Physical science he regarded as the enemy of Poetry. 'Do not all charms,' he asks—

> Do not all charms fly
> At the mere touch of cold philosophy?
> There was an awful rainbow once in heaven;
> We know her woof, her texture; she is given
> In the dull catalogue of common things.
> Philosophy will clip an angel's wings,
> Conquer all mysteries by rule and line,
> Empty the haunted air and gnomed mine,
> Unweave a rainbow.

These lines appear to me to contain a world of suggestion. They speak with equal force, artistically, to enthusiasts who, like Wordsworth, contend that the sphere of poetry is co-extensive with the sphere of Nature, and morally (in their pessimism and melancholy) to

O

those other optimists who hold that the resources of Art are boundless, so long as it is
pursued simply for its own sake.   To detach the
imagination from its proper sphere, from the
range of associations in which it can move with
natural freedom, and to plunge it into the midst
of common actual life, is to confuse the limits
that separate composition in verse from composition in prose ; while, on the other hand, to
struggle to get absolutely free from the world of
sense and reality in pursuit of mere Beauty of
Form, involves a relaxation of all the nerves and
fibres of manly thought, the growth of affectation, and the consequent encouragement of all
the emasculating influences that produce swift
deterioration and final decay.

CONCLUSION:

THE PROSPECTS OF POETRY

VI.

CONCLUSION: THE PROSPECTS OF POETRY.

AN attempt has been made in the foregoing papers to ascertain by an historical inquiry the origin of the movement described in the above title. Now that I am on the point of arriving at a conclusion, I may be permitted to dwell for a moment on the meaning of that title—since its propriety has been more than once questioned—to justify the critical method that I have pursued, and to recapitulate the general course of my argument.

And, in the first place, I think I need not waste many words in proving that during the present century there has been *a* movement—whatever we choose to call it—in literature, as distinct and definite as what are known in religion by the names of the Methodist and Tractarian movements, and in politics by the names of the Liberal and Radical movements. However much Wordsworth and Shelley and Keats may differ from each other in their individual characteristics, no one, I imagine, who considers the subject, will deny that in many important respects they were moved by common external impulses, and united by a common spirit of antagonism to their immediate predecessors.

In the next place, it is scarcely more open to dispute that this movement was a party movement. The present age is quick enough to recognize the fact that criticisms such as that in the ' Edinburgh Review ' on Coleridge's '' Christabel,' or that in the ' Quarterly ' on Keats' ' Endymion,' were founded on purely party principles, that the critics, starting as they did from certain axioms of their own as to the requisites of poetry, were quite insensible to the essential beauties of the poems they were considering ; but it is not sufficiently remembered that Wordsworth and Coleridge were no less dogmatic and no less narrow in their depreciation of such a poet as Gray, or that the perception of Keats was dead to the merits of the

famous writer whom he ridiculously speaks of
as ' one Boileau,' and whom with equal absurdity
he regarded as the progenitor of the English
poets of the eighteenth century. Besides, it is
easy enough to separate the critics of the first
thirty years of the present century into two
groups, one containing such men as Gifford, Sir
Walter Scott, George Ellis, Campbell, Jeffrey,
and Macaulay, all of whom (though two of them
certainly speak with very little gratitude of those
from whom they had learned the most) had evidently formed their taste on eighteenth-century
literature; the other including writers like
Wordsworth, Coleridge, Keats, Leigh Hunt,
and others who were bitterly opposed to the
eighteenth century and all its works.

Once more. Whereas sixty years ago the
critical principles of the eighteenth century were
still in the ascendent, and the apostles of the
new departure were suffering martyrdom or
struggling with a hostile public opinion, the
balance of taste has so entirely shifted that the
writers whom our grandfathers regarded with
the greatest esteem are now spoken of at most

with tolerance and often with contempt. Thus Mr. Swinburne, wishing to disparage Byron in comparison with Shelley, classes the former with Pope, and is so kind as to allow both to be ' poets after a fashion,' while Mr. Arnold goes still farther, and loftily decides : ' Though Dryden and Pope may write in verse, though they may in a certain sense be masters of the art of versification, Dryden and Pope are not classics of our poetry, they are classics of our prose.'

Now considering that nearly two hundred years have passed since the birth of Pope, and that, from his death up to the present time, he and. Dryden have unanimously been accounted ' classics of our poetry,' we have a right to expect that Mr. Arnold should support his para-doxical judgment with corresponding strength of demonstration. And at first sight it appears as if he were ready to satisfy our requirements. His reasoning is deduced from axioms and postu-lates almost Euclidean in their absoluteness. The poetry of Dryden and Pope, he says, lacks that ' high seriousness ' which is the mark of the true poetical classic, and which is to be found in a number of isolated passages from the poets selected by him as examples of the classical style. But when we ask him further to define this ' high seriousness,' he declines to do anything of the kind.

' The characters,' says he, ' of a high quality of poetry are what is expressed *there*. They are far better recognised by being felt in the verse of the master, by being perused in the verse of the master, than in the prose of the critic. Nevertheless, if we are urgently pressed to give some critical account of them, we may safely, perhaps, venture on laying down, not, indeed, how and why the characters arise, but where and in what they arise. They are in the matter and substance of the poetry, and they are in its manner and style. Both of them, the substance and the matter on the one hand, the style and manner on the other, have a mark, an accent of high beauty, worth, and power. But if we are asked to define this mark and accent in the abstract, our answer must be : No, for we should thereby be darkening the question, not clearing it. The mark and accent are as given by the substance and matter of that poetry, by the style and manner of that poetry, and of all other poetry which is akin to it in quality.'

It must, I should think, be apparent to every reader that, after delivering himself of the dis-

paraging judgment that two of the greatest
metrical writers in our language are 'not classics
of our poetry,' Mr. Arnold has chosen to main-
tain his thesis simply by proving that they do
not write in the same manner as other poets of
a totally different order, whose style commends
itself to his perception as possessing the exclusive hall-mark of 'high beauty, worth, and
power.' He makes not the slightest attempt to
explain why the two writers whom he allows to
be 'classics of our prose' should in nine-tenths
of their best known work have chosen to express
·themselves in a metrical form. .

.   So long as Mr. Arnold restricted himself to
judgments on writers who, whatever may be
their exact position in our literature, are allowed
to be classics of some kind, his paradoxes might
only have excited amusement. But he has
determined to apply his test to poets whose
merits have from the very first been the subject
of fierce controversy ; and happening to decide
that Shelley is not to be reckoned among our
poetical 'classics,' he has naturally aroused the
wrath of Mr. Swinburne. Mr. Swinburne tells

him roundly that his moral canons are good for nothing, and then makes as if he were about to establish an impregnable position of his own by reasoning and argument. He declines, he says, to discuss a question of poetical taste with any man who will not grant the assumption that ' the two primary and essential qualities of poetry are imagination and harmony.' Many of us would be very glad to concede thus much ; but, oddly enough, when this new critical method comes to be tested by application, the standard of ' imagination and harmony ' is found to be of just as much practical use as the standard of ' high poetic seriousness '—that is to say, for controversial purposes it is of no use at all.

' The test of the highest poetry,' we are informed, ' is that it eludes all tests. Poetry in which there is no element at once perceptible and indefinable by any reader or hearer of any poetic instinct . . . is not poetry—above all, it is not lyric poetry—of the first water.'

And then Mr. Swinburne quotes two lines from Wordsworth, which, as I have said, removed from their context, are absolutely devoid of

meaning, and declares in his own manner : ' If
not another word of the poem was left in which
these two lines occur, those two lines would
suffice to show the hand of a poet differing not
in degree but in kind from the tribe of Byron.'
No doubt ; but differing also from the tribe of
Homer, Virgil, and Milton, whose most sublime
passages can readily be analysed into their
elements, though the life and genius that inspires
them is, of course, beyond the reach of analysis.
All that Mr. Swinburne proves by his argument
is that the poetry of Byron is of a different kind
from the poetry of Wordsworth and Shelley, and
that he himself infinitely prefers the poetry of
the two latter.

Neither Mr. Arnold nor Mr. Swinburne
justifies the absolute test of poetry which they
respectively propose. Their principles of ' high
poetic seriousness,' and of ' imagination and
harmony,' do not carry them a single step in
advance of their own perceptions : *stat pro
ratione voluntas*. Must we, then, give up all
hopes of arriving at a general agreement about
the nature of poetry and the merits of individual

poets, and be content to acquiesce in the anarchical maxim, *De gustibus non est disputandum* ? I think not. Poetry, as I have already said—and I believe that for controversial purposes it is the only working definition that can be found—is the art of producing pleasure for the imagination by means of metrical language. The test of poetry, therefore, is the extent and quality of the pleasure it produces—a relative standard of judgment, no doubt. The man who can, by his metrical writing, produce pleasure in the mind of any reader is *pro tanto* a poet. But since we are all constituted more or less after the same fashion, metrical writing, if it is worth anything, must be capable of exciting general pleasure, and pleasure in the minds of good judges. If it can do this it is presumably good poetry. But, again, since contemporary judgment is liable to be distracted and confused by transitory currents of feeling, it is impossible to decide certainly whether metrical writing has in it the qualities that please permanently and generally until it has been tested by *time.* When it has secured the approval of generations of good judges, then we may be sure that the writer, whatever be the kind of pleasure which his verse excites, is a classic poet. Nor is it open to any critic, however distinguished, to challenge the position which these poets have acquired, because his opinion can weigh nothing against the verdict of time and common sense. All that he can do usefully is to observe and record the methods which the poet, whatever his kind, has employed, and to apply these as a test to the contemporary metrical writers who attempt composition of an analogous order.

But if there be one element in all classical poetry which is relative simply to the sense of the individual, there is another which is relative solely to the sense of the nation. We are apt to think of the genius of great poets as something original and *per se*, yet anyone who considers the matter will see that all genuine poetry springs out of the imagination of the people. If it be, as it is, the function of the poet to show ' the very age and body of the time his form and pressure,' he must, in order to do this,

first receive into his own mind the influences
that are operating on his age and time. These
he reproduces in an ideal form, and hence
poetry is as much the reflection of the growth
of the national mind and conscience, as history
is the record of national life and action. Spenser
shows a clear perception of this truth when he
says :

> For deeds do die, however nobly done,
>   And thoughts of men do as themselves decay ;
> But wise words, taught in numbers for to run,
>   Recorded by the Muses, live for aye.

To understand, therefore, the genius of
classical poets, their relations to each other, as
well as to the whole course of their nation's
literature, and the causes that made them write
in metre in the way they did, we ought to be
historically acquainted with the general laws that
seem everywhere to determine the progress of
popular imagination.

In the paper with which I opened this
series I examined the assertion of Macaulay that
' as civilisation advances poetry almost necessarily declines.' The proposition is contra-

dicted, as I showed, by universal experience, since the greatest poems of the world, the ' Æneid,' ' The Divine Comedy,' ' Paradise Lost,' the plays of the Greek dramatists and of Shakespeare, were all produced in the maturity of national life, while even the ' Iliad ' and the ' Odyssey ' argue a high degree of refinement in the surroundings of the poet. The fact is indisputable, and the explanation of it is simple. Early society lacks the power of *expression*. Language is then wanting in precise and philosophical terms, as well as in rhythmical harmony, and these, no less than the mental qualities which they imply, judgment, design, the power of selection and rejection, in a word, all that is involved in the word ' taste,' are essential to the composition of a really great poem.

But, in so far as what Macaulay is thinking of is poetical *conception*, I hold that his opinion is entirely right. The early ages of a nation's life are the ages of belief, and belief is the parent of poetry. It is then when primitive and warlike habits prevail ; when there are few facilities for communication and comparison of ideas ; before men have begun to observe and inquire into the nature of things ; that the unconscious life and liberty of Imagination is largest and fullest. Monarch of all it surveys, it employs its incomparable myth-making powers in investing the various appearances of nature with an atmosphere of marvel and mystery. As society becomes more orderly and refined, it is recognised that many of the phenomena hitherto ascribed to supernatural agencies are the effects of uniform causes ; and wherever this scientific observation extends there is so much territory conquered from the unconscious creative Imagination. Poets of genius at the same time arise who, perceiving the extraordinary wealth of material created for them by the unconscious imagination of their fathers, utilise this for the purposes of their own sublime inventions. It cannot be denied, for example, that all the great poems I enumerated in the last paragraph have their roots in national belief. But the subject-matter of Imagination, already encroached upon by science, is thus

P

largely appropriated by the poets themselves, so that, for the purposes of *creation*, the opportunities of the late poet being much diminished, his genius is naturally turned towards the ethical, didactic, and satiric orders of metrical composition—all of which have their origin in the religious instincts of the people ; and in this sphere he strives to compensate for the lower range of his thought by the polish and perfection of his language. It would appear, then, that, if Macaulay's proposition be amended so as to assert that as civilisation advances the matter for poetical creation diminishes, while the powers of poetical expression are multiplied, we shall have a correct description of an invariable phenomenon in the history of the art.

Applying this general law to the course of English literature, it seems to me we may arrive at some very definite conclusions. Throughout its history the genius of our poetry exhibits itself in two aspects. Viewed in one light, it is seen to be mystical, picturesque, romantic ; in the other, it appears real, positive, natural. The sources of English poetry are, on the one hand, the Catholic Church and the Feudal. System, those 'Gothic and Monkish founda- tions,' as Burke calls them in his vivid manner, of our national life ; and on the other, the spirit of the Renaissance, which has done so much to modify the form of the literary superstructure. Moreover, through the earlier and greater period of our literature, the period between Chaucer and Milton, we see these two apparently con- flicting elements harmoniously fused and blended in the work of the poets, though, as our litera- ture develops, each element appears mixed there in very different proportions.

Let me dwell on this point with a little more detail. Take the poetry of Chaucer for instance. With him romance, in our sense of the word, is reality. He writes from within a system or order of society which has long ceased to exist, and he reflects all the ideas and sentiments proper to that system with complete *naïveté* and good faith. In the 'Parson's Tale,' for instance, he speaks like a good Catholic in approval of auricular confession ; 'The Flower and the Leaf' is full of the mystical morality of the age ;

while of the thirty Canterbury pilgrims themselves, the names of at least two-thirds express
some ecclesiastical relation which has no longer
any meaning for English society. And yet the
mystical atmosphere in which he breathed has
had no power to obscure the clear imagination
of the poet. The figures and characters of his
imperishable ' Pilgrimage' stand out before us
with as much distinctness as if five hundred
years had not intervened. In this power of
looking through social fashions and institutions
at Nature, as she really is, we see the first
traces in our literature of the genius of the
Renaissance.

In Spenser all this is changed : the romantic
in his work predominates over the real. The
feudal system is no longer part and parcel of
the national life : it has become an *allegory*, a
philosophical ideal to be aimed at by every
gentleman who desires to cultivate inward perfection. Throughout the allegory Pagan myths
lie oddly jumbled with mediæval dogmas, and
legendary forms are employed to cloak political
allusions ; yet all is somehow blended so as to

seem natural and harmonious in the fairy-land
of Spenser's fancy.   In spite of the Protestantism of the poet and the nation, we feel, as we
read the splendid description of the procession
of the Seven Deadly Sins in the House of Pride,
how deeply Catholic theology had coloured the
English imagination, and can readily understand
that, though much of the sense of the allegory
is lost to the modern world, the knightly virtues
of Prince Arthur possessed a real significance
for men like Sidney, Raleigh, and Essex.

When we come to Shakespeare we find a
perfect balance of the opposing principles.
Many incidental expressions throughout his
plays, and notably his histories, prove his
sympathies to have been monarchical, and his
religious faith Catholic, in the broad sense of the
word ; while in all his judgments of men and
manners he speaks like a typical Englishman
of the age of Elizabeth.   These 'Gothic and
Monkish foundations,' however, are only the
ground on which, just as Scott did after him,
he took his stand to let his imagination build
with more facility ideal structures out of the

materials supplied to it by his all-embracing
observation. He does not, like Chaucer, write
as the representative of a particular order of
society ; he does not, like Spenser, inculcate any
special ideal ; he views nature as she appears in
the strongest light of reason, common-sense,
and imagination : in a word, we feel in his
genius, as in that of no other poet, the spirit of
Humanity.

Milton's work, too, shows a like harmonious
blending of opposites ; but in him the centre of
gravity has travelled far to the side of Realism.
His subject-matter is Catholic and Romantic ;
witness, the whole theme of ' Paradise Lost,'
and those numerous allusions to the books of
chivalry, survivals of his ideas when it was in
his mind to take King Arthur as the hero of an
epic poem. Who can forget the comparison of
the mustering of the fallen angels with

> What resounds,
> In fable or romance of Uther's son,
> Begirt with British and Armoric knights;
> And all who since, baptised or infidel,
> Jousted at Aspramont, or Montalban,
> Damasco, or Morocco, or Trebizond,

> Or whom Biserta sent from Afric shore,
> When Charlemagne with all his peerage fell
> At Fontarabia.

But the *form* of his imagination is completely classical, and the whole bent of his individual prejudice, strongly Calvinist and Republican, is against the feudal and ecclesiastical institutions which are the cradle of Romance.

Now it is a fact which I think will be acknowledged by every careful student of English literature, that the two opposing principles which, even as late as the production of 'Paradise Lost,' appear in harmonious fusion, are, from Milton's time up to our own, seen in perpetual antagonism. During the eighteenth century Realism completely overpowers Romance; in the present century Romanticism has shown a constantly increasing hostility to Reality. How is this remarkable phenomenon to be explained? What was it that made a poet like Pope reject on critical grounds the principle of romance, and men of such robust genius as Fielding and Johnson encounter anything like enthusiastic sentiment with dislike

and contempt ?   It will not do to-say that this
kind of spirit was in the air, that the eighteenth
century was an age of prose and reason, not of
poetry ; for that is merely restating the difficulty in other words, besides overlooking the
fact that the present century has been an epoch
far more scientific and critical even than the
eighteenth, and yet. the present century has
witnessed an extraordinary revival of romance.

The explanation of the phenomenon that
I have offered in the foregoing papers is that
men of letters, after the Restoration, found
themselves confronted by an imaginative problem exactly analogous to the political diffi-
culties that perplexed the statesman.   Just as
Somers and his allies perceived the decline of
the feudal system as a motive power in the
constitution of society, and sought to establish
a new order with the least possible sacrifice
of ancient principle, so Dryden, Addison, and
Pope, finding that Romance, the ideal reflection
of the feudal spirit, was no longer a fitting
form for the expression of the ideas of the age,

modelled their style exclusively on forms derived from the Renaissance.

I have called this movement *Conservative*, because it was, in the first place, a movement in behalf of Order. The last half of the seventeenth century was a period of political and imaginative anarchy. When government by prerogative passed from the Tudors to the Stuarts, the end of government by prerogative was evidently at hand. Similarly, no one can study the poetry of the merely fashionable writers of the seventeenth century without seeing that the spirit of old Romance had ceased to be a living influence on the imagination. Whether you turn to the rants of the romantic drama under Charles II. and James II., or to the witty conceits of the poets of gallantry, like Suckling and Rochester, or to the ghosts of chivalric sentiment in the love-poems of Cowley and Waller, everywhere you find a vapid idealism based on hollowness and unreality. The question for the creative genius of the new age was whether some natural ideal could not be constituted between this lifeless formalism and

realism of the loathsome kind that throve so
rankly in the comedies of Etherege and his contemporaries. The answer was provided by the
poets in the characters of Achitophel and Zimri;
of Atticus and Sporus and Atossa; in the
'Vanity of Human Wishes'; in 'The Traveller';
in 'The Village' and 'The Borough'; and by
the writers of fiction in the person of Sir Roger
de Coverley, and all that splendid series of
pictures representing contemporary life and
manners from 'Tom Jones' down to 'Vanity
Fair.' Throughout this series the spirit of the
Renaissance speaks as clearly in the new order
of society as it did in Chaucer under the feudal
system.

Again, the imaginative movement after the
Restoration and in the eighteenth century may
be justly called Conservative, because it aimed
at preserving the principle of literary continuity.
When Carlyle, in his anger with the shams and
conventionalities of English life, calls out in
'Sartor Resartus' for 'old sick society to be
burned,' and when in an analogous spirit, in
order to emphasise his own individuality and

genuineness, he imports into the language all
kinds of Teutonic monstrosities, we see that we
are face to face with literary Radicalism. The
Conservative reformers of the eighteenth century
never strained after individualism of this kind.
Though they felt that a great part of the old
religious and military framework of society was
gone for ever, they sought to establish the new
social ideals on historic foundations, and to preserve whatever was noble in the life of the past.
Everybody will acknowledge the truth of this
observation as applied to Addison. But it is
applicable even to Dryden, at least in his views
as to the development of language. The idea of
inheritance, which is so prominent in all the
political speculations of Burke, is constantly
cropping up in Dryden's literary criticism.
Here, for instance, is a passage strongly illus-
trative of the poetical Conservatism of which I
am speaking :—

Milton was the poetical son of Spenser and Mr.
Waller of Fairfax, for we have our lineal descents and
classes as well as other families. Spenser more than
once insinuates that the soul of Chaucer was transfused
into his body, and that he was begotten by him two

hundred years after his decease. Milton has acknowledged to me that Spenser was his original, and many
besides myself have heard our ʼmous Waller own that
he derived the harmony of his numbers from the God-
frey of Bulloigne, which was turned into English by ·
Mr. Fairfax.

Pope was, in like manner, the poetical son of
Dryden ; and when he announced ' correctness '
to be his aim in writing, he merely signified, by
an epigrammatic phrase, his view of the kind of
development which the language appeared to
him to be still capable of receiving at the historic
stage in which he found it.

Now, whatever judgment we may be inclined
to pass on the poetry of the present century, I
think it will be generally acknowledged that, in
all essential points, its spirit is radically opposed
to the spirit of eighteenth-century verse. The
latter reflects the taste of a national aristocracy,
and is coloured throughout by the political
genius of the men who effected the Revolution
of 1688 ; the former has a thousand points of
contact and sympathy with the democratic
movement culminating in the French Revolution, which roused such vehement antipathy in

the mind of a typical Englishman like Burke. The literary movement in the eighteenth century was a constructive movement in behalf of social order in the sphere of imagination ; the movement of the nineteenth century was a practical assertion of the unfettered liberties of the individual imagination. And while the eighteenth century employed the classical forms familiar to the Renaissance to embody its positive and direct judgments on life and manners, the nineteenth century has striven to express the vague and unsatisfied cravings of imagination, by reviving forms of romance peculiar to the language in the earlier stages of society. For all these reasons I have transferred from politics the term usually opposed to the word 'Conservative,' and have called the imaginative revolution of this century ' The Liberal Movement in English Literature.'

We are in the habit of thinking of this great change in taste as the work of a few men of genius, who arbitrarily turned the imagination into new channels ; but the closer we look into the question, the more clearly we see that there

was an influence 'in the air,' and the general
causes which were at work in society disclose
themselves as plainly as those which operated
after the Restoration. The ruling force of the
eighteenth century, as has been said, was Aristocracy, an aristocracy which preserved the social
order produced spontaneously under the feudal
régime, while it discarded the outward forms
which expressed the Catholic and chivalric conceptions of life. Dryden and Addison, and
Pope and Fielding and Johnson, are the faithful
representatives of their age : their style exhibits
many of the essential qualities of the elder
writers whose language they inherit ; vigour,
distinctness of outline, unerring observation of
Nature, brilliant wit, with an added finish and
accuracy of expression ; but it lacks certain
other qualities which the work of those predecessors also possessed, pathos, enthusiasm,
emotion, mystery, in a word—Romance. Moreover, we find that as the aristocratic *régime* of
the eighteenth century becomes settled, and its
action regular and mechanical, individual impulse and vitality decline ; forms and con-

ventions gradually predominate. So, too, in
literature. Comparing the work of Darwin and
Hayley and Pye—or even poems of merit like
the ' Pleasures of Memory ' and the ' Pleasures
of Hope '—with work like 'Absalom and
Achitophel' or the ' Epistle to Arbuthnot ' or
' The Traveller,' we feel how feeble has become
the impulse of the once abundant fountains of
the Classical School, and that the poets who
drink from them are in the same exhausted case
as the last representatives of mediævalism in the
seventeenth century.

Contrarily, one sees the germs of the new
Romantic School far back in the literature of
the eighteenth century. They are visible in
what I have called the school of the Dilettanti,
in the poetry of men of genius like Gray and
Collins, where the imagination appears brooding
fondly over the images of bygone times. The
active spirit of democracy glows in the provincial
poetry of Burns. Rousseau's spirit of philosophic
melancholy transforms itself in England into the
religious melancholy of Cowper. But all these
external impulses are at present qualified and

checked by that prevailing sense of form which distinguishes the style of the poets of the eighteenth century.

Then comes the French Revolution, and whatever forces are at work in the age to carry the individual away from society, or to influence his mind against existing institutions, acquire an enormous impetus. Individualism becomes rampant; Liberty is everywhere the watchword of generous spirits; it is the mark of genius to assail all kinds of tradition and established order. The spirit of the age embodies itself in the philosophic isolation of Wordsworth; in the rebellion of Byron against society; in the Utopianism of Shelley; in the artistic reaction of Coleridge and Keats. I have traced in previous papers the various imaginative channels into which the rising waters forced their way; it is needless to recapitulate here what has been said; and it now only remains to endeavour to estimate the general results of the movement and its probable influence on the future of English poetry.

The vein of mediæval Romance was ex-

hausted in the seventeenth century; the inspiration of the Classical School failed at the
end of the eighteenth century: have we grounds
for thinking that the poetry of the nineteenth
century is fed from more enduring fountains?
Mr. Arnold has no misgivings on the subject:—

'The future of poetry,' says he, 'is immense, because in poetry, when it is worthy of its high destinies,
our race, as time goes on, will find an ever surer and
surer stay. There is not a creed which is not shaken,
not an accredited dogma which is not shown to be
questionable, not a received tradition which does not
threaten to dissolve. Our religion has materialised
itself in the fact, in the supposed fact, and now the fact
is failing it. But for poetry the idea is everything;
the rest is a world of illusion, of divine illusion. Poetry
attaches its emotions to the idea; the idea *is* the fact.
The strongest part of our religion to-day is its unconscious poetry.'

Forbearing any criticism on the characteristic
paradox which places the power of religion in
poetry, whereas all history shows that poetry
springs out of religion, what, let me ask, are the
grounds for Mr. Arnold's extraordinary confidence? Holding, as he does, that the metrical
compositions of the eighteenth century are un-

Q

deserving of the name of poetry, and all his sympathies being given to the poetical move-ment originating with Wordsworth, it is plain that he must look for the supply of the poetical ideas of which he speaks to the Romantic sources in our literature. And yet I should think no one can take a survey of the poetry of this century without being impressed with the large amount of what is merely temporary, evanescent, particular, in the romantic ideas embodied in it. For instance, there was the Romance of what Carlyle calls Werterism. To Byron this was a reality ; for the society contemporary with Byron it possessed enough of reality to become a fashion ; but the poet who should now think of working the mine would hardly make his fortune. There was, again, the Romance of Jacobinism. This was, in Shelley's time, virgin soil, and, as Mr. Swinburne has shown us in his 'Songs before Sunrise,' it still produces ideas available for treatment in verse ; but anyone may see that the thoughts and feelings which filled the mind of the elder poet with something like religious belief have changed in the hands of his successor

into a mere theme for metrical rhetoric. Once
more, there was what Wordsworth conceived to
be the Romance of Common Life. Yet it is
evident that what really inspired Wordsworth
was not Common Life, but the particular group
of romantic and patriotic associations connected
with his own birthplace ; nor has anyone since
been able to bend the bow of the Ulysses of the
Lakes. Lastly, there was Romance pure and
simple, and those who would test the difference
in romantic temperature between the first and
last quarters of the century have only to compare Marmion and William of Deloraine with
the revived Knights of the Round Table. In
the one case we have the representative of the
feudal age in England, a real being, though
with a touch of melodrama—*impiger, iracundus,
inexorabilis, acer* ; in the other, ideal figures,
which had some verisimilitude for the feudal
times in which they were conceived, but which,
in these latter days, in spite of their admirably
picturesque equipment, can scarcely disguise the
democratic and commercial nature of their origin.
As far, therefore, as the materials of Romance

go, there scarcely seems to be promise of a boundless future for Poetry.

If we look at the Form in which the ideas of Romance are expressed, in other words, at the question of Poetical Diction, our conclusions will not be very different. Dryden, after the Restoration, had sought to fix the standard of poetic diction by modelling it on the style of the best authors in the language qualified by the language of the best society of the time. He thus provided for the principles both of stability and development. To Wordsworth, however, this literary and social standard appeared too artificial. He wanted a larger liberty. It was his object :—

> Along Life's common way
> With sympathetic heart to stray,
> And with a soul of power.

As a follower of Rousseau, he held that the language of poetry should be founded not on literature or the forms of refined society, but on the idiom of the peasantry. As a philosopher, desiring to make poetry reflective, he sought to break down the distinctions between the

language of poetry and the language of prose.
He has had many followers, and a generation
ago volumes of philosophy in verse were much
more common than they are at present.   But
the movement was contrary to the genius of the
art.   Of metrical compositions of this kind the
reader instinctively asks, ' Why were they not
written in prose ? '

The movement initiated by Coleridge and
Keats was also a rebound from the standard of
Dryden, but in a totally different direction.
Their aim was to set the imagination at liberty
by removing it from all contact with modern
life, and they, therefore, looked for literary
models as free as possible from contemporary
associations.   These they found in the early
romantic poetry of the nation, where the spirit
of feudal Romance is still strong, and the
language, highly charged with metaphor, has
not yet come to maturity.   Steeping themselves in this atmosphere, they sought to combine certain dream-like associations of romantic
ideas in musical movements of metre and
picturesque combinations of words.

One might, indeed, imagine that the inexhaustible variety of literary romantic themes would give scope for an almost boundless extension of the art of poetry to those who simply seek to develop in it the elements of painting and music.   Yet though the movement begun by Coleridge and Keats was continued with exquisite skill by Lord Tennyson in his earlier poems, and though it has received a yet further development in the hands of Mr. Swinburne and the late Mr. Rossetti, no one, I should think, can fail to be struck with the fact that in the works of the two latest representatives of the Romantic School there is far less liberty of imagination.   In 'The Ancient Mariner,' and in ' St. Agnes' Eve ' the rapid succession of musical ideas, or the rich colouring of the verbal imagery, carries us away into dreamland.   But in a ' Ballad ' of Mr. Swinburne or Mr. Rossetti, the effect is quite different.   What primarily impresses the reader is the extraordinary skill shown by the poet in the imitation of antique forms ; we are always conscious of the presence of the artist ; it is plain that he is thinking less of the theme itself than of its capacities for enabling him to display his powers of word-painting or of metre-music.

All these symptoms seem to me to point to but one conclusion. As the Classical and Conservative Movement in English Literature exhausted itself at the end of the last century, so the inspiration of the Romantic School is now failing, and the Liberal Movement in our Literature, as well as in our Politics, is beginning to languish. Nor are the causes of this decline at all difficult to comprehend. The Liberal Movement was a practical protest on behalf of liberty for the individual imagination—a protest against the trammels of form and convention which, at the end of the eighteenth century, were stifling life and nature and simplicity. But owing to the force of circumstances it has grown to be a revolt against society. Forgetful that the source of poetry, as of the language which is its vehicle, lies not only in himself, but in the nation to which he belongs, the latter-day poet has sought to turn poetry into the ideal of the individual, instead of being what it once was,

the ideal of society.   Hence the revival of forms
and methods of poetical diction proper to bygone
ages.   The present direction of the movement is
contrary to nature.   In its craving for unlimited
liberty of imagination our latest school of
metrical writing is aiming at an unattainable
ideal.   The author of ' Marius the Epicurean '
—a book full of fine genius and imagination—
himself a Liberal in the region of art, shows a
far truer perception of the nature of the problem
which the modern poet has to solve.

   ' Homer had said,' so he writes—

     Οἱ δ'ὅτε δὴ λιμένος πολυβενθέος ἐντὸς ἵκοντο,
     Ἱστία μὲν στείλαντο, θέσαν δ' ἐν νηὶ μελαίνῃ,
     Ἐκ δὲ καὶ αὐτοὶ βαῖνον ἐπὶ ῥηγμῖνι θαλάσσης.

' And how poetic the simple incident seemed told just
thus : Homer was always telling things in this manner.
And one might think there had been no effort there ;
that it was but the almost mechanical transcript of a
time intrinsically and naturally poetic, in which one
could hardly have spoken at all without ideal effect, or
the sailors have pulled down their boat without making
a picture " in the great style," against a sky charged
with marvels.   Must not an age, itself thus ideal, have
counted for more than half of the whole work ? '

Undoubtedly it must; in the early ages of

society the atmosphere of imagination is universal and its pressure is equal on all sides.   In
later times, as science and refinement advance,
the pressure diminishes; but in every age there
are certain ideal perceptions of nature which
are common to every individual ; and he who
realises these most strongly and expresses them
in metre most naturally is the classical poet.

It is this positive ideal spirit, prevailing in
the best poetry of the eighteenth century, which
all metrical composers of the rising generation
might study with advantage.   The men of
genius in that age felt that the spirit which had
produced the philosophy of Bacon, the psycho-
logical speculations of Locke, the discoveries of
Newton, as well as the Reformation and the
Revolution of 1688, could not find adequate
expression in those romantic forms which the
fashionable poets of the seventeenth century
employed to decorate the expiring spirit of
mediævalism.   They faced nature boldly, and
wrote about it in metre directly as they felt it :
hence their conception, such as it is, is founded
on reality ; the portraits of Zimri the statesman,

and Atticus the man of letters, are, in their own kind, as ideally true as Chaucer's Good Parson and Shakespeare's Hamlet. The ideal was, no doubt, too cold, unemotional, and repressive, nor is it at all wonderful that the men who lived through the fever of the Revolutionary period should have rebounded into Romanticism. That period was essentially a lyrical one, when poets were moved to write about their own feelings and ideas, rather than about things. But now that the atmosphere has sensibly cooled ; now that the poet is beginning to aim again at Invention and Creation ; it is all-important to be sure that we have solid and positive conceptions of Nature on which to build our ideal.

On the other hand, if we are simply and solely positive, we shall not be able to create at all. The exclusively scientific order which the philosophers who have appropriated the title of Positive would impose upon society is more remote from the reality of nature, or, at least, of human nature, than the wildest extravagances of the 'Arabian Nights.' The revolt of the Romantic school against the excessive realism of the eighteenth century, ought to prove, *à fortiori*, that men will not tolerate an intellectual system from which the mystical and religious element is altogether excluded.

In an ancient nation like ours, moved by instincts and beliefs of which the origin lies far beyond the reach of analysis, the progress of imagination keeps pace with the development of society; and just as in the political world it is becoming more and more evident that an union must be effected between the principles of Liberalism and Conservatism, so the best hopes for the future of Poetry seem to lie in a reconciliation between the Positive and Romantic elements of the Imagination. There is no essential contradiction between the two principles. Mr. William Morris, indeed, one of those who have done the most to develop the Romantic movement pure and simple, urges as an apology for reviving the external manner of Chaucer that the present is 'an empty day.' But of no society in which men retain, even in the lowest degree, the power of forming ideal conceptions can this justly be said. If the spirit of patriotic

action out of which spring the Epic and the Drama
languishes, if the ethical standard of society
decays, yet the historic conscience of the nation
has the Satiric Form in which to embody itself,
and Juvenal's scornful question *Quid magis
Heracleas?* has profound significance as an
answer to all those who, in a declining age, cry
to Poetry to 'simply tell the most heart-easing
things.' But we are not living under a Domi-
tian. We are all of us conscious, Mr. Morris as
much as any man, of imaginative impulses from
without; what is wanting is the genius to conceive and construct some Ideal which shall ' show
the very age and body of the time his form and
pressure.' Doubtless it is a matter of infinite
difficulty in an era of Steam, Electricity, and
Cheap Literature, in an Age of Appearances,
when everything seems to take a momentary
shape and then to be forgotten, to discover the
element of the real, the permanent, the classical
—the ideal element, that is to say, which is
relative not only to the individual but to society.
Yet such an element there must be somewhere;
and within this ideal region, whatever it may

be, are the limits of the just liberties of the
poet.

To attempt to define the boundaries of poetic
liberty would be foolish ; but, as a practical conclusion to these papers, I will venture to indicate
two points in which I think that the reappear-
ance of the Positive Element in poetic creation
and an increased attention to classical models
would exercise a vitalizing influence on the art.
In the first place we should recognize the soundness of Dryden's principle of poetic diction.   It
is true that the principle is essentially aristocratic, and that there is a danger of its proving
artificial in its application ; it is true, too, that
Wordsworth, yielding to the democratic impulse,
and to the desire to be *natural*, strove to break
down what he regarded as the arbitrary barriers
between the language of poetry and the language
of prose ; but it is no less true that the counter-
movement of Coleridge and Keats proves that
the poetical instinct insists on the distinction
between the two methods of expression.   The
purely literary standard erected by Coleridge
and Keats has been carried forward by succes-

sive modern poets with great artistic skill and invention ; the mischief of it is that those who hold by it, ignoring the *social* principle of Dryden, the ' usus ' of Horace, and concentrating their energies solely on the construction of new metres, or new metrical combinations of words, help to exhaust the virility and stunt the growth of the language. An attempt to restore the habit of writing naturally, yet with the distinctions proper to verse, would probably lead to a revival of the simpler iambic movements of English in metres historically established in our literature. How readily such metres mould themselves to the social idiom of the time may be seen from Byron's use of the Spenser stanza in his noble reflections on the Battle of Waterloo in ' Childe Harold,' and of the *ottava rima* in the description of the shipwreck in ' Don Juan.'

Again, a study of the classical poets would re-establish those habits of instinctive judgment which enable the metrical writer to discern the boundaries and relations between the sphere of poetry and the sphere of science. What one admires in the work of Homer and Æschylus and Aristophanes and Virgil and Juvenal, and in the English poets who most resemble them, in Chaucer and Shakespeare, and Dryden and Scott, is the power of reproducing the idea of external Nature, and the complete disappearance of the poet in his creation. In modern poetry one finds, on the contrary, perpetual self-consciousness—opinions, theories, philosophies, broken lights reflected from many minds, but not the distinct idea of an external world. Why is this ? Is it not that the old poets started from a basis of positive Acceptance, while the modern poet writes in an atmosphere of Doubt. Since Wordsworth's time, the poets have universally adopted the method of introspection, and have introduced into their art the principle of analysis which is the proper instrument of science. The man of science begins his investigation with doubt because he hopes to end with certainty ; but the poet whose object is to create must necessarily build on a foundation of belief. The ideal creator in prose or verse who seeks to represent the real character, the positive life, of the Nation—something necessarily very different from the kaleidoscopic thoughts about itself which it reads daily in the newspapers—will draw his inspiration not simply from his own individual mind, but from national Instinct, Conscience, Memory, fountains which lie far back in the infancy of the people, and beyond the reach of Analysis. In respect of this *inspiration*, poets are not free agents : the freedom of true Genius is shown by constructing from the conceptions of Nature with which the national Muse supplies her favourites, a form of expression unaffected in thought, masculine in diction, suitable to the growth of the language and the scientific requirements of the age.

PRINTED BY
SPOTTISWOODE AND CO., NEW-STREET SQUARE
LONDON

ALBEMARLE STREET, LONDON.
January, 1885.

MR. MURRAY'S
GENERAL LIST OF WORKS.

ALBERT MEMORIAL. A Descriptive and Illustrated Account of the National Monument erected to the PRINCE CONSORT at Kensington. Illustrated by Engravings of its Architecture, Decorations, Sculptured Groups, Statues, Mosaics, Metalwork, &c. With Descriptive Text. By DOYNE C. BELL. With 24 Plates. Folio. 12*l.* 12*s.*

—————————— HANDBOOK TO. Post 8vo. 1*s.*; or Illustrated Edition, 2*s.* 6*d.*

—————— (PRINCE) SPEECHES AND ADDRESSES. Fcap. 8vo. 1*s.*

ABBOTT (REV. J.). Memoirs of a Church of England Missionary in the North American Colonies. Post 8vo. 2*s.*

ABERCROMBIE (JOHN). Enquiries concerning the Intellectual Powers and the Investigation of Truth. Fcap. 8vo. 3*s.* 6*d.*

ACLAND (REV. CHARLES). Popular Account of the Manners and Customs of India. Post 8vo. 2*s.*

ADMIRALTY PUBLICATIONS; Issued by direction of the Lords Commissioners of the Admiralty:—

CHALLENGER EXPEDITION, 1873—1876: Report of the Scientific Results of. ZOOLOGY. Vol. I. 37*s.* 6*d.* Vol. II. 50*s.* Vol. III. 50*s.* Vol. IV. 50*s.* Vol. V. 50*s.* Vol. VI. 42*s.* Vol. VII. 30*s.* Vol. VIII. 40*s.*

A MANUAL OF SCIENTIFIC ENQUIRY, for the Use of Travellers. Edited by R. MAIN, M.A. Woodcuts. Post 8vo. 3*s.* 6*d.*

GREENWICH ASTRONOMICAL OBSERVATIONS, 1837 to 1880. Royal 4to. 20*s.* each.

GREENWICH ASTRONOMICAL RESULTS, 1847 to 1881. 4to. 3*s.* each.

MAGNETICAL AND METEOROLOGICAL OBSERVATIONS, 1841 to 1847. Royal 4to. 20*s.* each.

MAGNETICAL AND METEOROLOGICAL RESULTS, 1848 to 1881. 4to. 3*s.* each.

APPENDICES TO OBSERVATIONS.

1837. Logarithms of Sines and Cosines in Time. 3*s.*

1842. Catalogue of 1439 Stars, from Observations made in 1836, 1841. 4*s.*

1845. Longitude of Valentia (Chronometrical). 3*s.*

1847. I. Description of Altazimuth. 3*s.*
    III. Description of Photographic Apparatus. 2*s.*

1851. Maskelyne's Ledger of Stars. 3*s.*

1852. I. Description of the Transit Circle. 3*s.*

1853. Bessel's Refraction Tables. 3*s.*

1854. I. Description of the Reflex Zenith Tube. 3*s.*
    II. Six Years' Catalogue of Stars from Observations. 1848 to 1853. 4*s.*

1860. Reduction of Deep Thermometer Observations. 2*s.*

1862. II. Plan of Ground and Buildings of Royal Observatory, Greenwich. 3*s.*
    III. Longitude of Valentia (Galvanic). 2*s.*

1864. I. Moon's Semi-diameter, from Occultations. 2*s.*
    II. Reductions of Planetary Observations. 1831 to 1835. 2*s.*

1868. I. Corrections of Elements of Jupiter and Saturn. 2*s.*
    II. Second Seven Years' Catalogue of 2760 Stars. 1861-7. 4*s.*
    III. Description of the Great Equatorial. 3*s.*

1871. Description of Water Telescope. 3*s.*

1873. Regulations of the Royal Observatory. 2*s.*

1876. II. Nine Years' Catalogue of 2283 Stars. 1868-76. 6*s.*

1879. Description of Greenwich Time Signal System. 2*s.*

ADMIRALTY PUBLICATIONS—*continued.*

Cape of Good Hope Observations (Star Ledgers). 1856 to 1863. 2*s*.

——————————————————— 1856. 5*s*.

——————————— Astronomical Results. 1857 to 1858. 5*s*.

Cape Catalogue, 1834 to 1840, reduced to Epoch 1840. 7*s*. 6*d*.

—————— of 1159 Stars, 1856 to 1891, reduced to the Epoch 1860. 3*s*.

——————, 12,441 Stars for Epoch 1880. 31*s*. 6*d*.

Cape of Good Hope Astronomical Results. 1859 to 1860. 5*s*.

——————————————————— 1871 to 1873. 5*s*.

——————————————————— 1874 to 1876. 5*s*. each.

Report on Teneriffe Astronomical Experiment. 1856. 5*s*.

Observations on the Transit of Venus, 1874. 20*s*.

Paramatta Catalogue of 7385 Stars. 1822 to 1826. 4*s*.

REDUCTION OF THE OBSERVATIONS OF PLANETS. 1750 to 1830. Royal 4to. 20*s*. each.

———————————————— LUNAR OBSERVATIONS. 1750 to 1830. 2 Vols. Royal 4to. 20*s*. each.

———————————————— 1831 to 1851. 4to. 10*s*. each.

ARCTIC PAPERS. 13*s*. 6*d*.

BERNOULLI'S SEXCENTENARY TABLE. 1779. 4to. 5*s*.

BESSEL'S AUXILIARY TABLES FOR HIS METHOD OF CLEAR-ING LUNAR DISTANCES. 8vo. 2*s*.

ENCKE'S BERLINER JAHRBUCH, for 1830. *Berlin*, 1828. 8vo.

HANNYNGTON'S HAVERSINES. 21*s*.

HANSEN'S TABLES DE LA LUNE. 4to. 20*s*.

LAX'S TABLES FOR FINDING THE LATITUDE AND LONGI-TUDE. 1821. 8vo. 10*s*

LUNAR OBSERVATIONS at GREENWICH. 1783 to 1819. Compared with the Tables, 1821. 4to. 7*s*. 6*d*.

MACLEAR ON LACAILLE'S ARC OF MERIDIAN. 2 Vols. 20*s*. each.

MAYER'S DISTANCES of the MOON'S CENTRE from the PLANETS. 1822, 3*s*.; 1823, 4*s*. 6*d*. 1824 to 1835. 8vo. 4*s*. each.

MAYER'S TABULÆ MOTUUM SOLIS ET LUNÆ. 1770. 5*s*.

———— ASTRONOMICAL OBSERVATIONS MADE AT GÖT-TINGEN, from 1756 to 1761. 1826. Folio. 7*s*. 6*d*.

NAUTICAL ALMANACS, from 1767 to 1887. 2*s*. 6*d*. each.

———————————— SELECTIONS FROM, up to 1812. 8vo. 5*s*. 1834-54. 5*s*.

———————————— SUPPLEMENTS, 1828 to 1833, 1837 and 1838. 2*s*. each.

———————————— TABLE requisite to be used with the N.A. 1781. 8vo. 5*s*.

SABINE'S PENDULUM EXPERIMENTS to DETERMINE THE FIGURE OF THE EARTH. 1825. 4to. 40*s*.

SHEPHERD'S TABLES for CORRECTING LUNAR DISTANCES. 1772. Royal 4to. 21*s*.

———————————— TABLES, GENERAL, of the MOON'S DISTANCE from the SUN, and 10 STARS. 1787. Folio. 5*s*. 6*d*.

TAYLOR'S SEXAGESIMAL TABLE. 1780. 4to. 15*s*.

———————————— TABLES OF LOGARITHMS. 4to. 60*s*.

TIARK'S ASTRONOMICAL OBSERVATIONS for the LONGITUDE of MADEIRA. 1822. 4to. 5*s*.

———————————— CHRONOMETRICAL OBSERVATIONS for DIFFERENCES of LONGITUDE between DOVER, PORTSMOUTH, and FALMOUTH. 1823. 4to. 5*s*.

VENUS and JUPITER: OBSERVATIONS of, compared with the TABLES. *London*, 1822. 4to. 2*s*.

WALES AND BAYLY'S ASTRONOMICAL OBSERVATIONS. 1777. 4to. 21*s*.

———————————— REDUCTION OF ASTRONOMICAL OBSERVATIONS MADE IN THE SOUTHERN HEMISPHERE. 1764—1771. 1788. 4to. 10*s*. 6*d*.

ÆSOP'S FABLES. A New Version. By REV. THOMAS JAMES. With 100 Woodcuts, by TENNIEL and WOLFE. Post 8vo. 2*s*. 6*d*.

AGRICULTURAL (ROYAL) JOURNAL. (*Published half-yearly.*)

ALICE; GRAND DUCHESS OF HESSE, PRINCESS OF GREAT
BRITAIN AND IRELAND. Biographical Sketch and Letters, Edited by
H.R.H. Princess Christian. With portraits. Crown 8vo. 12s.

AMBER-WITCH (THE). A most interesting Trial for Witch-
craft. Translated by LADY DUFF GORDON. Post 8vo. 2s.

AMERICA. [See NADAILLAC.]

APOCRYPHA : With a Commentary Explanatory and Critical,
by various Writers. Edited by the REV. HENRY WACE, D.D.
2 vols. Medium 8vo.   [*In the Press.*

ARISTOTLE. [See GROTE, HATCH.]

ARMY LIST (THE). *Published Monthly by Authority.*

———— (THE QUARTERLY OFFICIAL). Royal 8vo. 15s.

ARTHUR'S (LITTLE) History of England. By LADY CALLCOTT.
New Edition, continued to 1878. With 36 Woodcuts. Fcap. 8vo. 1s. 6d.

————HISTORY OF FRANCE, from the earliest times to the
Fall of the Second Empire. With Map and Woodcuts. Fcp. 8vo. 2s. 6d.

AUSTIN (JOHN). LECTURES ON GENERAL JURISPRUDENCE; or, the
Philosophy of Positive Law. Edited by ROBERT CAMPBELL. 2 Vols.
8vo. 32s.

———— STUDENT'S EDITION, compiled from the above work,
by ROBERT CAMPBELL. Post 8vo. 12s.

———— Analysis of. By GORDON CAMPBELL. Post 8vo. 6s.

BABER (E. C.) Travels in W. China. Maps. Royal 8vo. 5s.

BARCLAY (BISHOP). Extracts from the Talmud, illustrating
the Teaching of the Bible. With an Introduction. 8vo. 14s.

BARKLEY (H. C.). Five Years among the Bulgarians and Turks
between the Danube and the Black Sea. Post 8vo. 10s. 6d.

———— Bulgaria Before the War; during a Seven Years'
Experience of European Turkey and its Inhabitants. Post 8vo. 10s. 6d.

———— My Boyhood : a True Story. Illustrations. Post
8vo. 6s.

BARROW (JOHN). Life, Exploits, and Voyages of Sir Francis
Drake. Post 8vo. 2s.

BARRY (EDW. M.), R.A. Lectures on Architecture. Edited,
with Memoir, by Canon Barry. Portrait and Illustrations. 8vo. 16s.

BATES (H. W.). Records of a Naturalist on the Amazons during
Eleven Years' Adventure and Travel. Illustrations. Post 8vo. 7s. 6d.

BAX (CAPT.). Russian Tartary, Eastern Siberia, China, Japan,
&c. Illustrations. Crown 8vo. 12s.

BECKETT (SIR EDMUND). "Should the Revised New Testament be Authorised?" Post 8vo. 6s.

BELL (SIR CHAS.). Familiar Letters. Portrait. Post 8vo. 12s.

———— (DOYNE C.). Notices of the Historic Persons buried in
the Chapel of St. Peter ad Vincula, in the Tower of London. Illustrations. Crown 8vo. 14s.

BENSON (ARCHBISHOP). The Cathedral; its necessary place in
the Life and Work of the Church. Post 8vo. 6s

BERTRAM (JAS. G.). Harvest of the Sea : an Account of British
Food Fishes, including Fisheries and Fisher Folk. Illustrations.
Post 8vo. 9s.

BESANT (WALTER). The Life and Achievements of Professor E.
H. Palmer, from his Birth to his Murder by the Arabs of the Desert
1882. With Portrait. Crown 8vo. 12s.

BIBLE COMMENTARY. THE OLD TESTAMENT. EXPLANATORY
and CRITICAL. With a REVISION of the TRANSLATION. By BISHOPS
and CLERGY of the ANGLICAN CHURCH. Edited by F. C. COOK,
M.A., Canon of Exeter. 6 VOLS. Medium 8vo. 6l. 15s.

Vol. I. 30s.	GENESIS, EXODUS, LEVI- TICUS, NUMBERS, DEU- TERONOMY.	VOL. IV. 24s.	JOB, PSALMS, PROVERBS, ECCLESIASTES, SONG OF SOLOMON.
Vols. II. and III. 36s.	JOSHUA, JUDGES, RUTH, SAMUEL, KINGS, CHRO- NICLES, EZRA, NEHEMIAH, ESTHER.	Vol. V. 20s. Vol. VI. 25s.	ISAIAH, JEREMIAH. EZEKIEL, DANIEL, MINOR PROPHETS.

THE NEW TESTAMENT. 4 VOLS. Medium 8vo.   4l. 14s.

Vol. I. 18s.	INTRODUCTION, ST. MAT- THEW, ST. MARK, ST. LUKE.	Vol. III. 28s.	ROMANS, CORINTHIANS, GALATIANS, PHILIPPIANS, EPHESIANS, COLOSSIANS, THESSALONIANS, PASTO- RAL EPISTLES, PHILEMON.
Vol. II. 20s.	ST. JOHN. ACTS OF THE APOSTLES.	Vol. IV. 28s.	HEBREWS, SS. JAMES, PETER, JOHN, JUDE, AND THE REVELATION.

——————— THE STUDENT'S EDITION. Abridged and Edited
by PROFESSOR J. M. FULLER, M.A., Crown 8vo. 7s. 6d. each Volume.
THE OLD TESTAMENT. 4 Vols.
THE NEW TESTAMENT. 2 vols.

BIGG-WITHER (T. P.). Pioneering in South Brazil; Three Years
of Forest and Prairie Life in the Province of Parana. Map and Illustrations. 2 vols. Crown 8vo. 24s.

BIRD (ISABELLA). Hawaiian Archipelago; or Six Months among
the Palm Groves, Coral Reefs, and Volcanoes of the Sandwich Islands.
Illustrations. Crown 8vo. 7s. 6d.

——————— Lady's Life in the Rocky Mountains.   Illustrations.
Post 8vo. 7s. 6d.

——————— The Golden Chersonese and the Way Thither. With Map
and Illustrations. Post 8vo. 14s.

——————— Unbeaten Tracts in Japan : Travels of a Lady in the
Interior of Japan, including Visits to the Aborigines of Yezo and the
Shrines of Nikko and Isé. New and Popular Edition. With Map and
Illustrations. Crown 8vo. .

BISSET (SIR JOHN). Sport and War in South Africa from 1834 to
1867, with a Narrative of the Duke of Edinburgh's Visit. Illustrations. Crown 8vo. 14s.

BLUNT (LADY ANNE). The Bedouins of the Euphrates Valley.
With some account of the Arabs and their Horses. Illustrations.
2 Vols. Crown 8vo. 24s.

——————— A Pilgrimage to Nejd, the Cradle of the Arab Race, and
a Visit to the Court of the Arab Emir. Illustrations. 2 Vols. Post
8vo. 24s.

BLUNT (REV. J. J.). Undesigned Coincidences in the Writings of
the Old and NewTestaments,anArgument of their Veracity. Post 8vo. 6s.

——————— History of the Christian Church in the First Three
Centuries. Post 8vo. 6s.

——————— The Parish Priest; His Duties, Acquirements, and
Obligations. Post 8vo. 6s.

——————— University Sermons.   Post 8vo.   6s.

BOOK OF COMMON PRAYER. Illustrated with Coloured
Borders, Initial Letters, and Woodcuts. 8vo. 18s.

BORROW (GEORGE). The Bible in Spain; Post 8vo. 5s.

———— Gypsies of Spain; their Manners and Customs. Portrait.
Post 8vo. 5s.

———— Lavengro ; The Scholar—The Gypsy—and the Priest.
Post 8vo. 5s.

———— Romany Rye. Post 8vo. 5s.

———— WILD WALES: its People, Language, and Scenery.
Post 8vo. 5s.

———— Romano Lavo-Lil ; Word-Book of the Romany, or
English Gypsy Language. Post 8vo. 10s. 6d.

BOSWELL'S Life of Samuel Johnson, LL.D. Including the
Tour to the Hebrides. Edited by Mr. CROKER. Seventh Edition.
Portraits. 1 vol. Medium 8vo. 12s.

BRADLEY (DEAN). Arthur Penrhyn Stanley ; Biographical
Lectures. Crown 8vo. 3s. 6d.

BREWER (REV. J. S.). The Reign of Henry VIII.; from his
Accession till the Death of Wolsey. Reviewed and Illustrated from
Original Documents. Edited by JAMES GAIRDNER, of the Record Office.
With portrait. 2 vols. 8vo. 30s.

BRIDGES (MRS. F. D.). A Lady's Travels in Japan, Thibet,
Yarkand, Kashmir, Java, the Straits of Malacca, Vancouver's Island,&c.
With Map and Illustrations from Sketches by the Author. Crown 8vo. 15s.

BRITISH ASSOCIATION REPORTS. 8vo.
₊ The reports for the years 1831 to 1875 may be obtained at the Offices
of the British Association.

Glasgow, 1876, 25s.	Swansea, 1880, 24s.
Plymouth, 1877, 24s.	York, 1881, 24s.
Dublin, 1878, 24s.	Southampton, 1882, 24s.
Sheffield, 1879, 24s.	Southport, 1883, 24s.

BROCKLEHURST (T. U.). Mexico To-day: A country with a
Great Future. With a Glance at the Prehistoric Remains and Antiquities of the Montezumas. Plates and Woodcuts. Medium 8vo. 21s.

BRUGSCH (PROFESSOR). A History of Egypt, under the
Pharaohs. Derived entirely from Monuments, with a Memoir on the
Exodus of the Israelites. Maps. 2 vols. 8vo. 32s.

BUNBURY (E. H.). A History of Ancient Geography, among the
Greeks and Romans, from the Earliest Ages till the Fall of the Roman
Empire. Maps. 2 Vols. 8vo. 21s.

BURBIDGE (F. W.). The Gardens of the Sun: or A Naturalist's
Journal in Borneo and the Sulu Archipelago. Illustrations. Cr. 8vo. 14s.

BURCKHARDT'S Cicerone ; or Art Guide to Painting in Italy.
New Edition, revised by J. A. CROWE. Post 8vo. 6s.

BURGES (SIR JAMES BLAND) BART. Selections from his Letters
and Papers, as Under-Secretary of State for Foreign Affairs. With
Notices of his Life. Edited by JAMES HUTTON. 8vo.

BURGON (J. W.), DEAN OF CHICHESTER. The Revision Revised :
(1.) The New Greek Text; (2.) The New English Version; (3.) Westcott and Hort's Textual Theory. 8vo. 14s.

BURN (Col.). Dictionary of Naval and Military Technical Terms, English and French—French and English. Crown 8vo. 15s.

BUTTMANN'S LEXILOGUS; a Critical Examination of the Meaning of numerous Greek Words, chiefly in Homer and Hesiod. By Rev. J. R. FISHLAKE. 8vo. 12s.

BUXTON (CHARLES). Memoirs of Sir Thomas Fowell Buxton, Bart. Portrait. 8vo. 16s. *Popular Edition.* Fcap. 8vo. 5s.

———— Notes of Thought. With a Biographical Notice by Rev. J. LLEWELLYN DAVIES, M.A. *Second Edition.* Post 8vo. 5s.

———— (SYDNEY C.). A Handbook to the Political Questions of the Day; with the Arguments on Either Side. Fourth Edition, revised and enlarged. 8vo. 6s.

BYLES (SIR JOHN). Foundations of Religion in the Mind and Heart of Man. Post 8vo. 6s.

BYRON'S (LORD) LIFE AND WORKS:—

LIFE, LETTERS, AND JOURNALS. By THOMAS MOORE. *Cabinet Edition.* Plates. 6 Vols. Fcap. 8vo. 18s.; or One Volume, Portraits. Royal 8vo., 7s. 6d.

LIFE AND POETICAL WORKS. *Popular Edition.* Portraits. 2 vols. Royal 8vo. 15s.

POETICAL WORKS. *Library Edition.* Portrait. 6 Vols. 8vo. 45s.

POETICAL WORKS. *Cabinet Edition.* Plates. 10 Vols. 12mo. 30s.

POETICAL WORKS. *Pocket Ed.* 8 Vols. 16mo. In a case. 21s.

POETICAL WORKS. *Popular Edition.* Plates. Royal 8vo. 7s. 6d.

POETICAL WORKS. *Pearl Edition.* Crown 8vo. 2s. 6d. Cloth Boards. 3s. 6d.

CHILDE HAROLD. With 80 Engravings. Crown 8vo. 12s.

CHILDE HAROLD. 16mo. 2s. 6d.

CHILDE HAROLD. Vignettes. 16mo. 1s.

CHILDE HAROLD. Portrait. 16mo. 6d.

TALES AND POEMS. 16mo. 2s. 6d.

MISCELLANEOUS. 2 Vols. 16mo. 5s.

DRAMAS AND PLAYS. 2 Vols. 16mo. 5s.

DON JUAN AND BEPPO. 2 Vols. 16mo. 5s.

BEAUTIES. Poetry and Prose. Portrait. Fcap. 8vo. 3s. 6d.

CAMPBELL (LORD). Life: Based on his Autobiography, with selections from Journals, and Correspondence. Edited by Mrs. Hardcastle. Portrait. 2 Vols. 8vo. 30s.

———— Lord Chancellors and Keepers of the Great Seal of England. From the Earliest Times to the Death of Lord Eldon in 1838. 10 Vols. Crown 8vo. 6s. each.

———— Chief Justices of England. From the Norman Conquest to the Death of Lord Tenterden. 4 Vols. Crown 8vo. 6s. each.

———— (THOS.) Essay on English Poetry. With Short Lives of the British Poets. Post 8vo. 3s. 6d.

CAREY (Life of). See GEORGE SMITH.

CARLISLE (BISHOP OF). Walks in the Regions of Science and Faith—a Series of Essays. Contents:—Connection between Mechanics and Geometry; Unity of Nature: a Speculation; God and Nature; Philosophy of Crayfishes; Man's Place in Nature; Law, Physical and Moral; Analogies and Contrasts between Human and Divine Science; Natural Theology; Pessimism; Evolution and Evolution; Charles

CARNARVON (Lord). Portugal, Gallicia, and the Basque Provinces. Post 8vo. 3s. 6d.

———————— The Agamemnon : Translated from Æschylus. 8m. 8vo. 6s.

CARNOTA (Conde da). The Life and Eventful Career of F.M. the Duke of Saldanha; Soldier and Statesman. 2 Vols 8vo. 32s.

CARTWRIGHT (W. C.). The Jesuits: their Constitution and Teaching. An Historical Sketch. 8vo. 9s.

CAVALCASELLE'S WORKS. [See Crowe.]

CESNOLA (Gen.). Cyprus; its Ancient Cities, Tombs, and Temples. With 400 Illustrations. Medium 8vo. 50s.

CHAMBERS (G. F.). A Practical and Conversational Pocket Dictionary of the English, French, and German Languages. Designed for Travellers and Students generally. Small 8vo. 6s.

CHILD-CHAPLIN (Dr.). Benedicite; or, Song of the Three Children; being Illustrations of the Power, Beneficence, and Design manifested by the Creator in his Works. Post 8vo. 6s.

CHISHOLM (Mrs.). Perils of the Polar Seas; True Stories of Arctic Discovery and Adventure. Illustrations. Post 8vo. 6s.

CHURTON (Archdeacon). Poetical Remains. Post 8vo. 7s. 6d.

CLASSIC PREACHERS OF THE ENGLISH CHURCH. Lectures delivered at St. James'. 2 Vols. Post 8vo. 7s. 6d. each.

CLIVE'S (Lord) Life. By Rev. G. R. Gleig. Post 8vo. 3s. 6d.

CLODE (C. M.). Military Forces of the Crown; their Administration and Government. 2 Vols. 8vo. 21s. each.

———————— Administration of Justice under Military and Martial Law, as applicable to the Army, Navy, and Auxiliary Forces. 8vo. 12s.

COLEBROOKE (Sir Edward, Bart.). Life of the Hon. Mountstuart Elphinstone. With Selections from his Correspondence and Papers. With Portrait and Plans. 2 vols. 8vo. 26s.

COLERIDGE'S (S. Taylor) Table-Talk. Portrait. 12mo. 3s. 6d.

COLES (John). Summer Travelling in Iceland. Being the Narrative of Two Journeys Across the Island by Unfrequented Routes. With a Chapter on Askja. By E. Delmar Morgan, F.R.G.S. With Map and Illustrations. 18s.

COLLINS (J. Churton). Bolingbroke: an Historical Study. Three Essays reprinted from the *Quarterly Review*, to which is added an Essay on Voltaire in England. Crown 8vo.

COLONIAL LIBRARY. [See Home and Colonial Library.]

COMPANIONS FOR THE DEVOUT LIFE. Lectures on well-known Devotional Works. Crown 8vo. 6s.

COOK (Canon F. C.). The Revised Version of the Three First Gospels, considered in its Bearings upon the Record of Our Lord's Words and Incidents in His Life. 8vo. 9s.

———————— The Origins of Language and Religion. Considered in Five Essays. 8vo. 15s.

COOKE (E. W.). Leaves from my Sketch-Book. With Descriptive Text. 50 Plates. 2 Vols. Small folio. 31s. 6d. each.

———————— (W. H.). Collections towards the History and Antiquities of the County of Hereford. In continuation of Duncumb's History, and forming the Third Volume of that Work. Illustrations. 4to. £2 12s. 6d.

COOKERY (Modern Domestic). Founded on Principles of Economy and Practical Knowledge, and Adapted for Private Families. By a Lady. Woodcuts. Fcap. 8vo. 5s.

CRABBE (Rev. George). Life & Poetical Works. Illustrations. Royal 8vo. 7s.

CRAIK (Henry). Life of Jonathan Swift. Portrait. 8vo. 18s.

CRIPPS (Wilfred). Old English Plate : Ecclesiastical, Decorative, and Domestic, its Makers and Marks. With a Complete Table of Date Letters, &c. New Edition. With 70 Illustrations. Medium 8vo. 16s.
. Tables of the Date Letters and Marks sold separately. 5s.

———— Old French Plate; With Paris Date Letters, and Other Marks. With Illustrations. 8vo. 8s. 6d.

CROKER (Rt. Hon. J. W.). Correspondence and Diaries, comprising Letters, Memoranda, and Journals relating to the chief Political and Social Events of the first half of the present century. Edited by Louis J. Jennings. With Portrait. 3 vols. 8vo. 45s.

———— Progressive Geography for Children. 18mo. 1s. 6d.

———— Boswell's Life of Johnson. Including the Tour to the Hebrides. *Seventh Edition.* Portraits. 8vo. 12s.

———— Historical Essay on the Guillotine. Fcap. 8vo. 1s.

CROWE AND CAVALCASELLE. Lives of the Early Flemish Painters. Woodcuts. Post 8vo, 7s. 6d.; or Large Paper 8vo, 15s.

———— History of Painting in North Italy, from 14th to 16th Century. With Illustrations. 2 Vols. 8vo. 42s.

———— Life and Times of Titian, with some Account of his Family, chiefly from new and unpublished records. With Portrait and Illustrations. 2 vols. 8vo. 21s.

———— Raphael; His Life and Works, with Particular Reference to recently discovered Records, and an exhaustive Study of Extant Drawings and Pictures. Vol. I. 8vo. 15s. Vol II. (*in the press.*)

CUMMING (R. Gordon). Five Years of a Hunter's Life in the Far Interior of South Africa. Woodcuts. Post 8vo. 6s.

CURRIE (C. L.) An Argument for the Divinity of Jesus Christ. Translated from the French of the Abbé Em. Bougaud. Post 8vo. 6s.

CURTIUS' (Professor) Student's Greek Grammar, for the Upper Forms. Edited by Dr. Wm. Smith. Post 8vo. 6s.

————Elucidations of the above Grammar. Translated by Evelyn Abbot. Post 8vo. 7s. 6d.

———— Smaller Greek Grammar for the Middle and Lower Forms. Abridged from the larger work. 12mo. 3s. 6d.

———— Accidence of the Greek Language. Extracted from the above work. 12mo. 2s. 6d.

———— Principles of Greek Etymology. Translated by A. S. Wilkins, M.A., and E. B. England, M.A. 2 vols. 8vo.

———— The Greek Verb, its Structure and Development. Translated by A. S. Wilkins, and E. B. England. 8vo. 12s.

CURZON (Hon. Robert). Visits to the Monasteries of the Levant. Illustrations. Post 8vo. 7s. 6d.

CUST (General). Warriors of the 17th Century—Civil Wars of France and England. 2 Vols. 16s. Commanders of Fleets and Armies. 2 Vols. 18s.

———— Annals of the Wars—18th & 19th Century. With Maps. 9 Vols. Post 8vo. 5s. each.

DAVY (Sir Humphry). Consolations in Travel; or, Last Days of a Philosopher. Woodcuts. Fcap. 8vo. 3s. 6d.

———— Salmonia; or, Days of Fly Fishing. Woodcuts. Fcap. 8vo. 3s. 6d.

DARWIN'S (CHARLES) WORKS :—

JOURNAL OF A NATURALIST DURING A VOYAGE ROUND THE WORLD. Crown 8vo. 9s.

ORIGIN OF SPECIES BY MEANS OF NATURAL SELECTION ; or, the Preservation of Favoured Races in the Struggle for Life. Woodcuts. Crown 8vo. 7s. 6d.

VARIATION OF ANIMALS AND PLANTS UNDER DOMESTICATION. Woodcuts. 2 Vols. Crown 8vo. 18s.

DESCENT OF MAN, AND SELECTION IN RELATION TO SEX. Woodcuts. Crown 8vo. 9s.

EXPRESSIONS OF THE EMOTIONS IN MAN AND ANIMALS. With Illustrations. Crown 8vo. 12s.

VARIOUS CONTRIVANCES BY WHICH ORCHIDS ARE FERTILIZED BY INSECTS. Woodcuts. Crown 8vo. 9s.

MOVEMENTS AND HABITS OF CLIMBING PLANTS. Woodcuts. Crown 8vo. 6s.

INSECTIVOROUS PLANTS. Woodcuts. Crown 8vo. 14s.

EFFECTS OF CROSS AND SELF-FERTILIZATION IN THE VEGETABLE KINGDOM. Crown 8vo. 12s.

DIFFERENT FORMS OF FLOWERS ON PLANTS OF THE SAME SPECIES. Crown 8vo. 10s. 6d.

POWER OF MOVEMENT IN PLANTS. Woodcuts. Cr. 8vo. 15s.

THE FORMATION OF VEGETABLE MOULD THROUGH THE ACTION OF WORMS. With Illustrations. Post 8vo. 9s.

LIFE OF ERASMUS DARWIN. With a Study of his Works by ERNEST KRAUSE. Portrait. Crown 8vo. 7s. 6d.

FACTS AND ARGUMENTS FOR DARWIN. By FRITZ MÜLLER. Translated by W. S. DALLAS. Woodcuts. Post 8vo. 6s.

DE COSSON (E. A.). The Cradle of the Blue Nile; a Journey through Abyssinia and Soudan. Map and Illustrations. 2 vols. Post 8vo. 21s.

DENNIS (GEORGE). The Cities and Cemeteries of Etruria. A new Edition. With 20 Plans and 200 Illustrations. 2 vols. Medium 8vo. 21s.

DERBY (EARL OF). Iliad of Homer rendered into English Blank Verse. With Portrait. 2 Vols. Post 8vo. 10s.

DERRY (BISHOP OF). Witness of the Psalms to Christ and Christianity. The Bampton Lectures for 1876. 8vo. 14s.

DEUTSCH (EMANUEL). Talmud, Islam, The Targums and other Literary Remains. With a brief Memoir. 8vo. 12s.

DILKE (SIR C. W.). Papers from the Writings of the late CHARLES DILKE. 2 Vols. 8vo. 24s.

DOG-BREAKING. [See HUTCHINSON.]

DOUGLAS'S (SIR HOWARD) Theory and Practice of Gunnery. Plates. 8vo. 21s.

DRAKE'S (SIR FRANCIS) Life, Voyages, and Exploits, by Sea and Land. By JOHN BARROW. Post 8vo. 2s.

DRINKWATER (JOHN). History of the Siege of Gibraltar, 1779-1783. With a Description of that Garrison. Post 8vo. 2s.

DU CHAILLU (PAUL B.). Land of the Midnight Sun; Journeys through Northern Scandinavia, with Descriptions of the Inner Life of the People. Illustrations. 2 Vols. 8vo. 36s.

————— Journey to Ashango Land; and Further Penetration into Equatorial Africa. Illustrations. 8vo. 21s.

DUFFERIN (LORD). Letters from High Latitudes; a Yacht voyage to Iceland, Jan Mayen, and Spitzbergen. Woodcuts. Post 8vo. 7s. 6d.

DUNCAN (Col.) History of the Royal Artillery. Compiled from the Original Records. Portraits. 2 Vols. 8vo. 18s.
————— English in Spain; or, The Story of the War of Succession, 1834-1840. With Illustrations. 8vo. 16s.

DÜRER (Albert); his Life and Work. By Dr. Thausing. Translated from the German. Edited by F. A. Eaton, M.A. With Portrait and Illustrations. 2 vols. Medium 8vo. 42s.

EASTLAKE (Sir Charles). Contributions to the Literature of the Fine Arts. With Memoir of the Author by Lady Eastlake. 2 Vols. 8vo. 24s.

EDWARDS (W. H.). Voyage up the River Amazon, including a Visit to Para. Post 8vo. 2s.

ELDON'S (Lord) Public and Private Life, with Selections from his Diaries, &c. By Horace Twiss. Portrait. 2 Vols. Post 8vo. 21s.

ELGIN (Lord). Letters and Journals. Edited by Theodore Walrond. With Preface by Dean Stanley. 8vo. 14s.

ELLESMERE (Lord). Two Sieges of Vienna by the Turks. Translated from the German. Post 8vo. 2s.

ELLIS (W.). Madagascar Revisited. The Persecutions and Heroic Sufferings of the Native Christians. Illustrations. 8vo. 16s.
————— Memoir. By His Son. Portrait. 8vo. 10s. 6d.
————— (Robinson) Poems and Fragments of Catullus. 16mo. 5s.

ELPHINSTONE (Hon. M.). History of India—the Hindoo and Mahomedan Periods. Edited by Professor Cowell. Map. 8vo. 18s.
————— Life of. [See Colebrooke.]
————— (H. W.). Patterns and Instructions for ornamental Turning. With 70 Illustrations. Small 4to. 15s.

ELTON (Capt.) and H. B. COTTERILL. Adventures and Discoveries Among the Lakes and Mountains of Eastern and Central Africa. With Map and Illustrations. 8vo. 21s.

ENGLAND. [See Arthur—Brewer—Croker—Hume—Markham —Smith—and Stanhope.]

ESSAYS ON CATHEDRALS. Edited, with an Introduction. By Dean Howson. 8vo. 12s.

FELTOE (Rev. J. Lett). Memorials of John Flint South, twice President of the Royal College of Surgeons and Surgeon to St. Thomas's Hospital (1841-63). With Portrait. Crown 8vo. 7s. 6d.

FERGUSSON (James). History of Architecture in all Countries from the Earliest Times. With 1,600 Illustrations. 4 Vols. Medium 8vo. Vols. I. & II. Ancient and Mediæval. 63s.
     III. Indian & Eastern. 42s.   IV. Modern. 31s. 6d.
————— Rude Stone Monuments in all Countries; their Age and Uses. With 230 Illustrations. Medium 8vo. 24s.
————— Holy Sepulchre and the Temple at Jerusalem. Woodcuts. 8vo. 7s. 6d.
————— Temples of the Jews and other buildings in the Haram Area at Jerusalem. With Illustrations. 4to. 42s.
————— The Parthenon. An Essay on the construction of Greek and Roman Temples, with especial reference to the mode in which light was introduced into their interiors. 4to. 21s.

FLEMING (Professor). Student's Manual of Moral Philosophy. With Quotations and References. Post 8vo. 7s. 6d.

FLOWER GARDEN. By Rev. Thos. James. Fcap. 8vo. 1s.

FORBES (Capt.). British Burma and its People; Native Manners, Customs, and Religion. Crown 8vo. 10s. 6d.

FORD (Richard). Gatherings from Spain. Post 8vo. 3s. 6d.

FORSTER (John). The Early Life of Jonathan Swift. 1667-1711.

FORSYTH (WILLIAM). Hortensius; an Historical Essay on the
Office and Duties of an Advocate. Illustrations. 8vo. 7s. 6d.
———————— Novels and Novelists of the 18th Century, in
Illustration of the Manners and Morals of the Age. Post 8vo. 10s. 6d.

FRANCE (HISTORY OF). [See ARTHUR — MARKHAM — SMITH — STUDENTS'—TOCQUEVILLE.]

FRENCH IN ALGIERS; The Soldier of the Foreign Legion—
and the Prisoners of Abd-el-Kadir. Translated by Lady DUFF GORDON.
Post 8vo. 2s.

FRERE (SIR BARTLE). Indian Missions. Small 8vo. 2s. 6d.
——————— Missionary Labour in Eastern Africa. Crown 8vo. 5s.
——————— Bengal Famine. How it will be Met and How to
Prevent Future Famines in India. With Maps. Crown 8vo. 5s.
——————— (MARY). Old Deccan Days, or Hindoo Fairy Legends
current in Southern India, with Introduction by Sir BARTLE FRERE.
With 50 Illustrations. Post 8vo. 7s. 6d.

GALTON (F.). Art of Travel; or, Hints on the Shifts and Contrivances available in Wild Countries. Woodcuts. Post 8vo. 7s. 6d.

GEOGRAPHY. [See BUNBURY—CROKER— RICHARDSON — SMITH
—STUDENTS'.]

GEOGRAPHICAL SOCIETY'S JOURNAL. (1846 to 1881.)
——————— Supplementary Papers (i), Travels and Researches in
Western China. By E. COLBORNE BABER. Maps. Royal 8vo. 5s.
——————— (ii) 1. Notes on the Recent Geography of Central
Asia; from Russian Sources. By E. DELMAR MORGAN.
——————— 2. Progress of Discovery on the Coasts of New Guinea.
By C. B. MARKHAM. With Bibliographical Appendix, by E. C. Rye.
Maps. Royal 8vo. 5s.

GEORGE (ERNEST). The Mosel; Twenty Etchings. Imperial 4to. 42s.
——————— Loire and South of France; Twenty etchings. Folio. 42s.

GERMANY (HISTORY OF). [See MARKHAM.]

GIBBON (EDWARD). History of the Decline and Fall of the
Roman Empire. Edited with notes by MILMAN, GUIZOT, and Dr.
WM. SMITH. Maps. 8 Vols. 8vo. 60s.
——————— The Student's Edition; an Epitome of the above
work, incorporating the Researches of Recent Commentators. By Dr.
WM. SMITH. Woodcuts. Post 8vo. 7s. 6d.

GIFFARD (EDWARD). Deeds of Naval Daring; or, Anecdotes of
the British Navy. Fcap. 8vo. 3s. 6d.

GILBERT (JOSIAH). Landscape in Art: before the days of Claude
and Salvator. With 150 Illustrations. Medium 8vo. 30s.

GILL (CAPT.). The River of Golden Sand. A Narrative of a
Journey through China to Burmah. An Abridged Edition, by E. COL-
BORNE BABER. With Memoir and Introductory Essay, by Colonel H.
YULE, C.B. With Portrait, Map, and Illustrations. Post 8vo. 7s. 6d.
——— (MRS.). Six Months in Ascension. An Unscientific Ac-
count of a Scientific Expedition. Map. Crown 8vo. 9s.

GLEIG (G. R.) Life of Lord Clive. Post 8vo. 3*s*. 6*d*.
—— Life of Sir Thomas Munro. Post 8vo. 3*s*. 6*d*.
GLYNNE (Sir Stephen). Notes on the Churches of Kent. With
Preface by W. H. Gladstone, M.P. Illustrations. 8vo. 12*s*.
GOLDSMITH'S (Oliver) Works. Edited with Notes by Peter
Cunningham. Vignettes. 4 Vols. 8vo. 30*s*.
GOMM (F. M. Sir Wm.). His Letters and Journals. 1799 to
1815. Edited by F. C. Carr Gomm. With Portrait. 8vo. 12*s*.
GORDON (Sir Alex.). Sketches of German Life, and Scenes
from the War of Liberation. Post 8vo. 3*s*. 6*d*.
—— (Lady Duff) Amber-Witch : A Trial for Witch-
craft. Post 8vo. 2*s*.
—— French in Algiers. 1. The Soldier of the Foreign
Legion. 2. The Prisoners of Abd-el-Kadir. Post 8vo. 2*s*.
GRAMMARS. [See Curtius—Hall—Hutton—King Edward—
Leathes—Maetzner—Matthiæ—Smith.]
GREECE (History of). [See Grote—Smith—Students'.]
GROTE'S (George) WORKS :—
History of Greece. From the Earliest Times to the close
of the generation contemporary with the Death of Alexander the Great.
Library Edition. Portrait, Maps, and Plans. 10 Vols. 8vo. 120*s*.
Cabinet Edition. Portrait and Plans. 12 Vols. Post 8vo. 4*s*. each.
Plato, and other Companions of Socrates. 3 Vols. 8vo. 45*s*.
Aristotle. With additional Essays. 8vo. 12*s*.
Minor Works. Portrait. 8vo. 14*s*.
Letters on Switzerland in 1847. 6*s*.
Personal Life. Portrait. 8vo. 12*s*.
GROTE (Mrs.). A Sketch. By Lady Eastlake. Crown 8vo. 6*s*.
HALL'S (T. D.) School Manual of English Grammar. With
Illustrations and Practical Exercises. 12mo. 3*s*. 6*d*.
—— Primary English Grammar for Elementary Schools.
With numerous Exercises, and graduated Parsing Lessons. 16mo. 1*s*.
—— Manual of English Composition. With Copious Illustra-
tions and Practical Exercises. 12mo. 3*s*. 6*d*.
—— Child's First Latin Book, comprising a full Practice of
Nouns, Pronouns, and Adjectives, with the Active Verbs. 16mo. 2*s*.
HALLAM'S (Henry) WORKS :—
The Constitutional History of England, from the Acces-
sion of Henry the Seventh to the Death of George the Second. *Library
Edition,* 3 Vols. 8vo. 30*s*. *Cabinet Edition,* 3 Vols. Post 8vo. 12*s*. *Stu-
dent's Edition,* Post 8vo. 7*s*. 6*d*.
History of Europe during the Middle Ages. *Library
Edition,* 3 Vols. 8vo. 30*s*. *Cabinet Edition,* 3 Vols. Post 8vo. 12*s*.
Student's Edition, Post 8vo. 7*s*. 6*d*.
Literary History of Europe during the 15th, 16th, and
17th Centuries. *Library Edition,* 3 Vols. 8vo. 36*s*. *Cabinet Edition,*
4 Vols. Post 8vo. 16*s*.
—— (Arthur) Literary Remains; in Verse and Prose.
Portrait. Fcap. 8vo. 3*s*. 6*d*.
HAMILTON (Andrew). Rheinsberg : Memorials of Frederick the
Great and Prince Henry of Prussia. 2 Vols. Crown 8vo. 21*s*.
HART'S ARMY LIST. (*Published Quarterly and Annually.*)
HATCH (W. M.). The Moral Philosophy of Aristotle,
a translation of the Nichomachean Ethics, and of the Paraphrase of
Andronicus, with an Introductory Analysis of each book. 8vo. 18*s*.

HATHERLEY (LORD). The Continuity of Scripture, as Declared by the Testimony of our Lord and of the Evangelists and Apostles. Post 8vo. 2s. 6d.

HAY (SIR J. H. DRUMMOND). Western Barbary, its Wild Tribes and Savage Animals. Post 8vo. 2s.

HAYWARD (A.). Sketches of Eminent Statesmen and Writers, Contents: Thiers, Bismarck, Cavour, Metternich, Montalembert, Melbourne, Wellesley, Byron and Tennyson, Venice, St. Simon, Sevigné, Du Deffand, Holland House, Strawberry Hill. 2 Vols. 8vo. 28s.

———— The Art of Dining, or Gastronomy and Gastronomers. Post 8vo. 2s.

HEAD'S (SIR FRANCIS) WORKS:—
THE ROYAL ENGINEER. Illustrations. 8vo. 12s.
LIFE OF SIR JOHN BURGOYNE. Post 8vo. 1s.
RAPID JOURNEYS ACROSS THE PAMPAS. Post 8vo. 2s.
BUBBLES FROM THE BRUNNEN. Illustrations. Post 8vo. 7s. 6d.
STOKERS AND POKERS; or, the London and North Western Railway. Post 8vo. 2s.

HEBER'S (BISHOP) Journals in India. 2 Vols. Post 8vo. 7s.

———— Poetical Works. Portrait. Fcap. 8vo. 3s. 6d.

HERODOTUS. A New English Version. Edited, with Notes and Essays, Historical, Ethnographical, and Geographical, by CANON RAWLINSON, SIR H. RAWLINSON and SIR J. G. WILKINSON. Maps and Woodcuts. 4 Vols. 8vo. 48s.

HERRIES (RT. HON. JOHN). Memoir of his Public Life. Founded on his Letters and other Unpublished Documents. By his son, Edward Herries, C.B. 2 Vols. 8vo. 24s.

HERSCHEL'S (CAROLINE) Memoir and Correspondence. By MRS. JOHN HERSCHEL. With Portrait. Crown 8vo. 7s. 6d.

FOREIGN HAND-BOOKS.

HAND-BOOK—TRAVEL-TALK. English, French, German, and Italian. New and Revised Edition. 18mo. 3s. 6d.

———— DICTIONARY: English, French, and German. Containing all the words and idiomatic phrases likely to be required by a traveller. Bound in leather. 16mo. 6s.

———— HOLLAND AND BELGIUM. Map and Plans. Post 8vo. 6s.

———— NORTH GERMANY and THE RHINE,— The Black Forest, the Hartz, Thüringerwald, Saxon Switzerland, Rügen, the Giant Mountains, Taunus, Odenwald, Elsass, and Lothringen. Map and Plans. Post 8vo. 10s.

———— SOUTH GERMANY,— Wurtemburg, Bavaria, Austria, Styria, Salzburg, the Alps, Tyrol, Hungary, and the Danube, from Ulm to the Black Sea. Maps and Plans. Post 8vo. 10s.

———— SWITZERLAND, Alps of Savoy, and Piedmont. In Two Parts. Maps and Plans. Post 8vo. 10s.

———— FRANCE, Part I. Normandy, Brittany, the French Alps, the Loire, Seine, Garonne, and Pyrenees. Maps and Plans. Post 8vo. 7s. 6d.

———— FRANCE, Part II. Central France, Auvergne, the Cevennes, Burgundy, the Rhone and Saone, Provence, Nimes, Arles, Marseilles, the French Alps, Alsace, Lorraine, Champagne, &c. Maps and Plans. Post 8vo. 7s. 6d.

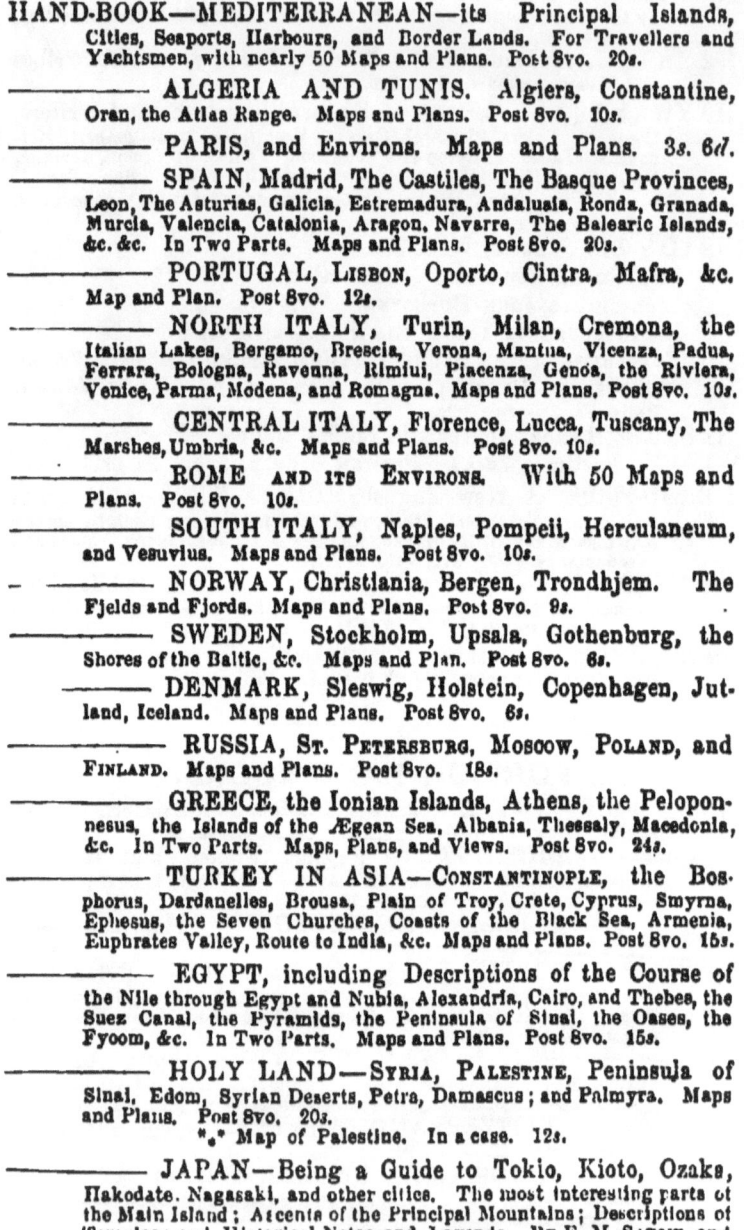

HAND-BOOK—MEDITERRANEAN—its Principal Islands,
Cities, Seaports, Harbours, and Border Lands. For Travellers and
Yachtsmen, with nearly 50 Maps and Plans. Post 8vo. 20s.

——— ALGERIA AND TUNIS. Algiers, Constantine,
Oran, the Atlas Range. Maps and Plans. Post 8vo. 10s.

——— PARIS, and Environs. Maps and Plans. 3s. 6d.

——— SPAIN, Madrid, The Castiles, The Basque Provinces,
Leon, The Asturias, Galicia, Estremadura, Andalusia, Ronda, Granada,
Murcia, Valencia, Catalonia, Aragon. Navarre, The Balearic Islands,
&c. &c. In Two Parts. Maps and Plans. Post 8vo. 20s.

——— PORTUGAL, LISBON, Oporto, Cintra, Mafra, &c.
Map and Plan. Post 8vo. 12s.

——— NORTH ITALY, Turin, Milan, Cremona, the
Italian Lakes, Bergamo, Brescia, Verona, Mantua, Vicenza, Padua,
Ferrara, Bologna, Ravenna, Rimini, Piacenza, Genóa, the Riviera,
Venice, Parma, Modena, and Romagna. Maps and Plans. Post 8vo. 10s.

——— CENTRAL ITALY, Florence, Lucca, Tuscany, The
Marshes, Umbria, &c. Maps and Plans. Post 8vo. 10s.

——— ROME AND ITS ENVIRONS. With 50 Maps and
Plans. Post 8vo. 10s.

——— SOUTH ITALY, Naples, Pompeii, Herculaneum,
and Vesuvius. Maps and Plans. Post 8vo. 10s.

——— NORWAY, Christiania, Bergen, Trondhjem. The
Fjelds and Fjords. Maps and Plans. Post 8vo. 9s.

——— SWEDEN, Stockholm, Upsala, Gothenburg, the
Shores of the Baltic, &c. Maps and Plan. Post 8vo. 6s.

——— DENMARK, Sleswig, Holstein, Copenhagen, Jut-
land, Iceland. Maps and Plans. Post 8vo. 6s.

——— RUSSIA, ST. PETERSBURG, MOSCOW, POLAND, and
FINLAND. Maps and Plans. Post 8vo. 18s.

——— GREECE, the Ionian Islands, Athens, the Pelopon-
nesus, the Islands of the Ægean Sea. Albania, Thessaly, Macedonia,
&c. In Two Parts. Maps, Plans, and Views. Post 8vo. 24s.

——— TURKEY IN ASIA—CONSTANTINOPLE, the Bos-
phorus, Dardanelles, Brousa, Plain of Troy, Crete, Cyprus, Smyrna,
Ephesus, the Seven Churches, Coasts of the Black Sea, Armenia,
Euphrates Valley, Route to India, &c. Maps and Plans. Post 8vo. 15s.

——— EGYPT, including Descriptions of the Course of
the Nile through Egypt and Nubia, Alexandria, Cairo, and Thebes, the
Suez Canal, the Pyramids, the Peninsula of Sinai, the Oases, the
Fyoom, &c. In Two Parts. Maps and Plans. Post 8vo. 15s.

——— HOLY LAND—SYRIA, PALESTINE, Peninsula of
Sinai. Edom, Syrian Deserts, Petra, Damascus ; and Palmyra. Maps
and Plans. Post 8vo. 20s.
     • Map of Palestine. In a case. 12s.

——— JAPAN—Being a Guide to Tokio, Kioto, Ozaka,
Hakodate, Nagasaki, and other cities. The most interesting parts of
the Main Island ; Ascents of the Principal Mountains ; Descriptions of
Temples ; and Historical Notes and Legends. By E. M. SATOW, and
Lieut. A. G. B. HAWES. With Maps and Plans. Post 8vo. 21s.

——— BOMBAY — Poonah, Beejapoor, Kolapoor, Goa,
Jubulpoor, Indore, Surat, Baroda, Ahmedabad, Somnauth, Kurrachee,
&c. Map and Plans. Post 8vo. 15s.

HANDBOOK—MADRAS—Trichinopoli, Madura, Tinnevelly, Tuti-
corin, Bangalore, Mysore, The Nilgiris, Wynaad, Ootacamund, Cellcut,
Hyderabad, Ajanta, Elura Caves, &c. Maps and Plans. Post 8vo. 15s.

———————— BENGAL — Calcutta, Orissa, British Burmah,
Rangoon, Moulmein, Mandalay, Darjiling, Dacca, Patna, Benares,
N.-W. Provinces, Allahabad, Cawnpore, Lucknow, Agra, Gwalior,
Naini Tal, Delhi, &c. Maps and Plans. Post 8vo. 20s

———————— THE PANJAB—Amraoti, Indore, Ajmir, Jaypur,
Rohtak, Saharanpur, Ambala, Lodiana, Lahore, Kulu, Simla, Sialkot,
Peshawar, Rawul Pindi, Attock, Karachi, Sibi, &c. Maps. 15s.

ENGLISH HAND-BOOKS.

HAND-BOOK—ENGLAND AND WALES. An Alphabetical
Hand-Book. Condensed into One Volume for the Use of Travellers.
With a Map. Post 8vo. 10s.

———————— LONDON. Maps and Plans. 16mo. 3s. 6d.

———————— ENVIRONS OF LONDON within a circuit of 20
miles. 2 Vols. Crown 8vo. 21s.

———————— ST. PAUL'S CATHEDRAL. 20 Woodcuts. 10s. 6d.

———————— EASTERN COUNTIES, Chelmsford, Harwich, Col-
chester, Maldon, Cambridge, Ely, Newmarket, Bury St. Edmunds,
Ipswich, Woodbridge, Felixstowe, Lowestoft, Norwich, Yarmouth,
Cromer, &c. Map and Plans. Post 8vo. 12s.

———————— CATHEDRALS of Oxford, Peterborough, Norwich,
Ely, and Lincoln. With 90 Illustrations. Crown 8vo. 21s.

———————— KENT, Canterbury, Dover, Ramsgate, Sheerness,
Rochester, Chatham, Woolwich. Maps and Plans. Post 8vo. 7s. 6d.

———————— SUSSEX, Brighton, Chichester, Worthing, Hastings,
Lewes, Arundel, &c. Maps and Plans. Post 8vo. 6s.

———————— SURREY AND HANTS, Kingston, Croydon, Rei-
gate, Guildford, Dorking, Winchester, Southampton, New Forest,
Portsmouth, ISLE OF WIGHT, &c. Maps and Plans. Post 8vo. 10s.

———————— BERKS, BUCKS, AND OXON, Windsor, Eton,
Reading, Aylesbury, Uxbridge, Wycombe, Henley, Oxford, Blenheim,
the Thames, &c. Maps and Plans. Post 8vo. 9s.

———————— WILTS, DORSET, AND SOMERSET, Salisbury,
Chippenham, Weymouth, Sherborne, Wells, Bath, Bristol, Taunton,
&c. Map. Post 8vo. 12s.

———————— DEVON, Exeter, Ilfracombe, Linton, Sidmouth,
Dawlish, Teignmouth, Plymouth, Devonport, Torquay. Maps and Plans.
Post 8vo. 7s. 6d.

———————— CORNWALL, Launceston, Penzance, Falmouth,
the Lizard, Land's End, &c. Maps. Post 8vo. 6s.

———————— CATHEDRALS of Winchester, Salisbury, Exeter,
Wells, Chichester, Rochester, Canterbury, and St. Albans. With 130
Illustrations. 2 Vols. Crown 8vo. 36s. St. Albans separately. 6s.

———————— GLOUCESTER, HEREFORD, AND WORCESTER,
Cirencester, Cheltenham, Stroud, Tewkesbury, Leominster, Ross, Mal-
vern, Kidderminster, Dudley, Evesham, &c. Map. Post 8vo. 9s.

———————— CATHEDRALS of Bristol, Gloucester, Hereford,
Worcester, and Lichfield. With 50 Illustrations. Crown 8vo. 16s.

———————— NORTH WALES, Bangor, Carnarvon, Beaumaris,
Snowdon, Llanberis, Dolgelly, Conway, &c. Map. Post 8vo.)

HAND-BOOK—SOUTH WALES, Monmouth, Llandaff, Merthyr, Vale of Neath, Pembroke, Carmarthen, Tenby, Swansea, The Wye, &c. Map. Post 8vo. 7s.

———————— CATHEDRALS OF BANGOR, ST. ASAPH, Llandaff, and St. David's. With Illustrations. Post 8vo. 15s.

———————— NORTHAMPTONSHIRE AND RUTLAND— Northampton, Peterborough, Towcester, Daventry, Market Harborough, Kettering, Wellingborough, Thrapston, Stamford, Uppingham, Oakham. Maps. Post 8vo. 7s. 6d.

———————— DERBY, NOTTS, LEICESTER, STAFFORD, Matlock, Bakewell, Chatsworth, The Peak, Buxton, Hardwick, Dove Dale, Ashborne, Southwell, Mansfield, Retford, Burton, Belvoir, Melton Mowbray, Wolverhampton, Lichfield, Walsall, Tamworth. Map. Post 8vo. 9s.

———————— SHROPSHIRE and CHESHIRE, Shrewsbury, Ludlow, Bridgnorth, Oswestry, Chester, Crewe, Alderley, Stockport, Birkenhead. Maps and Plans. Post 8vo. 6s.

———————— LANCASHIRE, Warrington, Bury, Manchester, Liverpool, Burnley, Clitheroe, Bolton, Blackburne, Wigan, Preston, Rochdale, Lancaster, Southport, Blackpool, &c. Maps & Plans. Post 8vo. 7s. 6d.

———————— YORKSHIRE, Doncaster, Hull, Selby, Beverley, Scarborough, Whitby, Harrogate, Ripon, Leeds, Wakefield, Bradford, Halifax, Huddersfield, Sheffield. Map and Plans. Post 8vo. 12s.

———————— CATHEDRALS of York, Ripon, Durham, Carlisle, Chester, and Manchester. With 60 Illustrations. 2 Vols. Cr. 8vo. 21s.

———————— DURHAM and NORTHUMBERLAND, Newcastle, Darlington, Stockton, Hartlepool, Shields, Berwick-on-Tweed, Morpeth, Tynemouth, Coldstream, Alnwick, &c. Map. Post 8vo. 9s.

———————— WESTMORELAND and CUMBERLAND—Map.

———————— SCOTLAND, Edinburgh, Melrose, Kelso, Glasgow, Dumfries, Ayr, Stirling, Arran, The Clyde, Oban, Inverary, Loch Lomond, Loch Katrine and Trossachs, Caledonian Canal, Inverness, Perth, Dundee, Aberdeen, Braemar, Skye, Caithness, Ross, Sutherland, &c. Maps and Plans. Post 8vo. 9s.

———————— IRELAND, Dublin, Belfast, the Giant's Causeway, Donegal, Galway, Wexford, Cork, Limerick, Waterford, Killarney, Bantry, Glengariff, &c. Maps and Plans. Post 8vo. 10s.

HOLLWAY (J. G.). A Month in Norway. Fcap. 8vo. 2s.

HONEY BEE. By Rev. Thomas James. Fcap. 8vo. 1s.

HOOK (Dean). Church Dictionary. 8vo. 16s.

——— (Theodore) Life. By J. G. Lockhart. Fcap. 8vo. 1s.

HOPE (A. J. Beresford). Worship in the Church of England. 8vo. 9s., or, Popular Selections from. 8vo. 2s. 6d.

———Worship and Order. 8vo. 9s.

HOPE-SCOTT (James), Memoir. [See Ornsby.]

HORACE; a New Edition of the Text. Edited by Dean Milman. With 100 Woodcuts. Crown 8vo. 7s. 6d.

HOSACK (John). The rise and growth of the Law of Nations: as established by general usage and by treaties, from the earliest times to the treaty of Utrecht. 8vo. 12s.

HOUGHTON'S (Lord) Monographs, Personal and Social. With Portraits. Crown 8vo. 10s. 6d.

———————— Poetical Works. Collected Edition. With Portrait. 2 Vols. Fcap. 8vo. 12s.

HOUSTOUN (Mrs.). Twenty Years in the Wild West of Ireland, or Life in Connaught. Post 8vo. 9s.

HOME AND COLONIAL LIBRARY. A Series of Works adapted for all circles and classes of Readers, having been selected for their acknowledged interest, and ability of the Authors. Post 8vo. Published at 2s. and 3s. 6d. each, and arranged under two distinctive heads as follows :—

CLASS A.
HISTORY, BIOGRAPHY, AND HISTORIC TALES.

1. SIEGE OF GIBRALTAR. By John Drinkwater. 2s.
2. THE AMBER-WITCH. By Lady Duff Gordon. 2s.
3. CROMWELL AND BUNYAN. By Robert Southey. 2s.
4. LIFE of Sir FRANCIS DRAKE. By John Barrow. 2s.
5. CAMPAIGNS AT WASHINGTON. By Rev. G. R. Gleig. 2s.
6. THE FRENCH IN ALGIERS. By Lady Duff Gordon. 2s.
7. THE FALL OF THE JESUITS. 2s.
8. LIVONIAN TALES. 2s.
9. LIFE OF CONDÉ. By Lord Mahon. 3s. 6d.
10. SALE'S BRIGADE. By Rev. G. R. Gleig. 2s.

11. THE SIEGES OF VIENNA. By Lord Ellesmere. 2s.
12. THE WAYSIDE CROSS. By Capt. Milman. 2s.
13. SKETCHES of GERMAN LIFE. By Sir A. Gordon. 3s. 6d.
14. THE BATTLE of WATERLOO By Rev. G. R. Gleig. 3s. 6d.
15. AUTOBIOGRAPHY OF STEFFENS. 2s.
16. THE BRITISH POETS. By Thomas Campbell. 3s. 6d.
17. HISTORICAL ESSAYS. By Lord Mahon. 3s. 6d.
18. LIFE OF LORD CLIVE. By Rev. G. R. Gleig. 3s. 6d.
19. NORTH - WESTERN RAILWAY. By Sir F. B. Head. 2s.
20. LIFE OF MUNRO. By Rev. G. R. Gleig. 3s. 6d.

CLASS B.
VOYAGES, TRAVELS, AND ADVENTURES.

1. BIBLE IN SPAIN. By George Borrow. 3s. 6d.
2. GYPSIES of SPAIN. By George Borrow. 3s. 6d.
3 & 4. JOURNALS IN INDIA. By Bishop Heber. 2 Vols. 7s.
5. TRAVELS in the HOLY LAND. By Irby and Mangles. 2s.
6. MOROCCO AND THE MOORS. By J. Drummond Hay. 2s.
7. LETTERS FROM the BALTIC. By A Lady. 2s.
8. NEW SOUTH WALES. By Mrs. Meredith. 2s.
9. THE WEST INDIES. By M. G. Lewis. 2s.
10. SKETCHES OF PERSIA. By Sir John Malcolm. 3s. 6d.
11. MEMOIRS OF FATHER RIPA. 2s.
12 & 13. TYPEE AND OMOO. By Hermann Melville. 2 Vols. 7s.
14. MISSIONARY LIFE IN CAN-

15. LETTERS FROM MADRAS. By A Lady. 2s.
16. HIGHLAND SPORTS. By Charles St. John. 3s. 6d.
17. PAMPAS JOURNEYS. By Sir F. B. Head. 2s.
18. GATHERINGS FROM SPAIN. By Richard Ford. 3s. 6d.
19. THE RIVER AMAZON. By W. H. Edwards. 2s.
20. MANNERS & CUSTOMS OF INDIA. By Rev. C. Acland. 2s.
21. ADVENTURES IN MEXICO. By G. F. Ruxton. 3s. 6d.
22. PORTUGAL AND GALICIA. By Lord Carnarvon. 3s. 6d.
23. BUSH LIFE IN AUSTRALIA. By Rev. H. W. Haygarth. 2s.
24. THE LIBYAN DESERT. By Bayle St. John. 2s.
25. SIERRA LEONE. By A Lady. 3s. 6d.

HUME (The Student's). A History of England, from the Invasion of Julius Cæsar to the Revolution of 1688. New Edition, revised, corrected, and continued to the Treaty of Berlin, 1878. By J. S. BREWER, M.A. With 7 Coloured Maps & 70 Woodcuts. Post 8vo. 7s. 6d. cach.
   . Sold also in 3 parts. Price 2s. 6d each.

HUTCHINSON (GEN.). Dog Breaking, with Odds and Ends for those who love the Dog and the Gun. With 40 Illustrations. Crown 8vo. 7s. 6d. *.* A Summary of the Rules for Gamekeepers. 1s.

HUTTON (H. E.). Principia Græca; an Introduction to the Study of Greek. Comprehending Grammar, Delectus, and Exercise-book, with Vocabularies. Sixth Edition. 12mo. 3s. 6d.

———— (JAMES). James and Philip van Artevelde. Two remarkable Episodes in the annals of Flanders: with a description of the state of Society in Flanders in the 14th Century. Cr. 8vo. 10s. 6d.

HYMNOLOGY, DICTIONARY OF. [See JULIAN.]

ICELAND. [See COLES—DUFFERIN.]

INDIA. [See ELPHINSTONE — HAND-BOOK — SMITH—TEMPLE— MONIER WILLIAMS—LYALL.]

IRBY AND MANGLES' Travels in Egypt, Nubia, Syria, and the Holy Land. Post 8vo. 2s.

JAMES (F. L.). The Wild Tribes of the Soudan : with an account of the route from Wady Halfah to Dongola and Berber. A new and cheaper edition with prefatory Chapter on the Condition of the Soudan, by SIR S. BAKER. With Map and Illustrations. Crown 8vo. 7s. 6d.

JAMESON (MRS.). Lives of the Early Italian Painters— and the Progress of Painting in Italy—Cimabue to Bassano. With 50 Portraits. Post 8vo. 12s.

JAPAN. [See BIRD—MOSSMAN—MOUNSEY—REED.]

JENNINGS (LOUIS J.). Rambles among the Hills in the Peak of Derbyshire and on the South Downs. With sketches of people by the way. With 23 Illustrations. Crown 8vo. 12s.

———— Field Paths and Green Lanes: or Walks in Surrey and Sussex. Fourth and Popular Edition. With Illustrations. Crown 8vo. 6s.

JERVIS (REV. W. H.). The Gallican Church, from the Concordat of Bologna, 1516, to the Revolution. With an Introduction. Portraits. 2 Vols. 8vo. 28s.

JESSE (EDWARD). Gleanings in Natural History. Fcp. 8vo. 3s. 6d.

JOHNSON'S (DR. SAMUEL) Life. See Boswell.

JULIAN (REV. JOHN J.). A Dictionary of Hymnology. A Companion to Existing Hymn Books. Setting forth the Origin and History of the Hymns contained in the Principal Hymnals, with Notices of their Authors. Medium 8vo. [In the Press.

JUNIUS' HANDWRITING Professionally investigated. Edited by the Hon. E. TWISLETON. With Facsimiles, Woodcuts, &c. 4to. £3 3s.

KING EDWARD VITH's Latin Grammar. 12mo. 3s. 6d.

———— First Latin Book. 12mo. 2s. 6d.

KIRK (J. FOSTER). History of Charles the Bold, Duke of Burgundy. Portrait. 3 Vols. 8vo. 45s.

KIRKES' Handbook of Physiology. Edited by W. MORRANT BAKER, F.R.C.S., and VINCENT D. HARRIS, M.D. With 500 Illustrations. Post 8vo. 14s.

KUGLER'S Handbook of Painting.—The Italian Schools. Revised and Remodelled from the most recent Researches. By LADY EASTLAKE. With 140 Illustrations. 2 Vols. Crown 8vo. 30s.

———— Handbook of Painting.—The German, Flemish, and Dutch Schools. Revised and in part re-written. By J. A. CROWE. With 60 Illustrations. 2 Vols. Crown 8vo. 24s.

LANE (E. W.). Account of the Manners and Customs of Modern
Egyptians. With Illustrations. 2 Vols. Post 8vo. 12s.

LAYARD (Sir A. H.). Nineveh and its Remains: Researches and
Discoveries amidst the Ruins of Assyria. With Illustrations. Post
8vo. 7s. 6d.
———— Nineveh and Babylon: Discoveries in the Ruins,
with Travels in Armenia, Kurdistan, and the Desert. With Illustrations. Post 8vo. 7s. 6d.

LEATHES (STANLEY). Practical Hebrew Grammar. With the
Hebrew Text of Genesis i.—vi., and Psalms i.—vi. Grammatical
Analysis and Vocabulary. Post 8vo. 7s. 6d.

LENNEP (REV. H. J. VAN). Missionary Travels in Asia Minor.
With Illustrations of Biblical History and Archæology. Map and
Woodcuts. 2 Vols. Post 8vo. 24s.
———— Modern Customs and Manners of Bible Lands in
Illustration of Scripture. Maps and Illustrations. 2 Vols. 8vo. 21s.

LESLIE (C. R.). Handbook for Young Painters. Illustrations.
Post 8vo. 7s. 6d.
———— Life and Works of Sir Joshua Reynolds. Portraits.
2 Vols. 8vo. 42s.

LETO (POMPONIO). Eight Months at Rome during the Vatican
Council. 8vo. 12s.

LETTERS FROM THE BALTIC. By A LADY. Post 8vo. 2s.
———— MADRAS. By A LADY. Post 8vo. 2s.
———— SIERRA LEONE. By A LADY. Post 8vo. 3s. 6d.

LEVI (LEONE). History of British Commerce; and Economic
Progress of the Nation, from 1763 to 1878. 8vo. 18s.

LEX SALICA; the Ten Texts with the Glosses and the Lex
Emendata. Synoptically edited by J. H. HESSELS. With Notes on
the Frankish Words in the Lex Salica by H. KERN, of Leyden. 4to. 42s.

LIDDELL (DEAN). Student's History of Rome, from the earliest
Times to the establishment of the Empire. Woodcuts. Post 8vo. 7s. 6d.

LISPINGS from LOW LATITUDES; or, the Journal of the Hon.
Impulsia Gushington. Edited by LORD DUFFERIN. With 24 Plates. 4to. 21s.

LIVINGSTONE (DR.). First Expedition to Africa, 1840–56.
Illustrations. Post 8vo. 7s. 6d.
———— Second Expedition to Africa, 1858–64. Illustra-
tions. Post 8vo. 7s. 6d.
———— Last Journals in Central Africa, from 1865 to
his Death. Continued by a Narrative of his last moments and sufferings.
By Rev. HORACE WALLER. Maps and Illustrations. 2 Vols. 8vo. 15s.
———— Personal Life. By Wm. G. Blaikie, D.D. With
Map and Portrait. 8vo. 6s.

LIVINGSTONIA. Journal of Adventures in Exploring Lake
Nyassa, and Establishing a Missionary Settlement there. By E. D.
YOUNG, R.N. Maps. Post 8vo. 7s. 6d.

LIVONIAN TALES. By the Author of "Letters from the
Baltic." Post 8vo. 2s.

LOCKHART (J. G.). Ancient Spanish Ballads. Historical and
Romantic. Translated, with Notes. Illustrations. Crown 8vo. 5s.
———— Life of Theodore Hook. Fcap. 8vo. 1s.

LONDON: its History, Antiquarian and Modern. Founded

LUTHER (MARTIN). The First Principles of the Reformation,
or the Ninety-five Theses and Three Primary Works of Dr. Martin
Luther. Translated and edited, with Introductions, by HENRY WACE,
D.D., and PROF. BUCHHEIM. Portrait. 8vo. 12s.

LYALL (SIR ALFRED C.), K.C.B. Asiatic Studies; Religious and
Social. 8vo. 12s.

LYELL (SIR CHARLES). Student's Elements of Geology. A new
Edition, entirely revised by PROFESSOR P. M. DUNCAN, F.R S. With
600 Illustrations. Post 8vo. 9s.

———— Life, Letters, and Journals. Edited by his sister-in-law,
MRS. LYELL. With Portraits. 2 Vols. 8vo. 30s.

———— (K. M.). Geographical Handbook of Ferns. With Tables
to show their Distribution. Post 8vo. 7s. 6d.

LYNDHURST (LORD). [See Martin.]   [8vo. 5s.

LYTTON (LORD). A Memoir of Julian Fane. With Portrait. Post

MᶜCLINTOCK (SIR L.). Narrative of the Discovery of the
Fate of Sir John Franklin and his Companions in the Arctic Seas.
With Illustrations. Post 8vo. 7s. 6d.

MACGREGOR (J.). Rob Roy on the Jordan, Nile, Red Sea, Gen-
nesareth, &c. A Canoe Cruise in Palestine and Egypt and the Waters
of Damascus. With 70 Illustrations. Crown 8vo. 7s. 6d.

MAETZNER'S ENGLISH GRAMMAR. A Methodical, Analytical,
and Historical Treatise on the Orthography, Prosody, Inflections, and
Syntax. By CLAIR J. GRECE, LL.D. 3 Vols. 8vo. 36s.

MAHON (LORD). [See STANHOPE.]

MAINE (SIR H. SUMNER). Ancient Law: its Connection with the
Early History of Society, and its Relation to Modern Ideas. 8vo. 12s.

———— Village Communities in the East and West. 8vo. 12s.

———— Early History of Institutions. 8vo. 12s.

———— Dissertations on Early Law and Custom. Chiefly
Selected from Lectures delivered at Oxford. 8vo. 12s.

MALCOLM (SIR JOHN). Sketches of Persia. Post 8vo. 3s. 6d.

MALLOCK (W. H.). Property and Progress : or, Facts against
Fallacies. A brief Enquiry into Contemporary Social Agitation in
England. Post 8vo. 6s.

MANSEL (DEAN). Letters, Lectures, and Reviews. 8vo. 12s.

MANUAL OF SCIENTIFIC ENQUIRY. For the Use of
Travellers. Edited by REV. R. MAIN. Post 8vo. 3s. 6d. (Published by
order of the Lords of the Admiralty.)

MARCO POLO. The Book of Ser Marco Polo, the Venetian. Con-
cerning the Kingdoms and Marvels of the East. A new English Version.
Illustrated by the light of the Oriental Writers and Modern Travels. By
COL. HENRY YULE. Maps and Illustrations. 2 Vols. Medium 8vo. 63s.

MARKHAM (MRS.). History of England. From the First Invasion by the Romans, continued down to 1880. Woodcuts. 12mo. 3s. 6d.

———— History of France. From the Conquest of Gaul by
Julius Cæsar, continued down to 1878. Woodcuts. 12mo. 3s. 6d.

———— History of Germany. From its Invasion by Marius,
continued down to the completion of Cologne Cathedral. Woodcuts.
12mo. 3s. 6d.

———— (CLEMENTS R.). A Popular Account of Peruvian Bark
and its Introduction into British India. With Maps. Post 8vo. 14s.

MARSH (G. P.). Student's Manual of the English Language.
Edited with Additions. By DR. WM. SMITH. Post 8vo. 7s. 6d.

MARTIN (Sir Theodore). Life of Lord Lyndhurst, three times Lord Chancellor of England. From Letters and Papers in possession of his family. With Portraits. 8vo. 16s.

MASTERS in English Theology. Lectures delivered at King's College, London, in 1877, by Eminent Divines. With Introduction by Canon Barry. Post 8vo. 7s. 6d.

MATTHIÆ'S Greek Grammar. Abridged by Blomfield. Revised by E. S. Crooke. 12mo. 4s.

MAUREL'S Character, Actions, and Writings of Wellington. Fcap. 8vo. 1s. 6d.

MAYO (Lord). Sport in Abyssinia; or, the Mareb and Tackazzee. With Illustrations. Crown 8vo. 12s.

MELVILLE (Hermann). Marquesas and South Sea Islands. 2 Vols. Post 8vo. 7s.

MEREDITH (Mrs. Charles). Notes and Sketches of New South Wales. Post 8vo. 2s.

MEXICO. [See Brooklehurst.]

MICHAEL ANGELO, Sculptor, Painter, and Architect. His Life and Works. By C. Heath Wilson. With Portrait, Illustrations, and Index. 8vo. 15s.

MIDDLETON (Chas. H.) A Descriptive Catalogue of the Etched Work of Rembrandt, with Life and Introductions. With Explanatory Cuts. Medium 8vo. 31s. 6d.

MILLER (Wm.). A Dictionary of English Names of Plants applied in England and among English-speaking People to Cultivated and Wild Plants, Trees, and Shrubs. In Two Parts. Latin-English and English-Latin. Medium 8vo. 12s.

MILLINGTON (Rev. T. S.). Signs and Wonders in the Land of Ham, or the Ten Plagues of Egypt, with Ancient and Modern Illustrations. Woodcuts. Post 8vo. 7s. 6d.

MILMAN'S (Dean) WORKS:—

History of the Jews, from the earliest Period down to Modern Times. 3 Vols. Post 8vo. 12s.

Early Christianity, from the Birth of Christ to the Abolition of Paganism in the Roman Empire. 3 Vols. Post 8vo. 12s.

Latin Christianity, including that of the Popes to the Pontificate of Nicholas V. 9 Vols. Post 8vo. 36s.

Handbook to St. Paul's Cathedral. Woodcuts. Crown 8vo. 10s. 6d.

Quinti Horatii Flacci Opera. Woodcuts. Sm. 8vo. 7s. 6d.

Fall of Jerusalem. Fcap. 8vo. 1s.

—— —— (Capt. E. A.) Wayside Cross. Post 8vo. 2s.

—————— (Bishop, D.D.,) Life. With a Selection from his Correspondence and Journals. By his Sister. Map. 8vo. 12s.

MIVART (St. George). Lessons from Nature; as manifested in Mind and Matter. 8vo. 15s.

— —— The Cat. An Introduction to the Study of Backboned Animals, especially Mammals. With 200 Illustrations. Medium 8vo. 30s.

MOGGRIDGE (M. W.). Method in Almsgiving. A Handbook for Helpers. Post 8vo. 3s. 6d.

MONTEFIORE (Sir Moses). A Centennial Biography. With Selections from Letters and Journals. By Lucien Wolf. With Portrait. Crown 8vo. 10s. 6d.

MOORE (Thomas). Life and Letters of Lord Byron. Cabinet Edition. With Plates. 6 Vols. Fcap. 8vo. 18s.; Popular Edition, with Portraits. Royal 8vo. 7s. 6d.

MOTLEY (J. L.). History of the United Netherlands: from the Death of William the Silent to the Twelve Years' Truce, 1609. Portraits. 4 Vols. Post 8vo. 6s. each.

———————— Life and Death of John of Barneveld. With a View of the Primary Causes and Movements of the Thirty Years' War. Illustrations. 2 Vols. Post 8vo. 12s.

MOZLEY (CANON). Treatise on the Augustinian doctrine of Predestination, with an Analysis of the Contents. Crown 8vo. 9s.

MUIRHEAD (JAS.). The Vaux-de-Vire of Maistre Jean Le Houx. With Portrait and Illustrations. 8vo, 21s.

MUNRO'S (GENERAL) Life and Letters. By REV. G. R. GLEIG. Post 8vo. 3s. 6d.

MURCHISON (SIR RODERICK). Siluria; or, a History of the Oldest Rocks containing Organic Remains. Map and Plates. 8vo. 18s.

———————— Memoirs. With Notices of his Contemporaries, and Rise and Progress of Palæozoic Geology. By ARCHIBALD GEIKIE. Portraits. 2 Vols. 8vo. 30s.

MURRAY (A. S.). A History of Greek Sculpture from the Earliest Times. With 130 Illustrations. 2 Vols. Royal 8vo. 52s. 6d.

MUSTERS' (CAPT.) Patagonians; a Year's Wanderings over Untrodden Ground from the Straits of Magellan to the Rio Negro. Illustrations. Post 8vo. 7s. 6d.

NADAILLAC (MARQUIS DE). Prehistoric America. Translated by N. D'ANVERS. With Illustrations. 8vo.

NAPIER (GENL. SIR GEORGE T.). Passages in his Early Military Life written by himself. Edited by his Son, GENERAL WM. C. E. NAPIER. With Portrait. Crown 8vo. 12s.

———————— (SIR WM.). English Battles and Sieges of the Peninsular War. Portrait. Post 8vo. 9s.

NAPOLEON AT FONTAINEBLEAU AND ELBA. Journals. Notes of Conversations. By SIR NEIL CAMPBELL. Portrait. 8vo. 15s.

NASMYTH (JAMES). An Autobiography. Edited by Samuel Smiles, LL.D., with Portrait, and 70 Illustrations. Crown 8vo. 16s.

NAUTICAL ALMANAC (THE). (By Authority.) 2s. 6d.

NAVY LIST. (Monthly and Quarterly.) Post 8vo.

NEW TESTAMENT. With Short Explanatory Commentary. By ARCHDEACON CHURTON, M.A., and the BISHOP OF ST. DAVID'S. With 110 authentic Views, &c. 2 Vols. Crown 8vo. 21s. bound.

NEWTH (SAMUEL). First Book of Natural Philosophy; an Introduction to the Study of Statics, Dynamics, Hydrostatics, Light, Heat, and Sound, with numerous Examples. Small 8vo. 8s. 6d.

———————— Elements of Mechanics, including Hydrostatics, with numerous Examples. Small 8vo. 8s. 6d.

———————— Mathematical Examples. A Graduated Series of Elementary Examples in Arithmetic, Algebra, Logarithms, Trigonometry, and Mechanics. Small 8vo. 8s. 6d.

NICOLAS (SIR HARRIS). Historic Peerage of England. Exhibiting the Origin, Descent, and Present State of every Title of Peerage which has existed in this Country since the Conquest. By WILLIAM COURTHOPE. 8vo. 30s.

NIMROD, On the Chace—Turf—and Road. With Portrait and Plates. Crown 8vo. 5s. Or with Coloured Plates, 7s. 6d.

NORDHOFF (CHAS.). Communistic Societies of the United States. With 40 Illustrations. 8vo. 15s.

NORTHCOTE'S (SIR JOHN) Notebook in the Long Parliament. Containing Proceedings during its First Session, 1640. Edited, with a Memoir, by A. H. A. Hamilton. Crown 8vo. 9s.

ORNSBY (PROF. R.). Memoirs of J. Hope Scott, Q. C. (of Abbotsford). With Selections from his Correspondence. 2 vols. 8vo, 24s.

OTTER (R. H.). Winters Abroad : Some Information respecting Places visited by the Author on account of his Health. Intended for the Use and Guidance of Invalids. 7s. 6d.

OVID LESSONS. [See WINTLE.]

OWEN (LIEUT.-COL.). Principles and Practice of Modern Artillery, including Artillery Material, Gunnery, and Organisation and Use of Artillery in Warfare. With Illustrations. 8vo. 15s.

OXENHAM (REV. W.). English Notes for Latin Elegiacs ; designed for early Proficients in the Art of Latin Versification, with Prefatory Rules of Composition in Elegiac Metre. 12mo. 3s. 6d.

PAGET (LORD GEORGE). The Light Cavalry Brigade in the Crimea. Map. Crown 8vo. 10s. 6d.

PALGRAVE (R. H. I.). Local Taxation of Great Britain and Ireland. 8vo. 5s.

PALLISER (MRS.). Mottoes for Monuments, or Epitaphs selected for General Use and Study. With Illustrations. Crown 8vo. 7s. 6d.

PALMER (PROFESSOR), Life of. [See BESANT.]

PARIS (DR.) Philosophy in Sport made Science in Earnest ; or, the First Principles of Natural Philosophy inculcated by aid of the Toys and Sports of Youth. Woodcuts. Post 8vo. 7s. 6d.

PARKYNS' (MANSFIELD) Three Years' Residence in Abyssinia ; with Travels in that Country. With Illustrations. Post 8vo. 7s. 6d.

PEEL'S (SIR ROBERT) Memoirs. 2 Vols. Post 8vo. 15s.

PENN (RICHARD). Maxims and Hints for an Angler and Chess-player. Woodcuts. Fcap. 8vo. 1s.

PERCY (JOHN, M.D.). METALLURGY. Fuel, Wood, Peat, Coal, Charcoal, Coke, Fire-Clays. Illustrations. 8vo. 30s.

———— Lead, including part of Silver. Illustrations. 8vo. 30s:

———— Silver and Gold. Part I. Illustrations. 8vo. 30s.

PERRY (REV. CANON). Life of St. Hugh of Avalon, Bishop of Lincoln. Post 8vo. 10s. 6d.

———— History of the English Church. See STUDENTS' Manuals.

PHILLIPS (SAMUEL). Literary Essays from " The Times." With Portrait. 2 Vols. Fcap. 8vo. 7s.

POLLOCK (C. E.). A book of Family Prayers. Selected from the Liturgy of the Church of England. 16mo. 3s. 6d.

POPE'S (ALEXANDER) Works. With Introductions and Notes, by REV. WHITWELL ELWIN, and W. J. COURTHOPE. Vols. I., II., III., IV., VI., VII., VIII. With Portraits. 8vo. 10s. 6d. each.

PORTER (REV. J. L.). Damascus, Palmyra, and Lebanon. With Travels among the Giant Cities of Bashan and the Hauran. Map and Woodcuts. Post 8vo. 7s. 6d.

PRAYER-BOOK (BEAUTIFULLY ILLUSTRATED). With Notes, by REV. THOS. JAMES. Medium 8vo. 18s. cloth.

PRINCESS CHARLOTTE OF WALES. A Brief Memoir. With Selections from her Correspondence and other unpublished Papers. By LADY ROSE WEIGALL. With Portrait. 8vo. 8s. 6d.

PRIVY COUNCIL JUDGMENTS in Ecclesiastical Cases relating to Doctrine and Discipline. With Historical Introduction by G. C. BRODRICK and W. H. FREMANTLE. 8vo. 10s. 6d.

PSALMS OF DAVID. With Notes Explanatory and Critical by Dean Johnson, Canon Elliott, and Canon Cook. Medium 8vo. 10s. 6d.

PUSS IN BOOTS. With 12 Illustrations. By OTTO SPECKTER. 16mo. 1s. 6d. Or coloured, 2s. 6d.

QUARTERLY REVIEW (THE). 8vo. 6s.

RAE (EDWARD). Country of the Moors. A Journey from Tripoli to the Holy City of Kairwan. Map and Etchings. Crown 8vo. 12s.

RAE (EDWARD). The White Sea Peninsula. Journey to the White
Sea, and the Kola Peninsula. With Map and Illustrations. Crown 8vo.
15s.

RAMBLES in the Syrian Deserts. Post 8vo. 10s. 6d.

RASSAM (HORMUZD). British Mission to Abyssinia. Illustrations. 2 Vols. 8vo. 28s.

RAWLINSON'S (CANON) Herodotus. A New English Version.
Edited with Notes and Essays. Maps and Woodcuts. 4 Vols. 8vo. 48s.

———— Five Great Monarchies of Chaldæa, Assyria, Media,
Babylonia, and Persia. With Maps and Illustrations. 3 Vols. 8vo. 42s.

———— (SIR HENRY) England and Russia in the East; a
Series of Papers on the Condition of Central Asia. Map. 8vo. 12s.

REED (Sir E. J.) Iron-Clad Ships; their Qualities, Performances,
and Cost. With Chapters on Turret Ships, Iron-Clad Rams, &c. With
Illustrations. 8vo. 12s.

———— Letters from Russia in 1875. 8vo. 5s.

———— Japan : Its History, Traditions, and Religions. With
Narrative of a Visit in 1879. Illustrations. 2 Vols. 8vo. 28s.

———— A Practical Treatise on Shipbuilding in Iron and Steel.
Second and revised edition with Plans and Woodcuts. 8vo.

REJECTED ADDRESSES (THE). By JAMES AND HORACE SMITH.
Woodcuts. Post 8vo. 3s. 6d.; or *Popular Edition*, Fcap. 8vo. 1s.

REMBRANDT. [See MIDDLETON.]

REVISED VERSION OF N. T. [See BECKETT—BURGON—COOK.]

REYNOLDS' (SIR JOSHUA) Life and Times. By C. R. LESLIE,
R.A. and TOM TAYLOR. Portraits. 2 Vols. 8vo. 42s.

RICARDO'S (DAVID) Works. With a Notice of his Life and
Writings. By J. R. M'CULLOCH. 8vo. 16s.

RIPA (FATHER). Residence at the Court of Peking. Post 8vo. 2s.

ROBERTSON (CANON). History of the Christian Church, from the
Apostolic Age to the Reformation, 1517. 8 Vols. Post 8vo. 6s. each.

ROBINSON (REV. DR.). Biblical Researches in Palestine and the
Adjacent Regions, 1838—52. Maps. 3 Vols. 8vo. 42s.

———— (WM.) Alpine Flowers for English Gardens. With
70 Illustrations. Crown 8vo. 7s. 6d.

———— English Flower Garden. Its Style and Posi-
tion. With an Illustrated Dictionary of all the Plants used, and
Directions for their Culture and Arrangement. With numerous
Illustrations. Medium 8vo. 15s.

———— Sub-Tropical Garden. Illustrations. Small 8vo. 5s.

———— Parks and Gardens of Paris, considered in
Relation to the Wants of other Cities and of Public and Private
Gardens. With 350 illustrations. 8vo. 18s.

———— Wild Garden ; or, Our Groves and Gardens
made Beautiful by the Naturalization of Hardy Exotic Plants. Being
one way onwards from the Dark Ages of Flower Gardening, with
Suggestions for the Regeneration of Bare Borders of the London
Parks. With 90 Illustrations. 8vo. 10s. 6d.

———— Hardy Flowers. Descriptions of upwards of 1300
of the most Ornamental Species ; with Directions for their Arrangement, Culture, &c. Post 8vo. 3s. 6d.

———— God's Acre Beautiful ; or, the Cemeteries of the
Future. With 8 Illustrations. 8vo. 7s. 6d.

ROBSON (E. R.). SCHOOL ARCHITECTURE. Remarks on the
Planning, Designing, Building, and Furnishing of School-houses.
Illustrations. Medium 8vo. 18s.

ROME (HISTORY OF). [See GIBBON—LIDDELL—SMITH—STUDENTS'.]

ROYAL SOCIETY CATALOGUE OF SCIENTIFIC PAPERS.
8 vols. 8vo. 20s. each. Half morocco, 28s. each.

RUXTON (GEO. F.). Travels in Mexico; with Adventures among Wild
Tribes and Animals of the Prairies and Rocky Mountains. Post 8vo. 3s.6d.

ST. HUGH OF AVALON, Bishop of Lincoln; his Life by G. G.
PEARY, Canon of Lincoln. Post 8vo. 10s. 6d.

ST. JOHN (CHARLES). Wild Sports and Natural History of the
Highlands of Scotland. Illustrated Edition. Crown 8vo. 15s. Cheap
Edition, Post 8vo. 3s. 6d.

———————— (BAYLE) Adventures in the Libyan Desert. Post 8vo. 2s.

SALDANHA (DUKE OF). [See CARNOTA.]

SALE'S (SIR ROBERT) Brigade in Affghanistan. With an Account of
the Defence of Jellalabad. By REV. G. R. GLEIG. Post 8vo. 2s.

SCEPTICISM IN GEOLOGY; and the Reasons for It. An
assemblage of facts from Nature combining to refute the theory of
"Causes now in Action." By VERIFIER. Woodcuts. Crown 8vo. 6s.

SCHLIEMANN (DR. HENRY). Ancient Mycenæ. With 500
Illustrations. Medium 8vo. 50s.

———————— Ilios; the City and Country of the Trojans,
including all Recent Discoveries and Researches made on the Site
of Troy and the Troad. With an Autobiography. With 2000 Illustrations. Imperial 8vo. 50s.

———————— Troja: Results of the Latest Researches and
Discoveries on the site of Homer's Troy, and in the Heroic Tumuli
and other sites made in 1882. With Maps, Plans, and Illustrations.
Medium 8vo. 42s.

———————— The Prehistoric Palace of the Kings of Tiryns;
Its Primeval Wall Paintings and Works of Art Excavated and
Described. With Coloured Lithographs, Woodcuts, Plans, &c.,
from Drawings taken on the spot. Medium 8vo.

SCHOMBERG (GENERAL). The Odyssey of Homer, rendered
into English verse. 2 vols. 8vo. 24s.

SCOTT (SIR GILBERT). The Rise and Development of Mediæval
Architecture. With 400 Illustrations. 2 Vols. Medium 8vo. 42s.

SCRUTTON (T. E.). The Laws of Copyright. An Examination
of the Principles which should Regulate Literary and Artistic Property in England and other Countries. 8vo. 10s. 6d.

SEEBOHM (HENRY) Siberia in Asia. A visit to the Valley of the
Yenesay in Eastern Siberia. With Descriptions of the Natural History,
Migrations of Birds, &c. Illustrations. Crown 8vo. 14s.

SELBORNE (LORD). Notes on some Passages in the Liturgical
History of the Reformed English Church. 8vo. 6s.

SHADOWS OF A SICK ROOM. Preface by Canon LIDDON.
16mo. 2s. 6d.

SHAH OF PERSIA'S Diary during his Tour through Europe in
1873. With Portrait. Crown 8vo. 12s.

SHAW (T. B.). Manual of English Literature. Post 8vo. 7s. 6d.

——— Specimens of English Literature. Selected from the
Chief Writers. Post 8vo. 7s. 6d.

——— (ROBERT). Visit to High Tartary, Yarkand, and Kashgar,
and Return Journey over the Karakorum Pass. With Map and
Illustrations. 8vo. 16s.

SIERRA LEONE; Described in Letters to Friends at Home. By
A LADY. Post 8vo. 3s. 6d.

SIMMONS (CAPT.). Constitution and Practice of Courts-Mar-
tial. 8vo. 15s.

SMILES' (SAMUEL, LL.D.) WORKS :—
BRITISH ENGINEERS; from the Earliest Period to the death of

SMILES' (Samuel, LL.D.) WORKS:—

George Stephenson. Post 8vo. 2s. 6d.
James Nasmyth. Portrait and Illustrations. Cr. 8vo. 16s.
Scotch Naturalist (Thos. Edward). Illustrations. Post 8vo. 6s.
Scotch Geologist (Robert Dick). Illustrations. Cr. 8vo. 12s.
Huguenots in England and Ireland. Crown 8vo. 7s. 6d.
Self-Help. With Illustrations of Conduct and Persever-
ance. Post 8vo. 6s.
Character. A Book of Noble Characteristics. Post 8vo. 6s.
Thrift. A Book of Domestic Counsel. Post 8vo. 6s.
Duty. With Illustrations of Courage, Patience, and Endurance.
Post 8vo. 6s.
Industrial Biography; or, Iron Workers and Tool Makers.
Post 8vo. 6s.
Boy's Voyage Round the World. Illustrations. Post 8vo. 6s.
Men of Invention and Industry. Post 8vo. 6s.

SMITH (Dr. George) Student's Manual of the Geography of British
India. Physical and Political. With Maps. Post 8vo. 7s. 6d.

—— Life of John Wilson, D.D. (Bombay), Missionary and
Philanthropist. Portrait. Post 8vo. 9s.

- —— Life of .Wm. Carey, DD., 1761—1834. Shoemaker and
Missionary. Professor of Sanscrit at the College of Fort William,
Calcutta. Crown 8vo.

——— (Philip). History of the Ancient World, from the Creation
to the Fall of the Roman Empire, A.D. 476. 3 Vols. 8vo. 31s. 6d.

SMITH'S (Dr. Wm.) DICTIONARIES:—

Dictionary of the Bible; its Antiquities, Biography,
Geography, and Natural History. Illustrations. 3 Vols. 8vo. 105s.
Concise Bible Dictionary. Illustrations. 8vo. 21s.
Smaller Bible Dictionary. Illustrations. Post 8vo. 7s. 6d.
Christian Antiquities. Comprising the History, Insti-
tutions, and Antiquities of the Christian Church. Illustrations. 2 Vols.
Medium 8vo. 3l. 13s. 6d.
Christian Biography, Literature, Sects, and Doctrines;
from the Times of the Apostles to the Age of Charlemagne. Medium 8vo.
Vols. I. II. & III. 31s 6d. each. (To be completed in 4 Vols.)
Greek and Roman Antiquities. Illustrations. Medium
8vo. 28s.
Greek and Roman Biography and Mythology. Illustrations.
3 Vols. Medium 8vo. 4l. 4s.
Greek and Roman Geography. 2 Vols. Illustrations.
Medium 8vo. 56s.
Atlas of Ancient Geography—Biblical and Classical.
Folio. 6l. 6s.
Classical Dictionary of Mythology, Biography, and
Geography. 1 Vol. With 750 Woodcuts. 8vo. 18s.
Smaller Classical Dict. Woodcuts. Crown 8vo. 7s. 6d.
Smaller Greek and Roman Antiquities. Woodcuts. Crown
8vo. 7s. 6d.
Complete Latin-English Dictionary. With Tables of the
Roman Calendar, Measures, Weights, and Money. 8vo. 21s.
Smaller Latin-English Dictionary. New and thoroughly
Revised Edition. 12mo. 7s. 6d.
Copious and Critical English-Latin Dictionary. 8vo. 21s.
Smaller English-Latin Dictionary. 12mo. 7s. 6d.

SMITH'S (Dr. Wm.) ENGLISH COURSE:—

SCHOOL MANUAL OF ENGLISH GRAMMAR, WITH COPIOUS EXERCISES and Appendices. Post 8vo. 3s. 6d.

PRIMARY ENGLISH GRAMMAR, for Elementary Schools, with carefully graduated parsing lessons. 16mo. 1s.

MANUAL OF ENGLISH COMPOSITION. With Copious Illustrations and Practical Exercises. 12mo. 3s. 6d.

PRIMARY HISTORY OF BRITAIN. 12mo. 2s. 6d.

SCHOOL MANUAL OF MODERN GEOGRAPHY, PHYSICAL AND Political. Post 8vo. 5s.

A SMALLER MANUAL OF MODERN GEOGRAPHY. 16mo. 2s. 6d.

SMITH'S (Dr. Wm.) FRENCH COURSE:—

FRENCH PRINCIPIA. Part I. A First Course, containing a Grammar, Delectus, Exercises, and Vocabularies. 12mo. 3s. 6d.'

APPENDIX TO FRENCH PRINCIPIA. Part I. Containing additional Exercises, with Examination Papers. 12mo. 2s. 6d.

FRENCH PRINCIPIA. Part II. A Reading Book, containing Fables, Stories, and Anecdotes, Natural History, and Scenes from the History of France. With Grammatical Questions, Notes and copious Etymological Dictionary. 12mo. 4s. 6d.

FRENCH PRINCIPIA. Part III. Prose Composition, containing a Systematic Course of Exercises on the Syntax, with the Principal Rules of Syntax. 12mo. [In the Press.

STUDENT'S FRENCH GRAMMAR. By C. HERON-WALL. With Introduction by M. Littré. Post 8vo. 6s.

SMALLER GRAMMAR OF THE FRENCH LANGUAGE. Abridged from the above. 12mo. 3s. 6d.

SMITH'S (Dr. Wm.) GERMAN COURSE:—

GERMAN PRINCIPIA. Part I. A First German Course, containing a Grammar, Delectus, Exercise Book, and Vocabularies. 12mo. 3s. 6d.

GERMAN PRINCIPIA. Part II. A Reading Book; containing Fables, Stories, and Anecdotes, Natural History, and Scenes from the History of Germany. With Grammatical Questions, Notes, and Dictionary. 12mo. 3s. 6d.

PRACTICAL GERMAN GRAMMAR. Post 8vo. 3s. 6d.

SMITH'S (Dr. Wm.) ITALIAN COURSE:—

ITALIAN PRINCIPIA. Part I. An Italian Course, containing a Grammar, Delectus, Exercise Book, with Vocabularies, and Materials for Italian Conversation. 12mo. 3s. 6d.

ITALIAN PRINCIPIA. Part II. A First Italian Reading Book, containing Fables, Anecdotes, History, and Passages from the best Italian Authors, with Grammatical Questions, Notes, and a Copious Etymological Dictionary. 12mo. 3s. 6d.

SMITH'S (Dr. Wm.) LATIN COURSE:—

THE YOUNG BEGINNER'S FIRST LATIN BOOK: Containing the Rudiments of Grammar, Easy Grammatical Questions and Exercises, with Vocabularies. Being a Stepping stone to Principia Latina, Part I. for Young Children. 12mo. 2s.

THE YOUNG BEGINNER'S SECOND LATIN BOOK: Containing an easy Latin Reading Book, with an Analysis of the Sentences, Notes, and a Dictionary. Being a Stepping-stone to Principia Latina, Part II. for Young Children. 12mo. 2s.

PRINCIPIA LATINA. Part I. First Latin Course, containing a Grammar, Delectus, and Exercise Book, with Vocabularies. 12mo. 3s. 6d.
    ⁎ In this Edition the Cases of the Nouns, Adjectives, and Pronouns are arranged both as in the ORDINARY GRAMMARS and as in the PUBLIC SCHOOL PRIMER, together with the corresponding Exercises.

SMITH'S (Dr. Wm.) Latin Course—*continued.*

APPENDIX TO PRINCIPIA LATINA. Part I.; being Additional Exercises, with Examination Papers. 12mo. 2s. 6d.

PRINCIPIA LATINA. Part II. A Reading-book of Mythology, Geography, Roman Antiquities, and History. With Notes and Dictionary. 12mo. 3s. 6d.

PRINOIPIA LATINA. Part III. A Poetry Book. Hexameters and Pentameters; Eclog. Ovidianæ; Latin Prosody. 12mo. 3s. 6d.

PRINCIPIA LATINA. Part IV. Prose Composition. Rules of Syntax with Examples, Explanations of Synonyms, and Exercises on the Syntax. 12mo. 3s. 6d.

PRINCIPIA LATINA. Part V. Short Tales and Anecdotes for Translation into Latin. 12mo. 3s.

LATIN-ENGLISH VOCABULARY AND FIRST LATIN-ENGLISH DICTIONARY FOR PHÆDRUS, CORNELIUS NEPOS, AND CÆSAR. 12mo. 3s. 6d.

STUDENT'S LATIN GRAMMAR. For the Higher Forms. Post 8vo. 6s.

SMALLER LATIN GRAMMAR. 12mo. 3s. 6d.

SMITH'S (Dr. Wm.) GREEK COURSE:—

INITIA GRÆCA. Part I. A First Greek Course, containing a Grammar, Delectus, and Exercise-book. With Vocabularies. 12mo. 3s. 6d.

APPENDIX TO INITIA GRÆCA. Part I. Containing additional Exercises. With Examination Papers. Post 8vo. 2s. 6d.

INITIA GRÆCA. Part II. A Reading Book. Containing Short Tales, Anecdotes, Fables, Mythology, and Grecian History. 12mo. 3s. 6d.

INITIA GRÆCA. Part III. Prose Composition. Containing the Rules of Syntax, with copious Examples and Exercises. 12mo. 3s. 6d.

STUDENT'S GREEK GRAMMAR. For the Higher Forms. By CURTIUS. Post 8vo. 6s.

SMALLER GREEK GRAMMAR. 12mo. 3s. 6d.

GREEK ACCIDENCE. 12mo. 2s. 6d.

PLATO, Apology of Socrates, &c. With Notes. 12mo. 3s. 6d.

SMITH'S (Dr. Wm.) SMALLER HISTORIES:—

SORIPTURE HISTORY. With Coloured Maps and Woodcuts. 16mo. 3s. 6d.

ANCIENT HISTORY. Woodcuts. 16mo. 3s. 6d.

ANCIENT GEOGRAPHY. Woodcuts. 16mo. 3s. 6d.

MODERN GEOGRAPHY. 16mo. 2s. 6d.

GREECE. With Coloured Map and Woodcuts. 16mo. 3s. 6d.

ROME. With Coloured Maps and Woodcuts. 16mo. 3s. 6d.

CLASSICAL MYTHOLOGY. Woodcuts. 16mo. 3s. 6d.

ENGLAND. With Coloured Maps and Woodcuts. 16mo. 3s 6d.

ENGLISH LITERATURE. 16mo. 3s. 6d.

SPECIMENS OF ENGLISH LITERATURE. 16mo. 3s. 6d.

SOMERVILLE (Mary). Personal Recollections from Early Life to Old Age. Portrait. Crown 8vo. 12s.

———— Physical Geography. Portrait. Post 8vo. 9s.

———— Connexion of the Physical Sciences. Post 8vo. 9s.

———— Molecular & Microscopic Science. Illustrations. 2 Vols. Post 8vo. 21s.

SOUTH (John F.). Household Surgery; or, Hints for Emergencies. With Woodcuts. Fcap. 8vo. 3s. 6d.

—— Memoirs of. [See Felton.]

SOUTHEY (Robt.). Lives of Bunyan and Cromwell. Post 8vo. 2s.

STANHOPE'S (Earl) WORKS :—

History of England from the Reign of Queen Anne to the Peace of Versailles, 1701-83. 9 vols. Post 8vo. 5s. each.

Life of William Pitt. Portraits. 3 Vols. 8vo. 36s.

Miscellanies. 2 Vols. Post 8vo. 13s.

British India, from its Origin to 1783. Post 8vo. 3s. 6d.

History of "Forty-Five." Post 8vo. 3s.

Historical and Critical Essays. Post 8vo. 3s. 6d.

The Retreat from Moscow, and other Essays. Post 8vo. 7s. 6d.

Life of Belisarius. Post 8vo. 10s. 6d.¡

Life of Condé. Post 8vo. 3s. 6d.

Story of Joan of Arc. Fcap. 8vo. 1s.

Addresses on Various Occasions. 16mo. 1s.

STANLEY'S (Dean) WORKS :—

Sinai and Palestine. Coloured Maps. 8vo. 12s.

Bible in the Holy Land; Extracted from the above Work. Woodcuts. Fcap. 8vo. 2s. 6d.

Eastern Church. Plans. Crown 8vo. 6s.

Jewish Church. From the Earliest Times to the Christian Era. Portrait and Maps. 3 Vols. Crown 8vo. 18s.

Church of Scotland. 8vo. 7s. 6d.

Epistles of St. Paul to the Corinthians. 8vo. 18s.

Life of Dr. Arnold. Portrait. 2 Vols. Cr. 8vo. 12s.

Canterbury. Illustrations. Crown 8vo. 6s.

Westminster Abbey. Illustrations. 8vo. 15s.

Sermons during a Tour in the East. 8vo. 9s.

—— on Special Occasions, Preached in Westminster Abbey. 8vo. 12s.

Memoir of Edward, Catherine, and Mary Stanley. Cr.8vo. 9s.

Christian Institutions. Essays on Ecclesiastical Subjects. 8vo. 12s. Or Crown 8vo. 6s.

Essays. Chiefly on Questions of Church and State; from 1850 to 1870. Revised Edition. Crown 8vo. 6s.

[See also Bradley.]

STEPHENS (Rev. W. R. W.). Life and Times of St. John Chrysostom. A Sketch of the Church and the Empire in the Fourth Century. Portrait. 8vo. 7s. 6d.

STRATFORD de REDCLIFFE (Lord). The Eastern Question. Being a Selection from his Writings during the last Five Years of his Life. With a Preface by Dean Stanley. With Map. 8vo. 9s

STREET (G. E.). Gothic Architecture in Spain. Illustrations. Royal 8vo. 30s.

—— Gothic Architecture in Brick and Marble. With Notes on North of Italy. Illustrations. Royal 8vo. 26s.

STUART (Villiers). Egypt after the War. Being the Narrative of a Tour of Inspection, including Experiences amongst the Natives, with Descriptions of their Homes and Habits; to which are adde Notes of the latest Archæological Discoveries and a revised Account of the Funeral Canopy of an Egyptian Queen, With interesting additions.

STUDENTS' MANUALS:—

OLD TESTAMENT HISTORY; from the Creation to the Return of the Jews from Captivity. Woodcuts. Post 8vo. 7s. 6d.

NEW TESTAMENT HISTORY. With an Introduction connecting the History of the Old and New Testaments. Woodcuts. Post 8vo. 7s.6d.

EVIDENCES OF CHRISTIANITY. By H. WACE, D.D. Post 8vo.
[In the Press.

ECCLESIASTICAL HISTORY; a History of the Christian Church from its foundation till after the Reformation. By PHILIP SMITH, B.A. With numerous Woodcuts. 2 Vols. 7s. 6d. each.
PART I. A.D. 30—1003. · PART II.—1003—1598.

ENGLISH CHURCH HISTORY; from the Planting of the Church in Great Britain to the Silencing of Convocation in the 18th Cent. By CANON PERRY. 2 Vols. Post 8vo. 7s. 6d. each.
First Period, A.D. 596—1509. Second Period, 1509—1717.

ANCIENT HISTORY OF THE EAST; Egypt, Assyria, Babylonia, Media, Persia, Asia Minor, and Phœnicia. By Philip Smith, B.A. Woodcuts. Post 8vo. 7s. 6d.

—————— GEOGRAPHY. By Canon BEVAN, M.A. Woodcuts. Post. 8vo. 7s. 6d.

HISTORY OF GREECE; from the Earliest Times to the Roman Conquest. By WM. SMITH, D.C.L. Woodcuts. Crown 8vo. 7s. 6d.
₊ Questions on the above Work, 12mo. 2s.

HISTORY OF ROME; from the Earliest Times to the Establishment of the Empire. By DEAN LIDDELL. Woodcuts. Crown 8vo. 7s. 6d

GIBBON'S DECLINE AND FALL OF THE ROMAN EMPIRE. Woodcuts. Post 8vo. 7s. 6d.

HALLAM'S HISTORY OF EUROPE during the Middle Ages. Post 8vo. 7s. 6d.

HISTORY OF MODERN EUROPE, from the end of the Middle Ages to the Treaty of Berlin, 1878. Post 8vo. [In the Press.

HALLAM'S HISTORY OF ENGLAND; from the Accession of Henry VII. to the Death of George II. Post 8vo. 7s. 6d.

HUME'S HISTORY OF ENGLAND from the Invasion of Julius Cæsar to the Revolution in 1688. Revised, and continued to the Treaty of Berlin, 1878. By J. S. BREWER, M.A. Coloured Maps and Woodcuts. Post 8vo. 7s. 6d. Or in 3 parts, price 2s. 6d each.
₊ Questions on the above Work, 12mo. 2s.

HISTORY OF FRANCE; from the Earliest Times to the Fall of the Second Empire. By H. W. JERVIS. With Coloured Maps and Woodcuts. Post 8vo. 7s. 6d.

ENGLISH LANGUAGE. By GEO. P. MARSH. Post 8vo. 7s. 6d.

ENGLISH LITERATURE. By T. B. SHAW, M.A. Post 8vo. 7s.6d.

SPECIMENS OF ENGLISH LITERATURE. By T.B.SHAW.Post 8vo. 7s.6d.

MODERN GEOGRAPHY; Mathematical, Physical and Descriptive. By Canon BEVAN, M A. Woodcuts. Post 8vo. 7s.6d.

GEOGRAPHY OF BRITISH INDIA. Political and Physical. By GEORGE SMITH, LL.D. Maps. Post 8vo. 7s. 6d.

MORAL PHILOSOPHY. By WM. FLEMING. Post 8vo. 7s. 6d.

SUMNER'S (BISHOP) Life and Episcopate during 40 Years. By Rev. G. H. SUMNER. Portrait. 8vo. 14s.

SWAINSON (CANON). Nicene and Apostles' Creeds; Their Literary History; together with some Account of "The Creed of St. Athanasius." 8vo. 16s.

SWIFT (JONATHAN). [See CRAIK—FORSTER.]

SYBEL (Von) History of Europe during the French Revolution, 1789—1795. 4 Vols. 8vo. 48s.

SYMONDS' (Rev. W.) Records of the Rocks; or Notes on the Geology of Wales, Devon, and Cornwall. Crown 8vo. 12s.

TALMUD. [See Barclay—Deutsch.]

TEMPLE (Sir Richard). India in 1880. With Maps. 8vo. 16s.

—————— Men and Events of My Time in India. 8vo. 16s.

—————————— Oriental Experience. Essays and Addresses delivered on Various Occasions. With Maps and Woodcuts. 8vo. 16s.

THIBAUT'S (Antoine) Purity in Musical Art. With Prefatory Memoir by W. H. Gladstone, M.P. Post 8vo. 7s. 6d.

THIELMANN (Baron). Journey through the Caucasus to Tabreez, Kurdistan, down the Tigris and Euphrates to Nineveh and Palmyra. Illustrations. 2 Vols. Post 8vo. 18s.

THOMSON (Archbishop). Lincoln's Inn Sermons. 8vo. 10s. 6d.

—————— Life in the Light of God's Word. Post 8vo. 5s.

—————— Word, Work, & Will : Collected Essays. Crown 8vo. 9s.

THORNHILL (Mark). The Personal Adventures and Experiences of a Magistrate during the Rise, Progress, and Suppression of the Indian Mutiny. With Frontispiece and Plan. Crown 8vo. 12s.

TITIAN'S LIFE AND TIMES. With some account of his Family, from unpublished Records. By Crowe and Cavalcaselle. Illustrations. 2 Vols. 8vo. 21s.

TOCQUEVILLE'S State of Society in France before the Revolution, 1789, and on the Causes which led to that Event. 8vo. 14s.

TOMLINSON (Chas.). The Sonnet: Its Origin, Structure, and Place in Poetry. Post 8vo. 9s.

TOZER (Rev. H. F.). Highlands of Turkey, with Visits to Mounts Ida, Athos, Olympus, and Pelion. 2 Vols. Crown 8vo. 24s.

—————— Lectures on the Geography of Greece. Post 8vo. 9s.

TRISTRAM (Canon). Great Sahara. Illustrations. Crown 8vo. 15s.

—————— Land of Moab : Travels and Discoveries on the East Side of the Dead Sea and the Jordan. Illustrations. Crown 8vo. 15s.

TWENTY YEARS' RESIDENCE among the Greeks, Albanians, Turks, Armenians, and Bulgarians. 2 Vols. Crown 8vo. 21s.

TWINING (Rev. Thos.). Recreations and Studies of a Country Clergyman of the Last Century. Crown 8vo. 9s.

TWISS' (Horace) Life of Lord Eldon. 2 Vols. Post 8vo. 21s.

TYLOR (E. B.). Researches into the Early History of Mankind, and Development of Civilization. 3rd Edition. 8vo. 12s.

—————— Primitive Culture : the Development of Mythology, Philosophy, Religion, Art, and Custom. 2 Vols. 8vo. 24s.

VATICAN COUNCIL. [See Leto.]

VIRCHOW (Professor). The Freedom of Science in the Modern State. Fcap. 8vo. 2s.

WACE (Rev. Henry), D.D. The Principal Facts in the Life of our Lord, and the Authority of the Evangelical Narratives. Post 8vo. 6s.

—————— Luther's Primary Works. (See Luther).

WELLINGTON'S Despatches in India, Denmark, Portugal, Spain, the Low Countries, and France. 8 Vols. 8vo. £8 8s.

——————————— Supplementary Despatches, relating to India, Ireland, Denmark, Spanish America, Spain, Portugal, France, Congress of Vienna, Waterloo, and Paris. 15 Vols. 8vo. 20s. each.

—————————— Civil and Political Correspondence. Vols. I. to VIII. 8vo. 20s. each.

—————— Speeches in Parliament. 2 Vols. 8vo. 42s.

WESTCOTT (Canon B. F.) The Gospel according to St. John, with
Notes and Dissertations (Reprinted from the Speaker's Commentary).
8vo. 10s. 6d.

WHARTON (Capt. W. J. L.), R.N. Hydrographical Surveying:
being a description of the means and methods employed in constructing
Marine Charts. With Illustrations. 8vo. 15s.

WHEELER (G.). Choice of a Dwelling. Post 8vo. 7s. 6d.

WHITE (W. H.). Manual of Naval Architecture, for the use of
Naval Officers, Shipowners, Shipbuilders, and Yachtsmen. Illustrations. 8vo. 24s.

WHYMPER (Edward). The Ascent of the Matterhorn. With
100 Illustrations. Medium 8vo. 10s. 6d.

WILBERFORCE'S (Bishop) Life of William Wilberforce. Portrait.
Crown 8vo. 6s.

———————— (Samuel, LL.D.), Lord Bishop of Oxford and
Winchester; his Life. By Canon Ashwell, D.D., and R. G. Wilberforce. With Portraits and Woodcuts. 3 Vols. 8vo. 15s. each.

WILKINSON (Sir J. G.). Manners and Customs of the Ancient
Egyptians, their Private Life, Laws, Arts, Religion, &c. A new edition
Edited by Samuel Birch, LL.D. Illustrations. 3 Vols. 8vo. 84s.

———————— Popular Account of the Ancient Egyptians. With
500 Woodcuts. 2 Vols. Post 8vo. 12s.

———————— (Hugh). Sunny Lands and Seas: A Cruise
Round the World in the S.S. "Ceylon." India, the Straits Settlements,
Manila, China, Japan, the Sandwich Islands, and California. With
Illustrations. Crown 8vo. 12s.

WILLIAMS (Monier). Religious Life and Thought in India. An
Account of the Religions of the Indian Peoples. Based on a Life's Study
of their Literature and on personal investigations in their own country.
2 Vols. 8vo.
Part I.—Vedism, Brahmanism, and Hinduism. Second Edition. 18s.
Part II.—Buddhism, Jainism, Zoroastrianism, Islam, and Indian
Christianity. [In preparation.

WILSON (John, D.D.). [See Smith, Geo.]

WINTLE (H. G.). Ovid Lessons, being Easy Passages selected
from the Elegiac Poems of Ovid and Tibullus, with Explanatory Notes
(in use at Eton College). Third Edition. 12mo. 2s. 6d.

WOOD'S (Captain) Source of the Oxus. With the Geography
of the Valley of the Oxus. By Col. Yule. Map. 8vo. 12s.

WORDS OF HUMAN WISDOM. Collected and Arranged by
E. S. With a Preface by Canon Liddon. Fcap. 8vo. 3s. 6d.

WORDSWORTH'S (Bishop) Greece; Pictorial, Descriptive, and
Historical. With an introduction on the Characteristics of Greek Art,
by Geo. Scharf. New Edition revised by the Rev. H. F. Tozer, M.A.
With 400 Illustrations. Royal 8vo. 31s. 6d.

YORK (Archbishop of). Collected Essays. Contents.—Synoptic
Gospels. Death of Christ. God Exists. Worth of Life. Design in
Nature. Sports and Pastimes. Emotions in Preaching. Defects in
Missionary Work. Limits of Philosophical Enquiry. Crown 8vo. 9s.

YULE (Colonel). Book of Marco Polo. Illustrated by the Light
of Oriental Writers and Modern Travels. With Maps and 80 Plates.
2 Vols. Medium 8vo. 63s.

———————— A Glossary of Peculiar Anglo-Indian Colloquial Words
and Phrases, Etymological, Historical, and Geographical. By Colonel
Yule and the late Arthur Burnell, Ph.D. 8vo.

———————— (A. F.) A Little Light on Cretan Insurrection. Post
8vo. 2s. 6d.